Wild

Written by
Dawn DeRamón

I want to dedicate this book to my husband. Without your support and belief, this might still be an idea in my head. Also a huge thank you to Kristen for your time and help.

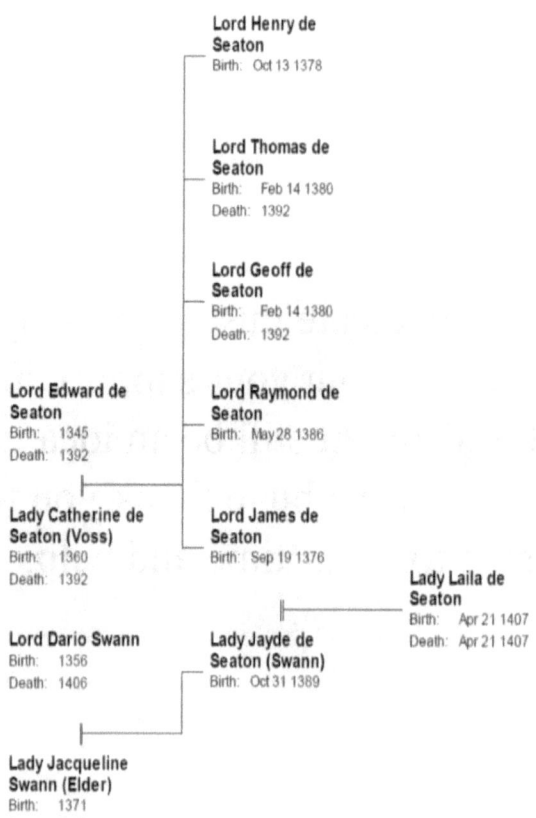

Lord Henry de Seaton
Birth: Oct 13 1378

Lord Thomas de Seaton
Birth: Feb 14 1380
Death: 1392

Lord Geoff de Seaton
Birth: Feb 14 1380
Death: 1392

Lord Edward de Seaton
Birth: 1345
Death: 1392

Lord Raymond de Seaton
Birth: May 28 1386

Lady Catherine de Seaton (Voss)
Birth: 1360
Death: 1392

Lord James de Seaton
Birth: Sep 19 1376

Lady Laila de Seaton
Birth: Apr 21 1407
Death: Apr 21 1407

Lord Dario Swann
Birth: 1356
Death: 1406

Lady Jayde de Seaton (Swann)
Birth: Oct 31 1389

Lady Jacqueline Swann (Elder)
Birth: 1371
Death: 1400

Chapter 1
November 1406

James had delayed his journey as long as possible. Now, sitting at the edge of the woods, he could see the Castle of Adonia and he was reminded that this was not a marriage for love, it was for wealth. Her dowry would bring him nearly as much land as his four estates and many knights' fees. James had heard that Lady Jayde of Adonia, his future bride, ran her Father's estate so tightly that the servants had taken to stealing scraps to feed their own families. He would secure their marriage and produce an heir, then send her to his farthest estate to live with whatever lover she wanted. Until he must face his fate however, he would remain outside the cold confining walls of matrimony every last moment that he could. Leaning back against the tree, he had just closed his eyes when he heard something to his right move. Without moving his head, he opened his eyes and glanced to his right and barely saw it. It? Her. She was running with her gown hitched high to her knees, barefoot, and hair flowing freely behind her. He jumped up and chased after her. She was fast, like a wild creature fleeing from danger. His long legs caught up to her quickly though and he slowed down as the gap between them became smaller. He watched in fascination as she reached the river bank and collapsed to the ground, her body consumed in sobs. Her hair seemed to go on forever, blanketing the soft mossy floor around her. James could not help but to stare at her hair as it was such an intriguing color; plain brown with wisps of gold and red.

Jayde was suddenly aware that she was not alone. She quickly stopped sobbing, slowly sat up gathering her skirts and then stood up. She wiped her tear stained face with her hands and struggled to push her wet hair back and off of her face and neck. Jayde turned around to face her attacker and was ready for the fight of her life. What was she thinking running outside of the castle walls into the woods! Hadn't she just overheard her maid talking of a young girl who was taken from these very woods recently?

James sucked in his breath so hard he nearly fell over. The eyes that stared back at him consumed him. Vibrant green, like nothing that nature could compare. They sparkled with defiance, and burned with life. Her shoulders were broad and delicate all at once, ample breasts, slight waist, and what had seemed like long strong legs, were now hidden under layers of the palest pink skirts he had ever seen.   The hair that had so intrigued him now cascaded down her back stopping just above her knees.   All he could do was stare.

"What do you want?" Jayde demanded, her heart racing. The man did nothing but stare, as though he were in a trance. Her anger was starting to rise and take the place of fear. Was he mute? She decided it would

2

be best to slowly side step around him and pray that her legs could carry her quickly to safety. She wouldn't dare say anything to her step-mother. She couldn't take another beating, especially on the eve of her wedding. Her WEDDING! To a stranger! Some old man marrying her for her land and estates. He was probably shorter than she, fat, and had ten moles with a long curling gray hair growing out of the center of each one. The man in front of her started to reach out to grab her...

Everything seemed to slow down. He watched as she side stepped away from him keeping her exquisite eyes on him rather than where she was going. He saw the stump too late and could say nothing to prevent her from tripping on it. Suddenly, his war reflexes kicked in and in a moment he had reached out to her gathering her in his arms. Her eyes were wild as she struggled against him trying to kick and claw at him, anything to get him to release her. When her teeth sank into his hand, he gave up trying to save her from the forest floor, immediately releasing her. Her body flew back to the ground forcing the air from her. She cried out in pain as the tree stump sliced into her calf.

"This is the last time I try to save someone not wanting to be saved. My apologies for trying to be a gentleman. I am sure you can manage to return within your castle walls without aide. Good evening my lady." James muttered before he stormed off to the tree where he had been peacefully contemplating his dire future and began to curse himself. He couldn't leave a lady alone in these woods, it was too dangerous. Now he would have to go back and try to convince her that he had no desire to paw her and take her on the forest floor. First he would need to convince himself.

Jayde was trying to find something she could use to wrap her cut leg with so she could get back before her step-mother started to look for her. A bit of fabric was dangled in front of her face. She looked up into the man's face. He was quite handsome. A perfectly chiseled chin and cheeks with a strong straight nose placed center of his face. Jayde noticed his unusual yet striking features. He had bright hazel eyes that clashed with his too blonde hair. There was a slight curl to it, and it looked as soft as a head of baby hair. He had broad shoulders that looked as though he could carry the world and not slow down. Why couldn't her husband to be look this handsome? Suddenly she realized that he had been speaking to her.

James had already asked the girl twice if she would like his aide. Her response had been nothing more than a blank look, not even acknowledging that he had spoken. Was she truly that afraid of him? This was a bad idea. He should have simply dropped the cloth in front of her and walked away.

"Would you like my aide in tending to your cut?" he paused to allow her to answer. "Is your home far within the walls? Do you think you can walk?"

"Yes," was all Jayde could manage. The pain in her calf was growing to a throb and she desperately wanted to soak her leg and get a poultice on it so it would not get infected.

"Yes? Yes, you want my aide? Yes, your home is not far? Yes, you can walk?" James asked.

"Yes, I would appreciate your aide, yes, my home is a short walk from here, and yes, and I believe I will be able to walk. Thank you for returning to aide me." Jayde watched as he kneeled down to her and could barely breathe as his hands gently pushed her skirts up to her knee to expose her cut.

"I am going to get this cloth wet at the river and then I will wipe the debris from your wound." James thought it might be wise to explain every detail so as to avoid her kicks and scratches again. "After I wrap your leg, would you like me to accompany you to the castle walls, or will you manage on your own?"

"Thank you. I should be well enough to walk on my own. Do you have a name or should I address you as stranger?" Jayde asked. What kind of "gentleman" did not introduce himself? What was he doing in the woods near the castle? Her fears began to nag at her again. She was being foolish. Allowing this stranger, albeit incredibly handsome, to be so close.

"James. May I ask for your name as well? Or shall I simply address you as Wild?"

Jayde couldn't help but laugh at the twinkle and sarcasm in his eyes and voice.

Jayde thought a moment before answering him. She did not want him to know her name, although she felt as though she could trust him, her trust for others had long since proven her wrong. "If Wild is what you wish, then Wild it should be." Jayde smiled up at the handsome face of James. "Are you going to wash the debris from my wound or just stand there?" Jayde asked with much amusement. James quickly kneeled down and bowed his head to clean her wound hoping she wouldn't see his unknightly blush. He could not help but notice how soft her muscular legs were as he cleaned and wrapped her wound.

"Your wound does not appear as deep as I thought it was, it should heal quickly. Let me help you stand." James reached down to Jayde to help her stand. She was much lighter than she seemed. James pulled her up too strongly and threw her against his chest. Their faces were less than an inch apart.

Jayde threw her arms around James's neck to keep from falling, reveling in how strong and tall he was while realizing how very close their bodies and lips were to one another. Without another thought, Jayde gently touched his lips with her own and gasped at the fire that ripped through her entire body...

James felt his lips burn the moment her lips touched his. Never had anything felt like this. Not any victory on the battlefield or in a lover's bed. Tangling one hand in her hair at the nape of her neck he supported her petite frame with his other hand wrapped securely around her tiny waist. He deepened their kiss tasting the sweet nectar that she offered, nearly losing control as she softly moaned.

Jayde was overwhelmed in this new sensation. It left her senseless, breathless and without any strength in her legs. As James gently touched his tongue to hers, she moaned with innocent pleasure. She felt James start to pull back and without further thought she laced her fingers into the curls that teased at the nape of his neck and drew him back to her.

Without warning, James dropped her to the ground, jarring her back into reality. Embarrassment seized Jayde as she sat on the cold damp moss covered ground.

Jayde struggled to her feet and hobbled towards the hidden passage in the castle wall as quickly as she could manage. Her lips still burning, and her skin tingling where his hands had been. How magnificent! At least life gifted her this small pleasure before the horrors of her future. As soon as Jayde was within the castle walls, her maid Anna rushed to her side hurrying her through the halls while whispering the hell that Lady Ethna, Jayde's step mother, had been causing in search of her. Quickly, Anna had Jayde sitting down on the little bench and was combing her hair moments before Lady Ethna stormed in demanding to know where Jayde was, threatening lashings for anyone whom dared to lie to her.

"Mother, please, calm down. Whatever is the matter? Are you okay?" Jayde was doing her best to ease her step mother's temper.

"Where have you been?!" Lady Ethna screamed. Turning and grabbing Anna by her already short hair, dragging the girl closer to the stairs threatening to push her down the dark and winding, cold stairwell.

"Please Mother! No! It was all my fault! I stormed off into the woods to be alone once more before my wedding tomorrow. I did not think of anyone but myself, I was selfish. If you must punish anyone, please, let it be me."

Lady Ethna paused, considering her punishment for her step daughter. "Get dressed and meet me in my private courtyard. I will give you your punishment there. Let this be your lesson, and the scars to remind you of your place in life. If you had been *my* daughter, you would know how to behave and accept your duties in life."

Jayde shuddered but did as she was told. Anna waited until Lady Ethna had left the room before giving in to her own sobs. Jayde's grief of losing her mother only 6 years earlier wrapped its fingers around her young heart. Marrying at 17 to a man whom was surely twice her age, her mother Lady Jacqueline, would never have allowed.

As Jayde dressed, her mind drifted to her last summer with her mother. They were in the garden, tending to her mother's beloved roses. Jayde couldn't help but fidget despite her mother reminding her that a Lady practices patience and restraint at all times. Sighing, Lady Jacqueline sat back on her heels and had suddenly stood up, walked to the grass dragging Jayde by the hand with her. Then, stretching her arms as wide as she could, palms upward and face lifted toward the sun she began to spin around and around calling to Jayde to join her letting out the sweet sounds of laughter. Jayde did as she was told and with her arms stretched out, tilting her face up to the sun and spinning with her mother until they both collapsed together on the grass laughing uncontrollably watching the world continue to spin without them. Her childhood died with her mother in the fall of that year.

Jayde's tight and churning stomach brought her back to reality. Quickly Jayde left her room and rushed into the very same courtyard where she used to read to her mother. The courtyard that now belonged to her step-mother. What had once been filled with flowers was now nothing more than dirt and weeds. A cold place to match the cold heart of the mistress whom now resided within the walls of Adonia. Jayde stood quietly in the cold courtyard doing her best not to shiver on the now frost covered ground. What could Ethna have planned for her? What did she mean when she said the scars to remind her of her place in life? She shuddered again at what horror awaited her.

James had waited until Wild had completely left his sight, disappearing into the wall of Adonia before he admitted defeat and walked through the gates. He was eagerly greeted by Lord Dario whom showed him the opulent stables were James left his horse to be cared for. Returning to the castle, Lady Ethna joined them, shooing away Lord Dario and taking James to his chamber for the evening. Once alone, James bathed and dressed for the evening meal hoping that he would wake up any moment delighting that this might very well be a dream. Despite not having eaten since his morning meal, he did not feel hungry and the thought of choking down food next to the troll that his future bride surely must be, made him feel ill. His grim fate ate away at the very life within him. James decided that he needed to take a walk. On his way to his room earlier he had seen a courtyard in a poor state and looking as miserable as he felt. Maybe he could find solace by surrounding himself with the pain that he felt. He passed the window that looked down into that courtyard and saw a woman standing there, barefoot and wearing a familiar pale pink gown in the November cold. He stood watching in stunned silence as he realized the petite frame standing in the cold belonged to that of his Wild creature from the woods. Why did she not tell him she was a servant at the castle? James was about to go down into the courtyard to speak with her when he saw Lady Ethna walking toward Wild while holding a whip. There was conversation between the two and he watched as Wild shook her head no vigorously and then drop to her knees shaking and reaching out to Lady

Ethna. Lady Ethna slapped the begging girl so hard she knocked her over, then taking a handful of the long, soft, hair, jerked his beautiful Wild to her feet. James watched in horror as Lady Ethna walked 15 paces from Wild's shaking body and raised the whip striking the tiny back. He counted 10 strikes across Wild's back but only counted 2 cries from her. Lady Ethna turned dragging the whip with her and disappeared from his view. He could hear her coming up the stairs, and quickly hid in a dark corner of the hall. Once she had passed, he ran to the window where he saw another maid rush out and cover Wild's blood drenched back and lead her out of sight. What could she have done that was so terrible to warrant such a punishment?

He stood there staring down into the cold courtyard praying for numbness to take over until he heard the bell ring for the evening meal. Reluctantly he made his way to the hall to choke down the meal with his soon to be in-laws and Soon-to-be Ogre Wife, Lady Jayde. When the meal started, there was an empty chair to his left, and his future Mother-in-Law to his right. Lady Ethna leaned over to him and apologized for her daughter's absence, citing that she was too nervous to attend this evening's meal.

The meal dragged on as did Lady Ethna. First explaining how grateful they were for him to accept their daughter in marriage, begging his pardon for her homely appearance, then boasting of how frequently they visit King Henry IV's court. James tuned Lady Ethna's voice out paying barely enough attention except to nod and make appropriate sounds to acknowledge the conversation. Instead, his mind focused on the sound of the whip as it cut through the air with a faint whistling sound landing with a sinking whish into the soft flesh of Wild. Finally, the meal ended and James pleaded exhaustion from his long travels, excusing him from any further celebrations.

Chapter 2

Anna gently led Jayde up to her room and ordered a plate of food be sent up while she carefully peeled away the embedded strips of clothing from the raw and gaping slashes across her mistress's back. Anna gently washed each of the ten cuts and then applied her mother's very own poultice to keep any infection away. Anna would have to find a way to dress Jayde for her morning wedding without further injuring her and without her bleeding again. Every day for the past month Anna had been counting the days until her mistress's wedding when she and Jayde would escape the hell that Adonia had become.

Anna stayed awake through the night nursing her dearest friend, desperately trying to stave off infection and fever. When dawn came, she knew she had lost the fight to both and that her darling friend and mistress would somehow have to suffer and bear the pain while she said her vows. She had no idea that Lady Ethna had dragged the whip through the stables, the manure, puddles of urine and dirt, guaranteeing this infection.

Jayde was vaguely aware that the sun had risen. She could barely think, consumed with pain from her wounds. Jayde twice refused the cool water that Anna had carefully boiled through the night and set aside to cool. Finally, she gave in and accepted the cool drink, wincing in pain as it carved its way down her throat. Anna helped her up to relieve herself and begin the process of preparing for her wedding. Her gown was truly beautiful, something her step-mother had not taken part of. Her gown was simple, unlike those traditionally worn. She dressed in a velvet gown the color of the pale blue winter sky. The shallow collar was of a heavy embroidered lace, with delicately entwined threads of gold. At her upper arms, were matching cuffs and a matching border on the hem of her skirt as well. About her waist was a belt made of the same embroidered lace, with small dark sapphires sewn on. Her sleeves ballooned open exposing a fitted sleeve of gold silk. Anna combed Jayde's hair then made two delicate braids, one at either temple, and tied them together with a matching gold silk ribbon. On her head was a crown of pearls and a veil that reached her fingertips and had small pearls and small dark sapphires sewn on. She was dressed. As Anna helped Jayde down the stairs to the waiting mare, she checked her mistress's head for fever. Jayde's flushed face gave away the raging fever making her already brilliant green eyes appear even brighter while her lips were as red as that of a winter rose. Jayde was lifted into the saddle of her black mare and the procession began through the streets of Adonia. Winding their way through the town, Lady Jayde's horse was led by the stable master. When they finally reached the steps of the church, Jayde was nearly delirious with fever, and was scarcely aware of the hands that touched her waist or the familiar face that searched hers with worry and pain.

It was his wedding day and standing alone at the steps of the church, James could only think about Wild. He had not seen her or the other maid from the night before all morning, and he hoped and prayed she was not ill. If there was only a way he could find out. Maybe he could find a way to bring her, and the other maid with him to his home and protect her from any further abuse. If only he could find her, and run off with her. He could almost hear his father's voice, telling him that would be irresponsible, that he must think beyond himself. The sound of people, horses and horns interrupted his thoughts. James finally looked up to his bride to be when her mare was led to him at the church steps. He had prepared himself to look upon the face of a troll, but the face he looked upon made him step back. Without thought he rushed forward and gently placed his hands on the tiny waist of his Wild. He remembered the scenes from yesterday in the woods, then in the courtyard and he struggled to keep his anger and tears controlled. Lady Ethna had lied to him when she had said Lady Jayde had been too nervous to come down to the evening meal on the eve of their wedding. Fighting the urge to vomit, he recalled the sickening scene of Lady Ethna whipping Wild, all the while searching her face in hopes she would respond to him. She didn't seem to recognize him, and her vibrant green eyes were brighter than he remembered and glazed over. He stared desperately into her eyes, he could see her bright red cheeks and knew the fever and likely infection were from yesterday's whipping. The priest cleared his throat. James softly turned Jayde to face the priest and guided her up the steps to begin their ceremony.

Jayde repeated words when told to do so, aware of only pain and exhaustion. If she could just lay down and sleep. Sleep. She would say or do just about anything right this moment if only she could rest. Something had happened. People cheered and she was being carried in some one's arms. Strong arms and a familiar scent... It was morning, her wedding day. Surely Ethna would not force her to wed when she was so ill, would she? Did she? There was something familiar about the arms that held her, something that was comforting and exciting all at once, then everything went dark.

James scooped up his wife and carried her limp body towards the maid he had seen tending to her last night. "Where can I take her?"

Anna knew that Lady Ethna's narrowed eyes bore into her back, but she did not care anymore. Her mistress was gravely ill. "We can take her up to her chamber my lord."

Lord Dario had managed to stay sober long enough to get through this day. Jacqueline would have loved James, he knew it. James was the son of an old friend of theirs that had passed several years back. When he happened upon James six months ago, he was thoroughly impressed with the man that James had grown into. He had heard that James had been in some serious trouble a while back, but appeared to have recovered from his folly. Lord Dario knew that he owed so much to his daughter to make up for the happiness she had been robbed of. If all he could do was secure his only child a good, honest and kind husband, then hopefully that would be enough. James seemed to be all of those qualities and more. Turning his attention towards the church, he watched as James scooped his beautiful daughter up in his arms and start to walk towards Anna, Jayde's maid.

Walking over to James, he placed a hand on his shoulder and said, "James, you will have her the rest of your life, your wedding night can wait until..." Dario looked down at his daughter and saw the fever that raged within her. "What has happened?" Lord Dario quietly asked through clenched teeth.

"My lord, before yesterday's evening meal, Lady Ethna whipped Lady Jayde for leaving the castle walls again. I tried everything I knew, but I could not prevent the infection and fever." Anna shook from the anger she felt of Lady Ethna and fear from the rage that consumed Lord Dario.

"Lord Dario, please let me take her from here, and heal her. We will ask you to visit with us after she has recovered." James prayed Lord Dario would see the sense in his decision.

"Take her and care for her James. I am counting on you to love her and treat her the way your mother would hope you would. Do not disappoint me. Go, leave now, and do not bring her back here. She has suffered too much already." Dario then kissed his precious daughter's forehead before turning to the crowd of people to search for Ethna.

James followed the thin woman as she ran through the crowds and up to her mistress's room. James laid down his wife and turned to his knight, Fendrel, "Prepare the wagons, and my men. We leave immediately, my wife is ill."

"My Lord, it would be most offensive if we were to leave now." Fendrel reminded James. James had a habit of not thinking of the consequences of his actions, especially when a lady was in need of protection.

"Fendrel, I said my wife is ill. She is gravely ill. I am leaving now with my wife. You ride with me or I ride alone. I need to get her home where I can care for and protect her." James turned to the maid, "What is your name?"

"Anna, my lord."

"How well can you ride?"

"I will be able to keep up with you my lord."

"Good, then let us not waste another minute." James scooped up his wife and strode down to the stables where his horse was saddled and waiting.

"Lord James, what do you think you are doing?" Lady Ethna asked.

Struggling to suppress the hate he felt, James replied, "I am taking my wife away from here and away from you."

"My Lord, the people of Adonia have been preparing for this celebration for seven days. It would be a great offense should you leave now and break tradition." Lady Ethna said crisply with her eyes narrowed.

"Lady Ethna, how do you think the good people of Adonia would feel if they knew you whipped their beloved Lady Jayde and that she was now fighting for her life, her body raging with fever and infection?" James waited a moment for Lady Ethna to answer. When she did not respond James continued. "I am leaving now with my wife. I am taking her home to Era."

Quickly closing her mouth, Lady Ethna chose to say nothing. How could he have known she had whipped Jayde? She would make that evil, conniving seductress pay for this.

James shifted his wife's frail body in his arms as he mounted his horse. He waited for Anna to mount a horse before spurring his horse forward with Anna and his knights following close behind him. The townspeople stood back and at either side of the street as the magnificent horses went thundering out of town. James rode hard, pushing his horse to a near breaking point. He pushed everyone to make the three day journey in one day. When they finally arrived at Era, all but James practically fell out of their saddles. James swiftly dismounted with Jayde in his arms running through the hall and up to his room calling for Maggie. When Maggie arrived, all she could do was gasp.

Maggie quickly went to the young woman lying on the bed. She was burning with fever, her breath shallow and her body limp. She looked into the eyes of the boy she had cared for so often when he was sick to prepare him for the worst. The anguish and hope she saw in his face and eyes forced her to not allow any doubt of the young lady's recovery. Maggie instructed James to help undress the young girl to begin to cool her off. When she rolled the young girl over to cool her back with a damp cloth she was so stunned she could do nothing but stare. The delicate back was covered in angry gaping wounds so swollen that there was not a space upon her back that could be touched that was not hot with infection.

James and Maggie took shifts during the next four days working to bring down Jayde's fever and applying a poultice of yarrow, cloves, and myrrh to the wounds on her back. James refused to leave the room choosing to sleep on the window seat. Maggie tried to talk to James during those four days, but James simply stared at the young woman and held her hand. They worked tirelessly those long four days until finally on that fourth night Maggie broke their silence.

"My lord, please, I am begging you, who is she?" Maggie tried once more.

James' only answer was the same as it had been for the last four days. Silence.

Sighing, Maggie spoke softly, "Lord James, there is nothing more we can do. She continues to be consumed with fever, and has not taken any tea in two days. I fear she will not live through the night." James did nothing but stare at her with hallowed eyes. "Who is she?" Maggie tried again to draw out words from James.

"Her name is Jayde. She is my wife, my Wild." James then turned his head back towards the frail figure in his large bed. The size of the bed engulfed her tiny frame, making her to look even more like a child than her petite frame already did.

Maggie laid her hand on his shoulder, then left the room to try and get some rest. She would need all of her strength to help Lord James manage his grief come morning.

Chapter 3

At dawn on the fifth day, Jayde awoke in a room unfamiliar to her. The room smelled of Thyme and Lavender, candle nubs were flickering around her and her body ached almost more than she could bare. She tried to look around to see more of the room she was in, if she was alone and to search for water but her body ached even too much for that.

"Please, water." Jayde tried to whisper, but not a noise was made. "Please, water." She spoke again, this time she used as much energy as she could gather. Something to her left stirred and she realized someone was holding her hand. She used what little energy she thought she had left to move her hand only managing to wiggle her fingers.

James slowly woke hearing something unusual, then something in his hands moved. She moved! My God, she was alive! Jumping to his feet, "Wild?" Quickly he placed his hand to her forehead and not feeling a fever, he grabbed the candle nearby and brought it closer to see that she was awake and staring at him. "Maggie! Maggie!" James called out.

Maggie came running into the chamber expecting to find the worst. Nothing they did could break the fever and she had run out of ideas and treatments. She had not expected for the young woman to survive this final night.

"Water." Jayde managed again. James dropped her hand and rushed to get a cup of the now cold tea of Rosemary Willow and helped support her head as she took small sips of the cool liquid then returned her head to the pillow. He was so relieved he began to cry and gently laugh together at once. He sank to his knees at her bedside, taking her hand back in his and laying his head on top of their hands as Maggie quietly left the chamber.

Jayde was desperately trying to understand why the man from the woods, James, was holding her hand and crying. She couldn't remember anything beyond painfully falling asleep after the incident in the courtyard with her step-mother.

James was so relieved! Maggie had said that there was nothing else that they could do, she had hinted that Jayde was not going to live. How could anything so wild and full of life *not* fight to survive? He felt slow hot tears begin to fall down his face and then he heard the deep laughter of his father escape his mouth. Bowing his head, giving thanks for her life, James closed his eyes and gave in to the sweet peaceful sleep that his body so desperately craved.

Listening to James drift off into sleep, Jayde's mind raced. How did she get here? She did not feel a ring on her finger, had this man taken her? Did her father know where she was? She had to remember something, anything! As she fell asleep, she vaguely remembered Anna dressing her, and there was the horse, people, cheers, and then darkness. Somewhere in the darkness there had been cool waves that seemed to soothe her but, those were fever dreams. Jayde closed her eyes tightly, there must be something. She could still smell the cold Rosemary Willow tea, the thyme and lavender too. There was something else though, roses maybe? The scent was familiar and comforting but it did not remind her of her mother, it simply made her feel safe and oddly, loved. Finally, Jayde could do nothing more other than softly drift off to sleep.

When Jayde awoke again, she felt the pang of hunger grip her stomach and then like thunder, heard her empty stomach rumble. It was dark outside and James was no longer at her side, but candles lit the room well. She looked to her right and saw a large door, a tapestry, and a wash basin. Looking to her left, she saw a shuttered window, a window seat and a figure curled up laying on the window seat. Just then, the door opened and Jayde saw the woman from earlier come in with a large tray laden with dishes. The room filled with delicious smells causing her stomach to growl even louder.

"Good! You are awake. If I sit you up on some pillows, do you think you could take a bit of broth?" Maggie asked with an enormous grin.

"Yes, I would love to try some broth. Thank you." Jayde managed to whisper.

James awoke to the sound of Jayde's voice and was amazed at how the sound of something so simple warmed his heart and gave him a smile from ear to ear. Maggie was talking to Jayde and the smell of Maria's food was intoxicating. He stood up and stretched, he had forgotten how small that window seat was. He had not fallen asleep on it since shortly after his mother had passed.

Walking over to Jayde, he asked "How are you feeling?"

"Terrible and hungry. Thank you for taking care of me." Jayde had so many questions she wanted to ask.

James gathered all of the pillows and used them to help Jayde sit up without tearing open the delicate wounds on her back.

Maggie carried over a small bowl of broth and handed it to James. She knew he would refuse to care for himself until Lady Jayde was fed and comfortable. She also knew that he would not leave his young wife's side until she was healed. Ever since Lord James was a child, he was loyal to a fault. Smiling at the memories, she could recall several instances where the truth was still not completely known since Lord James refused to turn his siblings in. Then when Lord Edward and Lady Catherine passed, Lord James stepped into the role of parent without question or hesitation.

James held the bowl while Jayde took her first drink. The broth was warm, and comforting and filled with spices.

"Maggie?" Jayde asked.

"Yes my lady?" Maggie was shocked at the soft and silky voice her new young mistress had.

"Thank you so much for caring for me and especially for this delicious broth."

Maggie simply smiled at the young woman, unable to speak and unable to trust that she would not cry at the gracious words. She turned to stoke the fire and light several new candles. James silently watched the scene between the two women with awe and pride. Never had anyone left Maggie speechless and never had he heard anyone outside his family speak so kindly to Maggie. Maggie was a gruff woman whom had grown accustomed to ordering others about since his parents had passed. She only had time for kindness towards him and his siblings and the blacksmith whom she flirted with shamelessly.

"Here, drink this, you need to heal and gain your strength. After you've eaten, Maggie will help you to relieve yourself, we will then apply a new poultice to your wounds and get you tucked back into bed. I would like it however, if you could finish this bowl of broth first." James spoke his orders softy, filled with the hope that the worst was behind them and she could heal quickly. He longed to kiss her lips again and hold her in his arms. He would protect her from all, and always be there to catch her should she stumble or fall. The sudden hate he felt for her mother must have shone in his eyes because Jayde gasped and drew back from him. He blinked away his thoughts and softly smiled at her, hoping he could gain her trust.

Jayde managed to finish the broth and swallowed her embarrassment for requiring Maggie's help to relieve herself and for her lack of clothing. She needed to talk to James and ask questions, but she would wait until Maggie had left the room.

James scooped Jayde up into his arms careful not to break open the wounds on her back and carried her back to the bed. There he and Maggie changed her poultice and tucked Jayde in with clean bedding. Maggie began to serve James and sensing that there needed to be some privacy between the two, quietly left.

Jayde waited until James had finished what looked to be lamb stew with enormous chunks of carrots, potatoes and onions with a side of bread. As he was drinking his wine, she began to ask her questions.

"Where are we?" Jayde had never seen a room so simple and clean yet still elegant.

"We are at my home, well, our home. Era." James softly replied, blushing slightly.

"How many days have I been here?" Jayde noticed the gentle blush that crept up on James' cheeks and felt her own cheeks start to pink as well. Before she could ask her next question, James spoke.

"We arrived five days ago. Do you not remember traveling with me?" James worried, she didn't seem to remember anything. What if she thought he was the one who caused her wounds? How could he tell her that he watched and could do nothing? "Jayde, can you tell me what you last remember?"

Jayde thought for a moment, shuddering at the memories, and took a deep breath to calm herself. "I remember meeting you in the woods. I remember returning home… Anna! Where is Anna?"

"She is safe. She is here and has already made herself quite at home. She has been helping Maggie to order everyone around. What else can you tell me?" James asked.

Jayde closed her eyes and relaxed a little. "I remember Anna trying to keep me from getting in trouble with my step-mother, I remember Ethna threatening to throw Anna down the stairs," She looked down at her hands and quietly continued, "I remember my punishment. I remember being carried to my room. I remember feeling safe. That is all. I do not remember anything else."

James's stomach tightened and he struggled to not be ill. He remembered Jayde's punishment and could actually hear the sickening sound of the cracking whip burying itself into the soft flesh on her back. Wait, her step-mother? Her step-mother! This brought up so many questions he needed to ask.

Gently, James asked, "When did your mother pass?" James was hoping that she would trust him enough to answer.

"Six years ago." Jayde quietly answered.

"What happened? Was she ill? Did you become ill as well?" James remembered his parents' and brothers' illness and deaths and remembered the fear that gripped him and his brothers.

"It was October when she passed. She loved her garden so much, there were roses, her favorite were the York Roses. She said they reminded her of true innocence and they should be loved accordingly. There was rosemary, thyme, sage, lemon balm, mint, lavender and violets just to name a few other herbs and flowers. She took pride in her work and often made poultice and teas for those that were ill. That morning, the blacksmith's wife went into labor and mother was rushing to get some herbs for her. She tripped on her skirts and fell down the stairs." Jayde spoke quietly and gently while talking about her mother, remembering each small detail as she spoke of them.

"When did your father remarry? What about Ethna enchanted him so?" James could not find anything good about a marriage to Ethna. Was there financial trouble?

"My father met and married Ethna two years after my mother's death. She was a widow as well with a daughter who was already married. She brought quite a bit of wealth to my father. At first she ignored me, then doted upon me when my father was near. My father truly did not care. He was too absorbed by his own grief to see anyone else's grief for my mother. After about a year, she quit trying to pretend she was a great step-mother. That is when the beatings started. I learned to stay out of her way and spend most of my time studying anything I could get my hands on. Anna tried her best to protect me, but she was no match for Ethna."

"Why did Ethna feel she could whip you?" James could barely get the question out. He was hoping that she would not question how he knew this and just answer. He was not sure he could bare the idea of her hating him.

Jayde sucked in her breath. "How did you know Ethna did this to me?"

"I… I… I saw her whip you in the courtyard." James watched her face change from pain to hate. He quickly tried explaining himself. "I was miserable at the thought of getting married. All I could think about was meeting you in the woods. Wishing I could marry for love and not for financial gain. I wanted to find some place I could sulk. I remembered seeing a courtyard filled with dead weeds and dirt and thought that would be a perfect place to wallow in my grief. I saw you standing there and before I could run down to you, I saw your mother, your step-mother, walk out with her whip. I could not believe what I was seeing. I could not move. Please do not hate me. I did not know where you had gone and I was worried I would make it worse if I said anything. When I saw you on your horse at the church, you did not recognize me. The only thing I could think of was to go through with the marriage so that I could get you away from her. Anna even helped me. I could not bear the idea of delaying our marriage so you could heal only to be harmed again by Ethna. Please, please. Jayde, Wild. Do not hate me." James waited quietly for Jayde to say something. Anything. To tell him she hated him and wished he were dead, or that he had just let her die. To scream, curse or maybe even thank him. Anything but the silence.

"Jayde?"

Jayde could barely breathe. He watched her being whipped and did nothing! How could he? How could anyone? The pain she felt, the humiliation she felt now. On the other hand, what exactly was he to do? Rush down to stop Ethna? She could have easily whipped him as well…

"Why did you not come down to me when Ethna left?" Jayde felt betrayed by this man she had only met in the woods and claiming to now be her husband. She did not remember saying any vows. Where was her wedding gown? Her random thoughts were interrupted by James.

James let out a sigh of relief. She spoke to him. Hopefully this was a sign that she could forgive him, if she wanted to. "I heard her coming up the stairs and had to duck into a corner to avoid being seen. Wild, do you hate me?"

Jayde sat in the bed for another moment before answering. "I do not hate you. I do not know what I feel except that I would like to see Anna. Would you please ask Anna to come here? I need to see her. I need… please, get her." Jayde tipped her head back against the pillows and closed her eyes. She just needed to choke back the tears until he left. The door opened, and there was silence. She let the tears start to slide. Slowly at first, then faster until she was on the verge of body shaking sobs. Anna would know what to do. Just hang on…

James watched her lean back and close her eyes. He opened the door, and turned to look at her. He saw the tears sliding down her cheeks, slow silent tears. He heard her choke on a sob and watched the tears start to flow faster. He turned and ran down the stairs to the hall to find Anna. If Jayde needed her maid to turn to, he wanted to make sure she had everything and everyone that she needed. He found Anna eating in the kitchen. He didn't have to say anything, she jumped up and turned him around and started to push him out of the kitchen. He ran back up to his room with Anna pushing him the whole way. James pushed the door open and Anna pushed past him running to Jayde with tears flowing down their faces. He could only watch for a moment before closing the door. He sank to the floor in the hall placed his head in his hands and began to cry.

Maggie had watched James go running through the hall for Anna and had decided to follow them up the stairs where she found James sitting with his knees to his chest sobbing. Maggie helped him to stand and led him to his parents' room. She always made sure it was clean. James sat in a chair and continued to cry. Hot, choking tears.

James struggled the first ten years after his parents had died. His parents had become ill and had sent the children to an Uncle's home to keep them from getting ill as well. His mother died first, his father just three days later. James was the oldest of five children, all boys. His youngest brother, Thomas, died four months later, followed by Geoff a month after that. James was sixteen then, and thirty now. His brothers Henry and Raymond were still alive and healthy refusing to settle down. Henry being twenty-eight and Raymond twenty. Each year the three brothers met for a week to honor their parents and brothers.

The three brothers had met just before James' wedding. James did not tell them of his impending marriage. He justified the secret with hoping there would be a way out of the agreed upon marriage. His marriage had been arranged six months ago after asking Lord Dario for ways to make his land more profitable. Lord Dario had offered some suggestions to reduce certain crops, increase others and to increase livestock. Then he invited James to have a few drinks with him. After many drinks, the two men shook hands and signed papers arranging the marriage. It took James a few days to recover from his evening before he remembered his engagement. This wedding would bring incredible wealth, land and security for James. Little did he know it would also bring him someone so incredible, beautiful and smart. Jayde had said she studied which meant that she could read. He was lucky. One thing he had not figured out yet was why Lord Dario would be so willing to give so much in dowry when there would be nothing to gain for himself? Unless Lord Dario knew of his daughter's pain and was trying to make up for his mistake of marrying Ethna? He would send word to his father-in-law. He should travel back to Adonia and ask. Then maybe apologize for leaving without warning. James immediately sent word with a messenger, stating that he would be arriving without Jayde in three days from the date of the message to speak with Lord Dario.

James walked down the hall to his room where Jayde was and found Anna sleeping on the window seat and Maggie preparing another poultice for his wild sleeping Jayde. He assumed Jayde would not want to see him, but he did not want her to think he abandoned her. He left her a note,

Wild

My dearest Wild,
I have some business to attend to at your
father's estate, Adonia. I am leaving in the
morning at dawn, will travel for three days and
will be gone for two weeks. I hope that will be
time enough for you to trust and believe in me
and my intentions. I fear that my actions have
caused distrust and hate from you and I cannot
say that your feelings are not warranted. I can
and do promise you though that everything I
have done and everything I do, will always be to
protect you. I travel to your father to have some
questions answered as well as pay for some
livestock that I asked for months ago. Should
you need anything, send a messenger for me. I
leave you in the care of Maggie and Anna. Rest,
heal and get strong. There is so much of Era
that I want to share with you. Maria is a
talented cook. She can make anything you
desire.
Be well my Wild.

Yours Truly,
James

James sealed the letter and left it on the table before
packing a few items and leaving the room. James got
very little sleep that night. The afternoon in the woods
of Adonia replayed itself in his dreams that night only to
be followed by the haunting scene in the courtyard that
evening. When dawn broke, James and three of his

knights left Era for Adonia. He hoped that when he returned, he would have some answers.

James returned to Adonia ten days after his marriage to Jayde. James and his knights sat outside the castle walls after arriving mid-morning waiting for the guard to call them in. Something was not right. It was as though everyone was gone. James, Fendrel, Luther and Walker sat uneasy on their horses. Cautiously with their swords drawn they entered into Adonia. There were no people walking the streets. Doors and windows were closed, not even the dogs walked the streets. The men rode their horses towards the stables and found a few horses still in their stalls and all appeared cared for. They dismounted and walked towards the hall. Once inside, they looked for signs of life. They found a servant cowering in a corner under a table. James asked where everyone was, but the servant just shook in terror and rocked back and forth. All four men heard a noise coming from upstairs. There were broken cups on the floor of the hall, as well as torn and barely hanging tapestries. The four men cautiously walked up the stairs to the chambers above. Jayde's door was wide open and the furniture in her room was thrown about, feathers from the bed covering the floor. There was blood smeared on the wall of the hallway and several candelabra's had been knocked to the floor, hot wax having spilled and cooled until solid.

"I will never let you live after what you have done to her! I will kill you myself if I must!" The men could hear Lord Dario shout.

James threw open the door to Lord Dario's chamber. Startled, Lord Dario turned to look at the group of intruders. In that moment of distraction, Lady Ethna picked up the dagger on the table and threw it at Lord Dario. The dagger sank deeply into Lord Dario's stomach.

Gasping in shock, Lord Dario touched the jeweled handle of the dagger that impaled his stomach. Disbelief shrouded his face and looking at James, he said "She got me."

Lady Ethna was covered in blood. Her hands were caked in dried blood and the men could see several cuts on her arms through her cut and bloody fabric. There was a set of daggers still sitting at the table, and Lady Ethna had already grabbed two more.

"What is the matter Lord James? Was Jayde not everything you hoped for? Are you here to beg for us to take her back? Did that worthless creature die in your arms? Go ahead. Tell her coward of a father the news. What is the matter? Cannot bring yourself to tell him? Here, let me! Dario, your weak creature of a daughter is dead! DEAD! You'll join her soon. You know, I have never loved you. I have hated the moment I laid eyes on you. I needed your money though. I couldn't be destitute. You are worthless!" Lady Ethna stood in front of the window facing the group. Drawing her hand back, she threw the other dagger at Lord Dario whom was now leaning against a wall.

James saw the flash of light off of the blade a second dagger before she threw it at Lord Dario. James did not think, he just reacted. He jumped in front of his Father-in-Law and felt astonishment when he saw the dagger sticking deep into his left thigh.

Lord Dario could not let the only good thing left in his only child's life be lost. Pushing James aside into the arms of one of the knights, Lord Dario grabbed the dagger in his own stomach and in one fluid motion threw it at Lady Ethna, hitting his target in the chest.

Lady Ethna barely felt the dagger sink into her chest as she began to gasp for air staggering backward falling out of the window and plunging to her death below.

Lord Dario slid to the ground and reached up to James. "Tell me James, is she safe now? Will you swear that you will keep her safe? Keep her happy? Will you promise to tell her that I am sorry I was not a better father and that I loved her always?" Lord Dario was pleading more than asking. These were the last words of a dying man.

"She is safe and she is healing from the whipping Ethna gave her the night before our wedding. I swear I will do everything within my power including giving my life to keep her safe and happy. May I ask you why you chose me?"

"I knew your father, Lord Edward. He was a good man. When your parents passed away, Lady Jacqueline and I were devastated. I was with your father when he passed. He asked me to promise to watch over you and your brothers. I tried my very best. After your eighteenth birthday, I stepped back and watched the man you were becoming. You look so much like your father, with your mother's heart. I recognized you when I saw you that day six months ago. You had grown to be an even stronger and kinder man than your father. I could not hope for a better husband for my daughter. Make up for the kindness and happiness I robbed her of. Promise me?"

"I promise." There was nothing else that James could say. He held the dying man's hand for his final breath. With the exhale came a single tear falling from Lord Dario's eye. James leaned back into Luther giving in to his own injury and pain. Luther dragged James back and onto the bed while Walker searched for cloth to wrap James's injury with. Fendrel examined the wound.

"My Lord, it seems as though the bleeding is slowing. Let us wrap your injury and return home where Maggie can heal you." Fendrel wanted nothing more than to just leave. He knew James too well though. He would want the estate secured before leaving. He would want a proper burial for Lady Ethna and Lord Dario. Fendrel and Walker wrapped James's wound and carried him down to the hall to lay on a table while Luther went in search for a messenger. The messenger was to ride at a neck breaking pace to Era, and send for 100 knights to come immediately to Adonia as well as poultice from Maggie for Lord James.

Chapter 4

Jayde woke up that morning to see that Anna slept at
the window. Maggie had already come in and changed
her bandages, this time leaving some lamb stew for her
at the bedside table. Jayde devoured it leaving not even
a drop of broth behind or crumb of bread. Shortly after
Jayde finished, Maggie appeared. Without speaking,
Maggie helped Jayde to her feet and walk to the
chamber pot to relieve herself. She cleared the dishes
and left without a single word being said. Jayde did not
understand what had caused such silence from Maggie,
but she would have to wait to find out until Maggie
came back. Jayde was feeling restless and needed a
walk. Quietly so as not to wake Anna, she slipped on a
loose gown and then out of her room and began to
wander the halls. Eventually she found herself outside
in a garden that had long since been tended to with a
gentle and loving hand. Without thought, she kneeled
on the frozen ground and began to pull weeds. The
exercise was invigorating and Jayde became so
absorbed that she did not feel the tiny tears from the
wounds on her back or the blood that began to soak
through her dress.

"Just what do you think you are doing?" Maggie
shouted as she ran across the garden to Jayde. Jayde
stood quickly spinning around to face Maggie. As
Maggie rushed to Jayde with her arms extended, Jayde
instinctively flinched from the blow that she knew was

coming. Maggie stopped right in front of the flinching Jayde. What had this child been through? With this reaction, this whipping was surely not the first time she had been punished so painfully. Now, after somehow surviving the worst infection Maggie had ever seen, she was outside pulling weeds like a servant and looking happy. It was as though she refused to let anything beat her. Maggie did not need to wonder why James had not mentioned he was going to be bringing back a bride, but she was beginning to understand why he held on to her for dear life. This young girl was his light in the dark. She gave him hope, Lady Jayde was the very breath he needed to live again. "Child, turn around and let me see your back." Maggie gently pulled Jayde's arms down to her sides and turned her around. "Come on now, time to go back in. You have torn open some of your wounds and are bleeding again. I cannot let you get sick again, I do not know that your frail body could survive. Come now, Lord James left you a note while you slept."

After Maggie undressed Jayde and began to investigate her back, Jayde read the note left by Lord James. She did not hate him. How could he think that? What questions did he need to ask her father? Maggie would know. She seemed very familiar and close with Lord James.

"Maggie, why does Lord James believe that I hate him, and what questions did he need to ask my father that he could not ask me?" Jayde asked.

"I do not know what questions Lord James needs to ask your father, but I believe that Lord James believes you to hate him because he hates himself for not doing more to protect you." Maggie recalled Lord James's tears last night. Maggie had not seen Lord James cry since his father and mother had passed, knowing he cried last night for his loss and pain, as well as the loss and pain of his new bride.

Jayde could do nothing but think about the words that Maggie had said and reread James letter over and over. Anna was gone when Jayde and Maggie returned from the garden. She came back to check on Jayde after the evening meal but did not stay and sleep. Jayde slept in the large room alone only waking when Maggie came in to stoke the fire and check her wounds.

After three more days of being required to stay indoors, Jayde could not stand it anymore. Maggie came in to clean around the wounds and help Jayde dress.

"Maggie, if you do not give me something to do outside of this room, I will escape when you leave and find trouble to get into." Jayde tilted her chin up with a look in her eyes that dared Maggie to deny her some freedom.

Laughing, Maggie agreed that Jayde should walk around a bit and asked if she would like to accompany her to the kitchen while she did some prep for the midday and evening meals. Jayde was giddy, nearly skipping down the stairs following Maggie down to the kitchen. She was sitting down with a basket pinching off the tips of green beans when the messenger came racing in.

"I am looking for a Lady Jayde." The messenger was breathing so hard he barely spoke his words.

"I am Lady Jayde." Jayde extended her hand out to the messenger and accepted the note.

"Please, sit and rest a bit. Get something to drink and stay for the midday meal." Jayde opened the note and read it slowly and carefully before standing sending the basket of beans to the floor. Maggie jumped up to steady the now ghost white young woman. She snatched the note from Lady Jayde's hands and read it herself. When she looked up, Lady Jayde was gone. "Where did she go?" Maggie asked the messenger. He could only point. Maggie looked out into the hall where the messenger had pointed the direction Lady Jayde had gone. She saw nothing but a bit of color at the top of the stairs. Chasing after her, Maggie found Jayde in James's room drawing a cloak closed over her shoulders. "Just where do you think you are going?"

"I am going to him. Either give me your poultice or go pack a few things. I will not abandon him when he needs us." Jayde called down to Corbett whom shadowed her every move since James had left. Corbett was one of James's trusted knights. "Corbett, gather 100 knights. We leave within the hour for Adonia. Lord James has been injured and has asked for knights."

"Yes my Lady. We will be ready to ride within minutes. Are you sure you are well enough to travel?"

Jayde answered with a flash from her green eyes. Corbett had never seen green like he was seeing in Jayde's eyes. He felt an icy chill run up his back leaving him with an unknown fear. Corbett ran to gather knights and sound the bell. Jayde was ready to ride and waiting when Corbett and Maggie joined her. Without any words, Jayde spurred her horse forward not looking back to see the thundering group that followed her. They rode hard all day and through the night. In the night they rode through a storm of pelting rain and ice only stopping once to let the horses drink water and rest. They reached Adonia by evening meal the next day.

The group slowed as they approached Adonia and only Jayde noticed the blood stain under her father's chamber window. Fear and panic gripped her entire body. Corbett began to tell the group of a plan to enter the castle walls after dark so as to not fall into a trap. Jayde dismounted her horse, hitched her skirts up and went running beyond the castle walls and into the hall up to her father's chamber. She opened the door to find a pool of blood too large for anyone to survive. Where was her father, James and Ethna? Jayde started to throw open each door searching for anyone. Finally getting to the door that was the chamber that James had stayed in briefly before they were married. Corbett was standing beside her, angry that she had defied him and put herself and everyone else in danger. He touched her shoulder to reprimand her but felt a wetness. Drawing his hand back, he noticed it was blood. Before he could say anything she opened the door. Standing there warming by a fire was Fendrel, Luther and Walker. James was laying in the bed, motionless. Jayde ran to his side, placing one hand against his forehead and taking his motionless hand in her other.

"James? Wake up. Please? I do not hate you, please do not die." Jayde sounded like a scared child. James slowly opened his eyes. There standing over him was his Wild. Her cheeks were pinked, her hair a wild mess and tears in her eyes. He was either dead or delirious because he knew she was home at Era. From over her shoulder he could see Maggie, Corbett and several of his knights.

"Wild?" James started to worry at his own delirium.

She smiled, closed her eyes and dropped her chin saying a quick prayer of thanks.

"Are you injured? What hurts?" Jayde started to feel his arms first the right then the left. James reached his hand up and held hers.

"I am okay now. I was stabbed, I am okay. Did you bring any of that poultice? I would not mind using it now." James watched her with concern and curiosity as she took a small dagger from her belt and cut the strip of cloth from his leg wound then began to cut away the

46

fabric of his pants. Maggie came forward and looked at the wound. It was not bad. It was clean, not infected and well on its way of healing. Jayde took the poultice that Maggie was holding and applied it to James wound then replaced the bandage. James sat up slowly, swinging his feet to the floor and gingerly standing up. Jayde stepped back to give him some room, desperately trying to blink back the tears of relief and fear while never taking her eyes from him. Her mind began to whirl. So much blood… James was okay, but she had not seen either her father or step-mother. The second pool of blood below her father's window. Oh God. No. NO NO NO!

James could see Jayde was struggling to keep it together. He signaled to Fendrel and everyone left them alone in the warm room.

"Jayde, I, your father, was… wounded. I think your father had been attacking Ethna for what she had done to you. She threw a dagger hitting your father in the stomach, then she threw a second dagger at me and it hit me in the leg. Your father pulled the dagger from himself and threw it at her. She fell back out the window." Taking a deep breath, James passed on Lord Dario's final words. "Lord Dario wanted to make sure that you knew he loved you. Your father knew your pain, he could do nothing to remedy the errors of his past. He found me instead, and arranged our marriage in hopes to give you a better future than your past." James looked into her eyes to tell her the last of it. "We buried your father next to your mother, and sent word to Ethna's daughter. They came for her body late that night. I am so sorry." James reached out to Jayde and pulled her to his chest.

The moment Jayde's cheek rested over James's strong beating heart she quit fighting back the tears. She held on to his shirt and cried. James stood still, holding onto this tiny angel, feeling helpless to shield her from all of the pain and heartache she must endure. He waited until her tears had subsided and she started to pull back from him. Looking into her eyes, all he wanted was to make everything better again for her. Tilting her chin up to face him, he gently brought his mouth down to hers. He had been dreaming of this for days. Waiting for the fire that would race through his body from their kiss. The kiss was even better than he remembered, it seemed as though the world exploded with this kiss. Her soft lips pressed against his, her arms reaching around and up his back pulling him closer to her. Her breasts pressed against his ribs, her hips just below his. James slipped one hand to the nape of her neck and slid his other hand from her hips to the edge of her breast where he gently caressed its soft roundness.

Jayde tried to stay focused and follow with her mind every feeling and sensation she was experiencing. Her knees began to shake when she felt James's hand caress her side and breast. When he touched her tongue with his though, her knees gave out and James had to support her weight against him to keep her from falling to the floor. His tongue demanded access to her mouth to explore and taste what it had craved since that day in the woods. Hungrily, he demanded more. Deeper and more desperate, he cupped her butt with his hand and pulled her to him even more tightly. Then he started to run his hand down from the nape of her neck, down her spine and ending on the other half of her butt. Something was wrong. Her back was wet and she cried out in pain. It took a moment for James to come back to reality and to make sense of everything. Realizing she was bleeding again, he called out for Maggie. A few moments later Maggie came in without asking any questions and began to strip away Jayde's now blood soaked dress to apply another poultice and bandage. She then ordered for Jayde to climb into bed and rest and not move until she checked on her at evening meal. James smiled, promising he'd keep her in bed making both Jayde and Maggie blush. James chuckled as Maggie huffed and puffed and hurried out of the room carrying Jayde's dress with her to wash. James undressed and sat back down onto the bed and gently pulled the now naked Jayde down with him. When Jayde began to protest, James silenced her with a kiss then pulled the bedding over them and pulled Jayde closer. Before either of them realized it, they had both fallen asleep clinging to each other as though their very lives depended on it.

Maggie quietly walked into the room holding a tray filled with heavenly smells that stirred the soul. Gently she set the tray down and stoked the fire then slipped out of the room as quietly as she entered. Soon the delectable scents from the tray filled the room and the roaring fire warmed the room wall to wall.

Jayde and James roused to the warmth of a fire and food. James climbed out of bed and walked over to the tray of meats, cheeses, bread, fruits and wine and picked it up and started to walk back to the bed only to stop, stand perfectly still and smile a most mischievous smile.

Jayde sat up and watched the perfect body walk around the foot of the bed, in front of the fire, and turn to face her. Never had Jayde seen a naked man before and she was fascinated. His back was molded with muscles that were the product of countless hours, weeks, years training with his knights. The muscles from his back tapered to a smooth and firm looking butt, which extended down to exquisitely sculpted thighs and calves. The muscles in the calves took turns flexing with each step. They turned around but no longer moved. Slowly Jayde traced the long golden legs up noting how thick the blonde hair covering them was. Her eyes continued to wander upward freezing on his shaft. To her delight and confusion, it began to move, and grow!

James could not help but to laugh. Jayde had been watching him strut across the room to the tray with their evening meal and when her eyes discovered his shaft, a look of fascination and confusion changed as did his flaccid shaft. When he felt his body responding to her eyes and her naked ample breasts, he watched the fascination on her face grow until she realized that he was watching her. Her lovely face burned red with embarrassment as she dropped her chin and eyes. James brought the tray to the bed, walked around and climbed back under the bedding. The discomfort was obvious and James was realizing that she had never seen a naked man before. To say that he was pleased with that notion was an understatement. James took her chin in his hand and guided her face towards his. He kissed her lips and smiled. "It is normal to be curious. We are husband and wife. You'll have an opportunity to gaze as much as you'd like every single day. I hope that eventually, we will do more than just gaze." Jayde turned an even deeper shade of red. "Are you as hungry as I am?"

Jayde's eyes grew wide, "I am famished… for the food on that tray."

James once again chuckled and began to serve his sweet, little, innocent wife. There was so much to show her, teach her and share with her. With time he hoped she would come to trust and love him too.

Jayde fell asleep in James's arms after eating the midday meal. When Maggie came in to check James's stab wound, James handed her a note requesting his brother Henry to join them at Adonia. He knew it would take a messenger two days to get to his brother, and nearly a week for him to prepare to travel and leave. This would give him a short amount of time to win the heart and trust of his new bride.

James spent the next two days convincing Jayde to stay indoors and read to him the books she had once read to her mother, Lady Jacqueline, and show him around

Adonia. The third and fourth days, Jayde took James out to the pond where she used to spend her afternoons and to the woods where she and Anna had learned to ride. On the fifth day, Jayde took James up the hill to a plateau that overlooked all of Adonia and even a few of the nearby estates. It was beautiful. They spent the entire afternoon up there bundled up and enjoyed a beautiful sunset before returning to Adonia where Maggie had been busy continuing to order people about to clean up the chaos that Lord Dario and Lady Ethna had caused.

Jayde gave Maggie a hug when they walked into the castle. Most signs of the struggle and pain had been removed from the Great Hall and the torn tapestries had been repaired, cleaned and hung again.

It had been six days since James had sent a messenger to his brother Henry, and James was becoming worried and impatient searching the horizon for any sign of his brother since yesterday morning. James and Jayde were enjoying their morning meal long after everyone else was in the fields training. James was telling Jayde about the garden that had been his mother's pride when she was alive. Describing the flowers and herbs she had once tended to so lovingly, James suddenly stopped.

"James, what is the matter?" Jayde watched as James turned his head slightly straining to hear. Jayde too strained to hear.

Jumping up with a grin from ear to ear, James grabbed Jayde's hand and pulled her behind him running towards the gate. In his excitement, James caused Jayde to trip on her skirts twice before realizing his haste and slowing down.

Once they reached the gate, James excitedly asked, "Jayde, do you hear it? Do you?"

Jayde paused and strained to hear some sound in the wind while catching her breath. She heard the sweet sound of a lone trumpet calling out and then heard the song of several trumpets ring loud and clear. It was beautiful. "What is the song they are trumpeting?"

"It was composed by my brother Geoff for our family. To be sounded anytime we came home, to announce our arrival to our family and town. It is something that I and my brothers, Henry and Raymond, continue. Look! Do you see our colors?" James pointed into the distance.

Jayde could see the beautiful green and gold banners waving in the sky. Then she saw what looked to be twenty horses and riders, followed by another row, and another row of horses and riders. Looking up at James, she watched as his smile grew even more and he raised his left arm in the air. Turning back to the army of men, horses and wagons, Jayde watched as one rider and horse broke formation and sprinted towards them. Before the horse and rider arrived at the gate, James had let go of Jayde and began to rush forward. The man on the horse unsaddled while his horse still ran and jumped to the ground rushing towards James. The two men embraced in a back slapping hug joking at each other. With arms around each other's shoulders, James turned the two of them towards Jayde, who stood awkwardly alone at the gate.

"Henry, I want you to meet someone. She is beautiful, kind, smart, and you are going to love her!" James said as the men approached Jayde.

"Brother, I am not interested in any of your damsels in distress! I am not interested in marriage! If you wish me to take her as a lover, well, that I can do, she is indeed beautiful, but she would be of no other use to me." By the time Henry noticed the tension in his brother's arm and the grip tighten on his shoulder, it was too late.

"Your lover? YOUR LOVER! I would not introduce you to the Queen of England! You are one of the most ungrateful, selfish men that I have ever known! How dare you speak of my wife in such a way! If you ever speak of her with such disrespect again, I swear, I will knock your teeth out!" James was seething.

Jayde was unaccustomed to seeing any anger from James and she did not like it. She saw the confusion and innocence in the other man's face and gently laid her tiny hands on James's forearm in hopes of calming him down. Immediately, the anger left James's body as he stepped back and wrapped his arm around Jayde's curvy waist.

"Hello, I am Lady Jayde. I am Lord James's wife. Welcome to Adoina." Jayde smiled at the man. He looked very familiar. "I am so sorry, but have we met before?"

Wife? When did James marry? Wow. Look at that smile. I bet her smile could melt ice. Her eyes were like nothing he had ever seen before. They were as deep green as summer grass and bright with life. They sparkled like an emerald and warmed his soul. She was looking at him as though she were expecting him to say something.

"Did you say something?" Henry asked.

Jayde looked up at James in confusion, how did he not hear anything she had just said?

James could not contain himself any longer. He roared with laughter embarrassing both his wife and brother. "Henry, I believe you have met your match. Someone more beautiful than you, and she has made you lose your senses. Henry, this is my *wife*, Lady Jayde. Jayde this is my brother, Lord Henry."

Jayde smiled warmly at Henry. He was familiar. He was a darker more petite image of James. Not quite as handsome though. His hair was not curly like James, nor did he have dimples like James.

Henry could not believe this. How did his brother find a woman as exquisite as this lovely little creature! Especially James. He was so different from himself and Raymond. Where the two younger brothers were dark haired and darker skinned, James had their mother's fair curly hair, and golden skin.

"Come, let us go in and sit. Your men can take their horses to the stables and get settled in." Taking Jayde's hand, they walked together to the hall where Maggie gave Henry a maternal hug, while wiping away tears.

Once the three were seated James explained how he came to be engaged, then married and that he had needed to return to Adonia to pay for some animals and to speak to Lord Dario. He told of the chaos, destruction and death that awaited him when he arrived. He left out the whipping that Lady Ethna had done to Jayde, he did not wish to humiliate her any further than she had already been humiliated.

Henry enjoyed the quiet conversations he shared with Jayde. It was a nice change from the boisterous voices of James and Raymond. He discovered that he and his little sister had a lot in common. Both loving music and chess, they agreed to a game after the evening meal.

James sat back watching and listening to Jayde and Henry talk. He could not help but feel a little bit of jealousy noticing that there was much in common between the two of them. Of course they had more in common, James had grown up and taken care of their family while Henry and Raymond played and enjoyed their childhood. James had never had time to enjoy chess, or literature.

Henry could feel the jealousy exuding from James. Unsure what had caused the sudden shift in mood, he excused himself and went to check on his men. Adonia was beautiful and he hoped to spend the afternoon wandering about. Standing, he gave Jayde a brotherly hug, slapped James on the shoulder and left the hall.

James grabbed Jayde by her waist and pulled her to him. Tilting her chin up, he touched his lips to hers, feeling the fire ignite within him while Jayde's hands rested on his biceps. Gently he traced her lips with his tongue before delicately slipping his tongue into her mouth. The moment his tongue found hers, Jayde's knees buckled, giving James a perfect excuse to scoop her up into his arms and carry her up to their chamber. He wanted to make love to her. To give her unimaginable pleasure, and hear her cry out his name. He wanted to touch every curve, taste every inch, and tease any part of her he could. He longed to take her firm round breasts in his hands and suckle her nipples, nibbling until they were hard peaks. Laying her down on their bed, James unlaced her shoes and pulled down her stockings. Sitting between her legs, he lifted one leg and starting at her small ankle and ran his hand up her strong muscular calf. Slowly, with his mouth he began to follow the path his hands took. Reaching her knee, he could hear her breathing quicken. Pushing his hand farther, he found her core. Anticipating his mouth reaching her hot wet virgin core, he barely heard the sound of horns above her gasps. Reaching mid-thigh with his mouth he finally heard the family song trumpeting again. Growling he pulled himself up and listened. Looking at Jayde's flushed face, his disappointment and frustration showed.

"My love, we must get up. If I am correct an uninvited brother is arriving." James reached down and picked up Jayde's stocking, putting it back on, covering up her beautiful legs inch by inch.

Embarrassed by her behavior and lack of self-control, Jayde tried to turn from James to lace her shoes and fix her hair. What does James think of her? She fought back the tears that were coming fast until she felt James's arm around her shoulders.

"Darling, do not cry! I promise, we will make time to start again what we could not finish and this time, I shall delight all of your senses. I had no idea I was so good!" James teased Jayde in hopes of lightening her mood and ceasing her tears.

Laughter erupted from Jayde's mouth. Giving way to tears and laughter, she let James take her shoes from her, slip them on her feet and lace them up. Wiping her face, Jayde smiled at James, grateful for his humor. Taking his offered hand she stood up and together, they walked quickly back down to the gate.

Waiting for them at the gate was Henry, looking a little sheepish. "I might have forgotten to mention that I sent a messenger to Raymond calling for reinforcements. You were cryptic in your message, simply stating you needed help. I hope this does not put strain on Adonia. My apologies little sister." Henry's heart nearly leaped out of his body when he received her smile.

Raymond did not make the entrance that Henry had. He rode with his knights as a group at a controlled pace to the gates of Adonia. Raymond dismounted and walked to each of his brothers giving them polite hugs, before turning his attention to Jayde.

"My lady, not even the stars in heaven could compete with such radiance as yours. It is an honor, I am Lord Raymond de Seaton. The youngest and most handsome, may I be so blessed to know your name?" Raymond had taken Jayde's hand in his and softly kissed the back of it looking up at her through his long lashes.

Jayde could not contain the giggles bubbling up from inside. "It is my pleasure to meet you Lord Raymond. I am Lady Jayde, the wife of Lord James de Seaton, perhaps you know of him?" Jayde could not help but tease the young man in front of her. James had not prepared her for his youngest and most charming brother.

Henry nearly died of laughter as he watched humility and embarrassment consume their baby brother.

Beaming with pride, James placed an arm around Jayde's shoulders in a possessive manner. "Baby brother, are you finished making a fool of yourself? Welcome to Adonia. Would you like to show your men to the stables and fields then join us for the midday meal?"

Nodding quietly, Raymond led his men through the gates and soon joined James, Jayde and Henry in the hall. Seeing James and Jayde sitting next to one another and Henry sitting next to James, left an empty seat next to Jayde. Raymond blushed as he walked around the table to sit and eat.

"Tell me Lord Raymond, what do you occupy your time with when you are not trying to sweep married women off of their feet?" Jayde could not turn down this opportunity to tease him yet again.

Laughing, Raymond replied, "Well, if my attempts to sweep married ladies off of their feet fail, I usually will settle for dining with darling little sisters."

Being so close in age, Jayde and Raymond found it easy to talk and got along quite well. While James and Henry were discussing war tactics, weapons, and what should be done to help Adonia recover and flourish, Raymond told Jayde all about his recent trip to the King's Court. Describing the hideous dresses and the hideous women who wore them and blushing and speaking quietly about one young lady in particular, Lady Helen Latham.

Jayde spent the rest of the day keeping busy trying to repair some of the damage that Lady Ethna had done over the years while sending servants to clean the rafters, windows and tapestries in the hall. Tomorrow she would explore each room and sort out what needed to be accomplished to guarantee that Henry and Raymond would have clean chambers to sleep in. Once Jayde had finished sending servants to various jobs of cleaning, she found Abigail and instructed her regarding the evening meal. Jayde wanted to make sure that every knight had food to fill his stomach.

James, Henry and Raymond spent the remainder of the day in the fields. James, still healing, could not train, but instead jested at his brothers and worked with the Falconers. Later, he would need to see that the stable had plenty of stable boys to tend to all of the horses for the night. Tomorrow he would need to make better arrangements for all of the horses and knights. He would need to speak with Jayde about asking the people of Adonia to offer their homes to some of the knights.

The hall was filled that evening with all one hundred and fifty knights for the evening meal. To James, the sound was deafening. Even the battle cries of war seemed quieter than the hall this evening. Jayde had insisted that everyone eat together, something about tradition. Jayde seemed at her most comfortable, almost seeming like second nature to have so many people around. James enjoyed seeing a light in her eyes that he had never seen before, and could feel her joy.

61

Everyone was tired after the evening meal and Jayde excused herself to retire early. Tomorrow was going to be busy for everyone in Adonia. Climbing the stairs alone, Jayde stopped at the door to the chamber she grew up in. Touching the door, she hesitated, then decided that tonight was not the time to address this room or the memories that lay in it. Suddenly feeling as though all of her energy had been taken from her, Jayde turned and made her way to hers and James chamber. Changing into her chemise, Jayde stoked the fire, and climbed into bed pulling the bedding up to her chin. Feeling complete for the first time since she was a young girl, Jayde closed her eyes sighing and within moments, she was sound asleep.

James enjoyed ale with his brothers and knights, reliving the past, and discussing the future. Henry spoke of hoping to be as lucky as James and to find a wife as beautiful, witty, and brave as Jayde someday. Both Henry and Raymond teased James asking when they should expect to be uncles. That was when James sobered, and explained what had happened to Jayde the night prior to their wedding and confessing that their marriage had not been consummated yet. He made his brothers swear to never discuss any of this with Jayde. Henry and Raymond looked at each other, both sharing a look and thought of true respect for their brave beautiful baby sister. Finally, the three men said goodnight, all of them going their own way feeling closer as a family than they had since their parents had passed fourteen years ago. Who would have thought that it would take so much tragedy and heart ache for this family to feel whole again?

James walked up to their chamber quietly so as to not wake his sleeping wife. Slowly opening the chamber door, he saw Jayde asleep with a smile upon her face. Crossing the room, James stoked the fire, stripped his clothes off and climbed into bed next to Jayde, leaning forward to kiss her cheek before tucking her against him and quickly falling asleep.

Chapter 5

James was delighted by the view of Jayde in bed next to him. Her chemise was thin and he could see the curve of her breast, the circle and tip of her nipple. Envisioning what he could start, he barely noticed Jayde's green eyes looking up at him.

Grabbing the bedding and tucking it up to her chin, giving him a look of warning Jayde said, "Do not start that again. My day is quite full and already the sun has risen and I am still in bed."

Smiling devilishly, James wiggled his eyebrows at Jayde and threw a large hairy leg across Jayde's waist and pulled her closer to him. Tipping his head to hers, he kissed her cheek, then her jaw, then her neck. Nibbling her ear lobes, he growled like a wild beast, whispering into her ear how hungry he was. Then he began to tickle her sides, while growling into her neck.

Jayde's laughter was contagious and soon they were both tickling each other, rolling in the bed laughing uncontrollably. Finally, Jayde begged for no more. Laying on their backs in one another's arms, catching their breath, James remembered he wanted to discuss Adonia with Jayde.

"Adonia deserves to have someone here, do you agree?" James asked.

"I do agree, but we cannot be in two places at once. What do you have in mind?" Jayde was worried about the future of her childhood home.

"I want to know what you would think about gifting Adonia to Henry. He wants to have a place of his own. Adonia is well established, needs change, and a strong level head to thrive under. I believe that Henry is that man and I believe he is ready." James studied Jayde as he spoke. He wanted to be able to read her true feelings in case she tried to lie to not hurt his feelings. Instead, James saw her face light up at the suggestion.

Jayde thought Henry would be exactly what Adonia needed. Adonia seemed to need Henry as much as it seemed that Henry needed Adonia. She agreed that a more perfect match would never be found. Excited about their plans for Adonia, they quickly dressed and went out to search for Henry to discuss with him their idea. Finding Henry in the field training with the other knights, Jayde and James pulled him aside.

"Henry, Jayde and I are worried about Adonia." James baited his brother.

"Why? What is wrong? Is there a threat to Adonia? I will help you fight." Henry's eager response made James and Jayde smile at one another.

"Well, Adonia needs change, guidance, and someone who will love the town and people. James and I cannot be here, we cannot care for Adonia the way it needs to be cared for." Jayde's love for Adonia poured out in her voice.

"Jayde and I have discussed the future of Adonia, and we believe that it needs you. We want to gift all of Adonia to you. What are your thoughts?" James was nearly as excited as Jayde and the seconds that it took for Henry to answer seemed like hours.

"Are you sure? I can manage it for you if you are not sure." Henry asked.

"I cannot think of anyone else I would rather to have here to love Adonia than you. Please, think about it?" Jayde's heart was pounding in her throat. What if Henry said no?

"I would be honored to take Adonia." Dropping down to one knee in front of Jayde and taking one of her hands in his, "Jayde, I promise to love all of Adonia the way it deserves, forever, you have my word."

Henry felt as though he had been rewarded when another smile from Jayde made his heart skip a beat with pride and loyalty. Jumping up he wrapped his hands on her waist, lifting her into the sky and twirling her in circles loving the sound of her laughter. Setting her down, Henry saw the scowl and jealousy on James face.

"Well, I should get back to training with my men. Tomorrow I would like to look over the books for

Adonia and review where the income is." With that statement, Henry turned and left, only stopping to look back after he had reached where he had been training.

Jayde and James turned towards the castle, joined hands and leaned into one another as they walked back to the castle. When James and Jayde reached their chamber, Maggie had already come and gone and left a tray of food for them. Their midday meal was simple, consisting of cold meats, cheeses and wine. James stoked the fire as Jayde prepared a plate for him. Jayde's back was no longer tearing open each time she moved and now Maggie came to check James's injury in the mornings only. They were healing both inside and out.

James tried everything he could think of to keep Jayde with him in their chamber after their midday meal. He wanted to start again what they had not finished yesterday. He wanted to discover every hidden curve, find each sensitive spot and taste her sweetness. He longed to lay in bed all day touching her bare skin and stroke her long soft hair.

Jayde found it hard to resist James's hands as they teased down her back and arms. James had untied the laces of her dress twice now. If she did not leave this room, she knew she would find herself without a single stitch of clothing on. There was so much to do still before the day ended. Rushing downstairs, she found Maggie and asked her if she could gather some servants and to meet her at her father's chamber door. Jayde wanted at least her father's room to be clean and available for Henry after the evening meal. He would be Lord of Adonia when Jayde and James finally left.

Discussing what needed to be accomplished in Henry's new room with Maggie, Jayde left Maggie to manage the servants and divide chores. Jayde took four servants to her old chamber. She had not been in her chamber since she left two and a half weeks ago and the tipped over bench, ripped bedding and broken statuette were evidence of the destruction of Ethna's rage. The broken bench was sent for repair. The bedding was sent for laundering, clean bedding was put on, the window was cleaned and the floors were to be scrubbed. Moving on, Jayde and the last two women went to the solar. Ethna rarely spent time in here, so it still looked the way it had when her mother had used it. It was filthy though. Three panes of glass from the window had long since been broken and birds had used that as an entrance to come in and nest. The two women began to carefully take down the tapestries and set them aside to be cleaned. Jayde began to dust the small book collection that her mother kept. These were her mother's most prized possessions. Gently touching the binding of each book, Jayde smiled remembering many afternoons and evenings spent listening to her mother read from these very books. She would make sure to take these back to Era with her. She hoped that one day when she was a mother, she too would sit down and read books to her children teaching them to read and write. Working with the women in the solar, Jayde began to wipe down the books, shelves, and table. Finally, after hours of cleaning, the three ladies finished by scrubbing the floor. Tomorrow, a craftsman would come to the castle and inventory all of the panes of stained glass that would need to be repaired but today, the two servants would start cleaning the first of the three tapestries. Slowly making her way to the room that would now become Lord Henry's, Jayde sank to her knees and began to help scrub the blood stain off of the floor.

Maggie watched as Jayde lowered to her knees and began to scrub her father's blood stain from the stone floor. She did not cry. She simply scrubbed. Maggie stretched her arthritic back, then knelt down next to Jayde and began to scrub again.

"Maggie, you know Lord Henry much better than I, what do you think he would like to have in this room?" Jayde wanted to make sure that before she left, that Henry felt completely at home here.

Maggie was startled. Was she not devastated at what she was cleaning? "My Lady, I recall that Lord Henry is quite fond of shades of blue and green." There was an awkward silence before Maggie continued. "My Lady, are you not pained at the scene before you? You should be down in the hall, eating with your family, not cleaning the stains of your father's death."

Sitting back on her knees, Jayde asked, "Maggie, what can I do? I cannot change the past. I must accept this reality, and learn to live my life." Sighing, "My father would not have wanted me to spend one more day crying. He would want me to be laughing and spending time with family and those that love me. I believe I am in the company of someone who is family." Jayde smiled at Maggie, then grabbed a clean, wet linen and wiped the floor of any bubbles. Standing, Jayde and Maggie stood back and looked at all of the hard work that had been done. The room was clean.

Stepping out of the room, Maggie handed the bucket and linens to one of the servants. She then ordered a bath to be taken to Lady Jayde's chamber and a plate of food. At Jayde's protests, Maggie took her arm and hooked her arm around it.

"My Lady, you must go and rest now. You have worked harder than any Lady should, although I suspect it is not the first time you have worked so hard. You must think of your strength and health. Your back is healing very well, but if you exert yourself, you could become very ill again." Maggie did not want to take any chances with Jayde's health. She still thought that Jayde was too thin and too pale. "My Lady, I will show Lord Henry to his chamber this evening. You go to your room and I will have a bath and evening meal sent up for you." If Lady Catherine were still alive, she would have loved having Lady Jayde as a daughter. The thought brought tears to Maggie's eyes.

Too tired and hungry to argue, Jayde smiled and gave Maggie a hug, then turned and went to her own chamber where a bath was already being prepared. Within minutes, Jayde was soaking in a hot bath, a fire cast dancing shadows on the walls, thinking about how much her life had changed in the last three weeks. So involved in her thoughts and memories, Jayde did not hear Maggie come in with a tray of food.

"Oh! Maggie! I did not hear you come in! Thank you for the bath and for preparing a plate for me. Did James ask where I was?" Jayde was so relaxed, she had not felt this calm in such a very long time.

"I hope I did not startle you Lady Jayde. I am glad you are enjoying your bath and I hope you enjoy your meal while it is still hot. Lord James was entertaining Raymond and Henry, but I reassured him you were fine. Everyone seems happy and enjoying themselves in the hall. I suspect the men will be up late, but I promise to ensure that Lord Henry is shown his chamber and Lord Raymond to a guest chamber. Do you need anything else Lady Jayde? Would you like me to wash or comb your hair?" Maggie again could not help but to think about Lady Catherine. Lady Jayde was kind like Lady Catherine. Maybe Lady Jayde reminded her of Lady Catherine. Lady Catherine was known to have a slight temper though.

"That is kind of you, I will manage on my own though. Thank you." Jayde was famished and ready to climb into bed and succumb to blissful sleep.

Turning to face Jayde, Maggie said, "very well My Lady. I shall send in Anna to help you dress. Shall I leave the bath for Lord James?"

"That would be wonderful. Thank you again." Jayde submerged under the water once more as Maggie left to send Anna in. Standing up, Jayde began to squeeze the water out of her long hair before stepping out to dry off and put on her chemise and eat dinner. Just then, there was a familiar soft knock on the door as Anna entered the room.

Anna winced seeing Jayde's back as she crossed the room to help dry Jayde's hair. The wounds were now scars, angry reminders of the pain and power wielded by Lady Ethna. Once Jayde was dressed, Anna sat Jayde down to eat while she combed her never ending hair. It took nearly an hour but it was finally free of all tangles. Bidding Jayde good night, Anna took the nearly empty tray from the room.

Climbing into bed it took only moments before Jayde was asleep.

James, Henry and Raymond were yet again the last of the men to be in the hall drinking and joking. Standing and stretching, James saw Maggie standing quietly in a corner looking exhausted.

"Well brothers, I believe it is time to end our stories. Sleep well." James turned and saying good night to Maggie, he walked up the stairs to his chamber.

Stepping forward, Maggie said, "Excuse me Lord Henry and Lord Raymond, your chambers are ready. Please follow me."

Henry and Raymond looked at each other sharing a look of surprise before following Maggie upstairs where she stopped at the first door.

"Lord Henry, this is your new chambers. Lady Jayde has tapestries to be hung tomorrow and paintings as well, she hopes it is to your liking. Will there be anything that I may get for you My Lord?" Maggie was proud of the work that had been done.

"Thank you," Lord Henry was amazed at the size of the room. There was a desk and chair in a corner, two sitting chairs, a fireplace in the corner near the desk and a second fireplace in the corner opposite. The four post bed was enormous, with white linen draping around the frame. It was beautiful. Turning around, Henry realized he was alone.

While Lord Henry stood open mouthed, taking in his new chamber, Maggie escorted Lord Raymond to his guest chamber. Opening the door, the room was simple, but quite adequate. The four post bed was draped with cream linen and the bedding was the same color. There was a seat at the window, and a fire roaring in the fireplace on the wall opposite the bed.

"Can I get you anything else Lord Raymond?" Maggie was exhausted. Hopefully tomorrow would be an easier day.

"No, thank you. Good night Maggie." Lord Henry was appreciative for the change in sleeping quarters.

"Very well, good night My Lord." Maggie closed the door as she left and retired to her own sleeping quarters for the night.

Chapter 6

The people of Adonia awoke to a chill in the air that could only mean snow was coming. By the midday meal, the snow began to fall and there was rush throughout Adonia, to prepare livestock and cupboards for the snowfall. The snow fell steadily for three days until the snow was knee deep.

One the first day of snowfall, there was plenty to do within the castle walls. The now clean tapestries were dry and Jayde had decorated Henry's and Raymond's chambers with the tapestries as well as adding more furniture to Raymond's guest chambers. Jayde finally handed over all of the keys to the rooms of Adonia to Henry. It felt both suffocating and lifting all at once. The finality of her Father's death, weighing her down, yet freeing her from the grief that had imprisoned her after her mother's death. The second day Jayde won game after game of chess with her brothers and James, while growing more comfortable with teasing her husband. Her brothers seemed to be enjoying teasing James as well. Anytime James was watching, either Henry or Raymond made it a point to stand too close, hold her hand, and even push strands of fallen hair back from her face.

Despite the past two days of being a pawn for abuse of James, Jayde was still not accustomed to men holding her hand and was most uncomfortable with the hugs and kisses her brothers constantly showered upon her. By the time the evening meal was finished, Jayde could see the storm brewing in James's eyes and could feel the tension in the air.

James had been watching his brothers make fools of themselves these past two days, showering his wife with kisses, hugs and whispering words of poetry. He tried to let it go, tried to not be upset by their affections to his wife, but his brothers pushed their limits when they insisted that James let them sit on either side of their darling little sister during evening meal. Finally when he felt he could be tortured no more, Raymond offered his arm to Jayde to escort her to the room where she and James slept, securing her hand before she could answer and pulling her forward as though they were two lovers, slipping off to explore one another. James strode forward spinning Raymond around by the shoulders and punched him in his jaw so hard Raymond fell to the floor. Turning around, James jerked Jayde into his arms and kissed her hard nearly bruising her lips.

Confused, and angry, Jayde pushed and kicked at James until he released her. Fire burned in her eyes as she glared at James. She walked to the bottom of the stairs and turned to face the three men. "The three of you are shameful! How dare you two use me as a pawn in some game against your brother! And you! You act like you own me! I am not owned by anyone regardless of what the church says. Enjoy sleeping with your brothers as you will not find warmth with me tonight!" Henry and Raymond burst with laughter while James simply stood there bewildered not quite understanding what he had done wrong. Jayde then turned and stormed up the stairs to the warm and empty room. She dressed in a sleeping gown, and for the first time in days climbed into bed to be alone all night. Curling up into a ball, Jayde cried herself to sleep.

The three men awoke with the hopes of apologizing and begging for forgiveness at breakfast. Jayde did not join them for the meal though. Instead, the men sat silently, eating, trying to plan a way to win a smile from her. They decided it would be best if Jayde had time to be angry but when she did not join them for their midday meal James's embarrassment became anger. He took the steps two at a time throwing their chamber door open. The room was empty and cold. The fire had died hours before and the room gave no inclination that Jayde had been there at all this day. James ran down the stairs in a panic and raced to the kitchen to find Maggie. "Where is she?" He demanded. "Where is Jayde?"

"My Lord, Lady Jayde left at dawn this morning with a pack full of food and some wool blankets. Maybe you boys will learn how to treat a lady! Before you ask again, she did not say where she was going." Maggie for the first time, did not feel afraid of the temper of Lord James. In truth she hoped that Lady Jayde could teach all three of those boys a lesson. James was so consumed with anger and concern he did not even think to remind Maggie of whom she was speaking to. He strode back out to the hall and then out to the stables his brothers close on his heels.

"What has happened?" Raymond asked of James.

"James, is everything okay?" Henry worried.

"Damn that foolish girl! She left at dawn with food and blankets, did not tell anyone where she was going and the newly fallen snow has covered any tracks left by her horse. She is going to freeze to death." James began walking to the stables with his brothers following close behind him. "We will start at the river in the woods, I know she likes to be there when she is upset." James hoped and prayed that she would be by the river where he had first met her. What was she thinking?

The three men saddled and mounted their horses and raced at a neck breaking pace through the gates and woods to the river side. Jayde was not there and there was no sign of her. James's anger was growing and he struggled to keep his panic suppressed. They had only been out in the snow for a short time and were shivering, Jayde had been out all day. What if something had happened? She could be laying hurt in the snow, unable to call for help.

Henry saw the anger and growing concern on his brother's face. Suddenly, he remembered something Jayde had said a few days ago. "The other day when Jayde was showing me Adonia, she pointed out a plateau that overlooked the woods. She may have gone there?" Henry spoke cautiously. He knew his brother had a temper that he rarely showed, but the few times he had seen James angry, he had been grateful it was directed at someone else. It took just one look from

James when Henry offered, "Follow me, I'll take you in that direction."

It took the men nearly an hour of hard riding before they reached the base of a cliff that had a narrow path twisting up into the rocks. James led the small group up the cliff slipping several times before finally finding Jayde's horse waiting patiently in the mouth of a shallow cave. Despite the lengthy hike, James could not stop to rest. He could see that the plateau was above them and accessible only by foot. Pushing on, the three men dismounted and started the climb up to where they hoped Jayde safely sat. Finally, after another hour of treacherous hiking, they reached the plateau and the scene they came upon left them silent and still. They found Jayde kneeling next to a rare winter rose looking out beyond Adonia and the woods below. You could see the river, and hills and a few other estates.

Without turning, Jayde spoke. "After my mother passed, I found this place. As I continued to visit here, I noticed that each winter a single red rose grew. I took comfort believing that it was my mother's way of telling me she loved me and watched over me." James walked to her and kneeled down beside her. Letting go of his anger, he took her hand in his but remained silent. While he understood her pain, it was different. After his parents' death, James had not had the time for grief the way his brothers had. He had been forced to support his brothers and run his estates. Raymond and Henry however, understood Jayde's grief exactly. They understood the pain that consumed her and left a raw gaping wound in her heart. They had not had the responsibilities of needing to provide for a family and run an estate as James had. Stepping forward, both Henry and Raymond knelt on the cold hard ground behind Jayde where they silently said a prayer for their parents and two brothers. Not another word was spoken until finally Jayde broke the silence. "We should go, it is cold and the snow looks to start to fall heavily again soon."

The four of them made their way down the cliff and back to the castle. When Maggie saw the group approaching, she ordered that a hot bath be brought up to each room for all of them to bathe and set about to light the fire in each room. With the bath, hot food and wine were brought up to help warm them all.

Once in their room, James helped Jayde to remove her frozen clothes and set them near the fire to melt the ice off. After undressing himself, he picked up his stiff and cold wife and set her in his lap in the tub filled with hot water.

"I do not know what I did yesterday that upset you so. I wish you would tell me so that I do not offend you again." James then kissed her cheek and pulled her back to rest against his chest.

Jayde took a moment to calm her temper. How does he not know what he did wrong? "I am not your property. You cannot walk up and kiss me to mark me as your territory like a dog peeing on a tree. I will not tolerate that behavior."

Tolerate that behavior? Tolerate! James tilted his head back and roared with laughter. He laughed so hard that tears began to stream down his cheeks. He felt Jayde trying to squirm out of his arms, her round butt rubbing against his shaft making him sober and quiet. Turning her chin to face him he calmly kissed her. Jayde did not like fighting his kisses and loved how they made every inch of her entire body come to life. Jayde turned her body to face his, resting her breasts on his chest that was covered in thick blonde curling hair. To get more comfortable, Jayde sat between James's legs placing one leg of hers on either side of his hips pausing only a moment when she felt the tip of his hard shaft touch against her hot core. The jolt of lightning the touch elicited made her hungrier for his mouth and craving his hands to caress her body as he had nights before.

Jayde's innocence only made the desire James felt in his heart and through his body stronger. He nearly lost his mind when Jayde turned and straddled him and it took more effort than he knew he had to keep from plunging deep into her. Instead, he wrapped his hands around her rib cage feeling the fresh scars across her back and began teasing her nipples with his thumbs. Jayde's kisses became more frantic and bruising as James continue to rub and trace her nipples sending jolts through her body. After hearing Jayde moan through their kiss as her nipples became hard little buds, he wanted to bring her to ecstasy in every way he knew how. He pulled his mouth from hers and began to nibble down her neck tracing her collar bone with his tongue. Grabbing one of her breasts, he tilted her nipple upward towards his mouth and hungrily descended upon it.

Jayde gasped aloud as she felt James's warm wet mouth engulf her nipple. Her body was alive and tingling with each slight touch. Tipping her head back, she arched her back towards him calling out his name as he sucked on her nipple.

James nearly died watching her pleasure. He picked her up and carried her to the rug before the fire, careful to spread her long hair out beside her. He returned his mouth to her breast, licking, then gently blowing on one before tending to the other breast. With one hand supporting her breast, his other hand began to explore the rest of her body. Softly caressing her stomach, then down to her hips and finally her thigh. He drew his hand back to her hip and reached underneath her to cup and squeeze her butt.

Jayde's body was on fire, moving and acting on its own. After James had squeezed her butt his hands ran down the back of her thigh curling his fingers up towards her core. Jayde nearly choked on her gasp when she felt James slide his fingers into her at first. Gently stroking deeper each time, he felt her begin to relax as he began to move faster within her. She felt her hips thrusting up to meet his hand until finally she screamed out as she felt her senses explode.

James lay next to her, breathing shallow and rasping breaths, enamored with the beauty of what Jayde had just experienced. Slowly he kissed her shoulders, neck and mouth before kneeling between her legs. Placing a hand on either side of her shoulders, James bent his arms and slowly brought his shaft to the tip of her center. Jayde's eyes flew open and she solemnly watched as James began to slip himself into her where his fingers had just been. James was able to thrust into her completely, groaning with pleasure feeling the tight warmth deep within. Pulling out and thrusting again, he heard Jayde gasp. Opening his eyes, he saw hers were closed and her head tilted back slightly. Slowly he continued to thrust watching her and feeling her learn to move with him to their own rhythm. Placing one hand behind her back, he pulled her to a sitting position without breaking apart and stood up walking her to the tapestry covered wall. Bracing her back against the tapestry, he cupped her butt and began to lift her up and down on his shaft faster and harder until they both cried out with pleasure.

Weak and shaking, Jayde clung to James as he turned and carried her to their bed sitting down still deep inside of her, he pulled her head to his chest as he laid down. Within moments, they had fallen fast asleep.

James awoke feeling Jayde shiver still laying on top of him. The fire was nothing more than glowing embers and the room had grown cold. Carefully rolling Jayde from him, he walked to the fire and added wood warming the room quickly. James quickly climbed back into the bed next to Jayde covering them up with the bedding. He laid next to Jayde watching her sleep and remembering their evening. She was worth waiting until she was ready for him. Finally, nearly a month after they were married, they had their wedding night. James pulled Jayde's curled body to his chest holding her close and drifted back to sleep.

Jayde woke up at dawn with James hairy arm across her waist and cupping one breast. She escaped his arm to get up and stoke the fire, and relieve herself. As Jayde tip toed past James back to the bed, she felt a strong arm reach around her waist and throw her down upon the bed. James began to tickle Jayde until she begged for him to stop.

James nuzzled her neck growling under her ear starting her giggles again. "Where has my Wild wife gone? Hmm?" Nipping her breasts, running his hands down her ribs, stomach and hips, James began to caress and tease her body again and Jayde's body reacted instantly. The deep ache and throbbing in her core was so strong it practically hurt. Spreading her legs she arched her hips to him, consumed in seeking the pleasure they had experienced the night before.

James's lust was too strong to hold back this time. Sliding his fingers into her, feeling how wet she was, knowing she was ready for him, he could not control himself. Supporting his body with his hands, he slammed into her, blind with desire. He was surprised when he felt Jayde's body match his own frantic pace as she clawed at his back and arms as though only he could save her. Jayde cried out first and James just a moment after. Covered in beads of sweat, James kissed her mouth sweetly before rolling to her side. Slowly he caressed her arm, then breast, and down to her soft smooth stomach. He could nearly cover her entire stomach with the span of his hand. Looking up at her smiling face, with complete seriousness, he asked, "What would you think about us having a family. Lots of children. Do you want that with me?"

Jayde's breathe caught, and her smile faded. Although she had always dreamed of having children of her own, she had yet to consider that those children would be with James. Sitting up, Jayde spoke her mind honestly, "I do not know. I want children, I just had not stopped to think of them with you. I suppose that our actions could have created a child though."

James did not think before speaking. "I love you Jayde, I think I have loved you since the moment I met you in the woods. Do you love me?"

Love? Fear flashed in Jayde's eyes and she held her breath. What did she say back? She was frozen, unable to move, unable to breath, and unable to speak. All she could do was stare at him.

James began to feel foolish for professing his love. She was still a child, and a child who had lived a painful lonely life. But she had not shut him out. She did not draw back from him, she looked scared. "Is it truly so horrible that I love you Jayde?" James whispered, desperate to hide the hurt his heart began to feel.

"I do not know what to say, please forgive me." Jayde was near tears. She could see the pain she was causing him and wished she could tell him she loved him too.

James kissed her forehead and stood up. He needed to walk away before he lashed out. A beautiful perfect moment and now, this. Without looking back, James dressed and left their room colliding with Henry not even stopping to excuse himself.

Jayde heard the door close behind James just moments before she felt the hot tears slide down her cheeks. She curled her knees to her chest, and buried her face into her hands allowing herself to be consumed by her emotions. Finally, Jayde got up and dressed, slowly making her way down to the hall for breakfast. Her eyes were swollen from crying and she only picked at her food. Henry and Raymond tried to make conversation with Jayde and understand what had happened. Jayde just sat there pushing her food around unable to speak or look at her brothers. She spent her day introducing the people of Adonia to Henry and reassuring them that he would be fair and honest. Jayde skipped the midday and evening meal, retreating finally to her room falling into bed crying herself to sleep.

After James had left that morning, he had paced along the outer wall until he stumbled on a brick. Looking closer, he found a hole in the wall, well covered by foliage on both the inside and outside of the wall. He spent the day repairing the hole in the wall and searching for any other weaknesses or holes. When he came in at the end of the day for the evening meal, Jayde was not there and neither Henry nor Raymond were very interested in conversation

Henry and Raymond had discussed the little problem between their brother and new sister and decided they should make them no longer needed. It was agreed that the newlyweds needed to return to their own home and sort out their own problems.

James finished his meal and requested a bath be sent up. If Jayde wanted to stay in their room all day hiding from him so be it, but he would not hide from her. If she could not bear to see him without his clothes, she could find a different room to sleep in. He was not going to use her for intimacy or be used by her. When he walked into their room, all of his anger left him. There, curled up on the bed was Jayde's petite body, sound asleep dressed in the clothes she had worn earlier. When Maggie opened the door to begin the process of bringing up his bath, James quickly placed his finger to his lips and then looked again at the sleeping form on the bed. His bath was quietly filled and more wood was brought up for the fire. James quietly bathed, keeping watch over Jayde and remembering again the evening they shared the night before.

James climbed into bed beside Jayde pulling up a blanket over her before turning over and falling into a fitful sleep.

Jayde woke up to an empty bed and the sounds of wagons down below. Quickly she changed and ran through the hall out to courtyard below. There she saw Henry and Raymond ordering trunks be loaded into one wagon and fabrics into another. When they turned to see Jayde standing with her mouth hanging open, Henry turned Jayde around and ordered her to the hall to eat a morning meal.

Jayde ate quickly and went in search of Henry or Raymond to ask what was going on and where these wagons were going to. When she finally found them, they were hugging and shaking hands with James, and promising to visit soon. Where was James going? Why had he not told her? Was he planning on leaving her here? She knew she had hurt him, but she had hoped they could work through this! Maybe he was not the kind man she had once believed him to be. Maybe it was a good thing she had not been able to tell him she loved him.

"Where are *you* traveling to on this calm winter day?" Jayde demanded as she marched up to the three men. Both Henry and Raymond could feel the anger from her words. Never had they feared anyone's temper more than their brother's, but this time, both men took a step back as if to avoid a punch. The two men exchanged a glance that said more than words possibly could.

James also sensed her anger. Rather than back down, James bristled and was ready to fight back. "Oh, not hiding from me today? Splendid. I have been informed by my brothers that our presence here is no longer needed. Anything else that they need to learn they will learn as they go. If it pleases you My Lady, we can return to Era, *our* home." James's sarcasm was so thick Henry and Raymond nearly choked on it.

"Try to be patient with him Jayde, he has much to learn about women, and much to learn about being wrong." Henry said as he gave Jayde a hug then kissed each cheek.

Raymond then approached and gave Jayde a hug and kisses on the cheeks as well saying, "Be kind to one another. I sense that you both have much to learn about love and compromise. James has never had to compromise, it will be an especially difficult task for him." Instead of their words diffusing her anger, it fueled it.

Chapter 7

The group had been traveling for two days. Still, the tension between Jayde and James prevailed, and the weather seemed to match their mood. James sarcasm continued to fuel Jayde's anger, which of course fueled James sarcasm. Jayde refused to sit on a wagon and instead saddled her own horse and rode it. She wanted nothing to do with James. To prove even further that she did not need him, instead of slowing her horse down to rest with the wagons, she kicked her horse forward leaving everyone behind. Hearing James call out for her to stop she pushed her horse harder and slipped into the forest. She could hear a horse behind her gaining on her and before she could turn around she felt an arm reach around her and seat her in front of a foul smelling body. Panic filled Jayde and she screamed out only once before a fist came down on her temple and her world went black.

"Jayde! Stop! We need to go around the woods!" Damn her stubborn self! She was going to get herself lost, then he'd have to go find her. Maybe then she'd stop being so determined to hate him. He watched as she veered into the woods and felt his stomach sink as he heard another horse's feet racing into the woods. Kicking his beast forward he chased after them. As he entered the wooded space, he heard a single scream cut short. Halting his war horse, he strained to listen. He heard a single horse galloping away in the distance. "JAYDE! JAYDE!" Jayde's darling mare came thru the brush slowly walking towards James. James turned his horse towards the brush that the mare had just come from and pushed his horse to gallop. Fendrel, Luther and Walker were close on James's heals through the woods. The four knights cleared the woods and saw nothing at first. Then Fendrel saw it and pointed it out to James. Dismounting, James ran to the tree pulling the dagger and note from the tree. Reading it to himself, he nearly passed out only steadying himself on the tree that had held the note. Fendrel dismounted and approached James, taking the note and reading it for himself.

James de Seaton

I told you to watch your back. You once took what was mine, and now I return the favor. I have been watching you and finally have found something you love that is worth taking.

Blaxton

Fendrel had grown up with James and therefore knew what Blaxton was speaking of, Luther and Walker however, had no idea what they were dealing with.

"Luther and Walker, go back to the wagons and continue the journey home. Fendrel, return to the wagons with them and collect provisions for you and me. We will make a camp just inside the woods here tonight and plan our next move." James gave his orders and the men dispersed to do as they were told.

James found a well-hidden spot and cleared away some branches then sat patiently, waiting for Fendrel to return. James remembered the summer well. He and Fendrel had celebrated their eighteenth birthdays just two days apart and were thirsting for adventure. James and Fendrel decided to travel for one month to get a taste of life. James was still learning how to grieve for the loss of his parents and was looking for a way to spend his anger. They traveled through many towns until finally they could smell their own stench. After getting baths and eating hot meals, they found a couple of women to enjoy some more personal pleasures with. In the morning, the two men bought wine and more food and went out to the river bank. There they ate, then drank both growlers of wine while contemplating life and the responsibilities they had. Soon they heard women nearby and decided to sneak around and take a peek. They came upon two beautiful ladies nearly nude wading into the cool slow river. In their drunken stupor, both men decided that neither women would be able to resist their looks or charms and would be grateful for the pleasure that they could bestow upon them. The blonde woman that Fendrel decided to claim did not even fight him as he raped her. The other woman had hair the color of honey. When James tried to claim her, she fought him desperately. To silence her screams, he covered her mouth with his hand. When he had pleasured himself, he rolled over and fell asleep. Fendrel awoke James several hours later noting that both women were gone. The drunken haze began to clear and their actions from that afternoon made their stomachs churn. Deciding that they needed to leave immediately, the two men quickly went back to the Inn to collect their belongings and horses. When they arrived back at the Inn, people began to gather in the streets. There were shouts of men and the crying of women. As they entered into the Inn, people were staring at them and whispering. A woman crying in the corner looked up, and pointed at them. In was the blonde woman Fendrel had raped. Soon men were descending upon them grabbing, punching and kicking them. Lord Simon's guards saved them from certain death and instead threw them into the dungeon. After spending two days in the dungeon of Lord Simon's, they were released and told to collect their belongings, leave and never to return. James had opened his mouth trying to explain what had happened, Lord Simon placed his hand in the air to silence him.

"The girl your friend took explained their, ah, situation at the river. The other young lady, hung herself in her brother's home." Lord Simon turned and walked away. James and Fendrel collected their belongings and went to the stables to leave. That is where they met Blaxton. Blaxton was the brother of the young girl who hung herself.

"I vow to you now, I will take someone who is precious to you. One day. Watch your back James, I'll be there." Blaxton then stepped back and allowed the two young men to saddle their horses and leave, never taking his eyes from James.

The memory haunted James and his fear for Jayde's safety grew. What would a vengeful man do to a young and innocent girl?

Fendrel saw James's face as he rode up. "Remembering that summer? Worried about Lady Jayde? We'll find her, I know we will."

"I am worried that it will be too late when we find her. We need a plan, and we need to act quickly. Where should we start?" James mind was racing.

"I think we should start where it all happened." Fendrel offered. "We should rest tonight, we'll be of no use if we are not rested."

Jayde woke up freezing. Her head hurt and she was scared. Where was James? Why did she have to prove she did not need him? Who had grabbed her and where was she? What should she do? Scream or sit here and wait? Just then there was a whistling and the sound of keys jingling, distant initially, then closer.

"Hello… are you awake yet little flower? I have been waiting for you for twelve years. Did you know that? You are much younger than I would have expected. You are probably close to how old Ann was. Tell me, was he kind to you or did he take you the way he took dear Ann?" Blaxton felt his anger growing watching her look of confusion and fear. Was it possible he made a mistake and taken the wrong girl?

Jayde was now even more scared than she had been before. This man seemed crazy and was reliving some memory at her expense. Her head was killing her! She should try to make him feel more comfortable with her. Then maybe she could escape. "I do not want to be a bother to you, but I am very thirsty and need to take care of some personal things."

Blaxton just laughed. "Did he ever tell you what he did to my precious baby sister? Did James ever tell you that he raped my innocent sixteen year old baby sister with his hand covering her mouth? How about that she was so ashamed that she came home and hung herself?" Laughing an even crazier laugh, he continued, "looks like he has left out some important details. See you in the morning Flower."

Jayde cringed at the sound of his laughter. There was something else about this man that was not right. What was he talking about? James? James raped a young girl? Jayde curled up on the bench she awoke on and looked out the slot in the wall allowing minimal light in. She could see the moon as it slowly rose into the sky. Finally succumbing to her fears she began to cry. She would let herself cry this one time. Only this one time. She needed to be strong, she needed to find a way out of here.

Morning could not come fast enough for Jayde. With the dawn, she was able to find a place to relieve herself and get a better idea of the room she was in. Jayde went to the window to attempt to see how high up she actually was, but was unable to see much. She heard the whistling and keys again. This time she walked to the door and waited for him

Blaxton saw her waiting at the door for him this morning. She was so young and innocent looking. That bastard probably had no idea of the darling beauty that she was. He probably used her much in the same way he had used Ann. This time however, it would be different. There would be no shame, no death. She looked scared and desperate. He would rescue her from James de Seaton.

James and Fendrel were awake and riding by dawn toward the little town that haunted each of them daily for the last 12 years. Neither man had realized how close they were, both not wanting to remember the pain they caused. James and Fendrel rode at a neck breaking pace through town to Lord Simon's gates. They announced themselves and were quickly escorted in. Lord Simon greeted them at the stables, obviously remembering who they were.

"I recall telling you to never return. There will be consequences." Lord Simon then signaled to his guards.

James thrust the note out towards Lord Simon. "Please, I have spent the last 12 years repenting, praying and changing who I am. There is not a day that goes by that I have not thought of the devastation I have caused and the good that I have robbed this town of."

Lord Simon took the note and after reading it asked, "Who is she to you?"

"She is my young wife. She has survived her mother, father and abusive step-mother. I think she even loved me at some point, but like everything else, I fear my stubbornness has managed to even kill that. If I had just let go of my pride, she would not have ridden ahead and into the woods, Blaxton would not have her somewhere, and instead, I could be showing her the garden in the courtyard below our room where she could plant what ever made her happy. I could be holding her hand right now, keeping her warm. Instead, she is probably cold, alone and scared. She is but seventeen, and everything is my fault. Please, help me before Blaxton makes mistakes that will haunt him too for the rest of his life." James was nearly in tears and ready to drop to his knees to beg if need be.

Lord Simon held his hand up to his guard and motioned for all of them to follow him into the hall. James and Fendrel followed the aged Lord Simon thru the hall to his private chamber. Lord Simon sat down, motioning for Fendrel and James to do the same. "Blaxton has not been the same since that day. He withdrew from everyone in town, and has not been around in weeks. There was rumor that he was spending quite a bit of time in an old castle that is falling apart, but I cannot be sure. If you would like, we can ride there today and search for them. To be honest though, there are many places nearby that he could be. What do you plan to do when you find him?"

James spoke carefully, "I do not wish to kill or harm him. I just want Jayde back. I will however, do what I must to keep my wife safe and rescue her from Blaxton." What James spoke and what he truly thought were completely different. If that man harmed even one perfect hair on her head, he would kill the man with his bare hands!

"I see, well, then we should ride. Let us hope that it is not too late." With that, Lord Simon stood up and walked out of the room with James and Fendrel close behind.

James, Fendrel and Lord Simon rode to the discussed castle. There was no shelter, just walls and there was no sign that anyone had been here in years. His heart sank. Lord Simon turned to James and could see the devastation on his face. Without a word, he spurred his horse onto the next place he could think of, Blaxton's home. The scene of the three men trailed by fifteen knights racing through the country sent shivers up the backs of those who witnessed it. Lord Simon motioned to the two men. "This is Blaxton's home. It looks cold and dark, so I am not sure when the last time he was home. As you can tell, he has nothing to tie him to his home."

Both James and Fendrel dismounted and walked to the home. James opened the door and found the home to be empty of all life. Anger surged through his veins as he scanned the home for any clue that would help him understand where Blaxton would have taken her. James and Fendrel left the tiny home and quietly mounted their horses. Lord Simon led the men back to his castle where the evening meal was hot and waiting. James and Fendrel graciously accepted the meal, a bath and beds to sleep on for the night.

Chapter 8

Minutes passed into hours, into days, into weeks for Jayde. Every day was the same. The man would whistle on his way to visit, slide a tray of stale bread and left over cheese and tell her the horrible story of James and Fendrel and her captor's perfect sister. This morning she made another mark on the wall. It had been ninety-eight days since she had been taken prisoner. Jayde was barely skin and bones, but still her tiny stomach was starting to grow. If she counted her weeks correctly, she was due mid to late August. She was beginning to give up hope for James to ever find her. What if he was not even looking for her! This recurring thought sent her into another round of tears that streaked her dirty face. It was midday and the rain was coming down hard. She heard the distinct sound of whistling from down the hall. Odd, he usually never visited twice in one day.

"Why do you think James has not come looking for you? He must not have loved you or he would have been here weeks ago. Do you think he has already taken another woman to his bed? Hmm, I believe I shall go find out. I should be gone for several days. I sure hope this tray of bread will sustain you while I'm gone. Although I doubt it. When I return, if you are dead, which you will most likely be, I will leave your dead body at his door. Then I shall kill him in the most slow and painful ways. What do you think? Shall I break his fingers before I cut them off, or should I begin with his toes?" Blaxton's laugh was a demonic sound that made even the fleas on her scalp be still. "Sweet dreams Flower."

"Wait! Please! Do not hurt him! Do not leave me in here to die! Please! I shall do anything!" Jayde's screams echoed down the hall chasing Blaxton's cackling laugh. "PLEASE!"

Jayde watched through the narrow window as her captor rode out of sight. Slowly sinking to the floor, Jayde gave in to the body shaking sobs, the sounds echoing into the empty castle.

James and Fendrel had been wandering for weeks. Lord Simon had been kind enough to allow them to return to his castle when needed, but James could only think of the pain and misery Jayde must be feeling. James and Fendrel were so near exhaustion they were practically falling off of their horses. The rain was pouring down in sheets so heavy they could not see. They decided to seek shelter in the nearby woods. Finally finding shelter under a tree, the two men sat on the cold wet ground. Looking up, from the ground, James saw what appeared to be the top of a wall. Jumping to his feet, he began to run towards it. It took a minute for Fendrel to react and chase after James. They came to a clearing and saw a castle kept well hidden in the trees. It looked abandoned. James's heart jumped to his throat. Silently he prayed that this was it. Slowly walking into the ruins of the castle, they found signs that someone had been here recently. Both men stood still, straining to hear any noise. A chill ran up their spines as they heard a ghostly sound echoing from somewhere within the castle walls. Fendrel touched James on the arm and motioned to go back outside. Something about the sound compelled James to stay within the walls however. Slowly, he started to walk along the wall to the stairs that led to the bed chambers above. Once upstairs, James and Fendrel started to open the doors one at a time. Each room only had broken furniture in it. Stopping to listen again, the sounds had stopped. Maybe they had gone in the wrong direction? Maybe they were both just so tired they imagined it all.

Jayde heard doors opening and closing below, and heard people whispering. Then all the noise stopped. No! They were leaving! No!

"Please! Please! Help me! Please! Do not leave me here! Please…" too weak to stand, Jayde lay across the floor trying to catch her breath.

Fendrel barely heard the quiet cries for help that James somehow heard. "JAYDE! JAYDE! I am here! Keep calling! Help me find you!"

"Here! I am up here! Please! James!" He was here! He came for her! "James! I am here! Do not leave me! I am here!" Jayde began to laugh she was so relieved. He made it! He had found her!

"Wild! I am here! I am here!" James began to cry as he realized that his search was near an end. A window along the wall let in enough light to spot the small staircase in the corner. James ran up the stairs and found a wooden door with bars on it. Looking in he could see a child laying on the floor laughing and crying all at once. "Jayde?" The person on the floor did not resemble his wife. This was but a girl. A small child filthy beyond imagination.

Jayde looked up from the floor to see James standing at the door staring at her as though she were a complete stranger. "James, you came for me."

James stepped back and rammed the door with his shoulder. It did not budge. Fendrel joined James and still there was no hope. James in a fit of desperation, kicked at the lock of the door. The door began to splinter. James and Fendrel each kicked the door once more when the door broke open. Rushing in James was appalled at the condition of the room. The room was small, with a chamber pot in one corner, a small pile of straw in the other corner and the odor unbearable. Without hesitation he scooped her up into his arms and ran outside all the way to their horses. Sitting down with Jayde still in his arms he started to rock with her in his arms and began to shake. "I did not think I was going to be able to find you. I have searched and searched. Are you okay? Did he hurt you?"

Jayde was so tired and relieved that this terror was finally over. She tucked her head against James's chest and fell asleep.

James looked up at Fendrel in panic but Fendrel just smiled. "My Lord, she is asleep. She is so thin and frail looking. Do you think she will be well enough to travel? I believe it would be best for us to travel now as I do not think it would be wise for us to camp here. We need to leave here immediately. We do not know where he is, or when he will come back. I think we should try to ride to Lord Simon." Fendrel was nervous and began to stammer. There was something about this castle that him feel as though he was being watched.

James thought about this for only a moment before standing up and mounting his horse without ever letting go of Jayde. They rode through the day and well into the night arriving at the gates of Lord Simon's castle just before dawn.

Lord Simon awoke to greet the two men and was shocked when he saw a child curled up in James arms. Ordering their rooms to have a blazing fire, baths and food, Lord Simon followed James and Fendrel into the chamber James was using. James laid Jayde down on a bench near the fire. "Lord Simon, I thank you again for your generosity and help. We could not have found her had you not been of assistance. We are in your debt."

"This is she? She looks to be a child!" Lord Simon was still in disbelief. "Did you find Blaxton? What did you do to him?"

James felt a surge of anger course through him, is that all the man was concerned with?

"Yes, this is my wife, Lady Jayde. Blaxton was not there, so I could not do anything to him." James could barely keep the hate and contempt from his voice.

"I am grateful you found her and welcome you to stay as long as you need to recover. Should you need anything, just ask. Rest well." Lord Simon turned and left.

Fendrel left as well to go bathe, eat, rest and give privacy to James and Jayde. James turned his attention to Jayde. She was so thin, it scared him. "Jayde, wake up Wild. I have a hot bath for you and food. Wild darling, please. Wake up my love."

Jayde was dreaming. She felt warm and could hear James talking to her. She was dead. She died! Her baby! Oh no. This was not right. He was louder now. Slowly Jayde opened her eyes.

James was so relieved when Jayde finally awoke. Trying to still the shaking he closed his eyes. Taking deep breaths, he was nearly composed when he felt Jayde's tiny cold hands touch his face. Bending down, resting his head on her breast, he cried letting out all of the grief he'd held for his parents, letting out the anger of growing up, and letting go of his past mistakes.

After moments that seemed to pass as hours, the foul odor emanating from her was more than he could take. "Jayde darling, when was the last time you bathed, I do not want to hurt your feelings, but darling, you smell."

Jayde burst out laughing. "Help me undress and into the bath."

James was struggling so much to help Jayde undress and not touch her clothes any more than he already had. Giving up, he grabbed his dagger and cut her clothes completely off and threw them into the fire. Picking up Jayde he walked her to the bath and gently lowered her into the tub. James scrubbed her hair while she soaked in the warm bath. Finally after an hour of scrubbing, Jayde felt clean enough to eat and sleep. James helped her climb out and begin to dry off. Drying her legs and butt, then her back, and finally turning her around to face him to dry her breasts and stomach, he froze. Slowly looking up into Jayde's eyes, he extended his hand out to rest on the small but firm bump.

"Jayde, are you... with child?" James asked so quietly Jayde almost could not hear him.
Without taking her eyes from him, she laid her own hand atop of his and nodded. Fresh tears filled his eye as he wrapped his arms around her naked body and laid his head on the small bump where his child grew.
"When?" was all that James was able to choke out.

"The end of August." The moment was more intimate than anything Jayde had ever experienced. Gently, Jayde tilted James's chin to look up at her. Softly, she said, "James, I must tell you something though. I am not sure how long you have gone without bathing, but your stench is starting to make me ill."

James leaned his head back and roared with laughter. He quickly undressed, climbed into the bath and scrubbed every inch of his filthy body. August was barely five months away! Never in his life could he remember being this happy.

Jayde sat on the bed in a clean chemise sampling all the delicious bites of food on their tray, except for the bread and cheese. Even looking at it made her feel ill. So many months of eating only stale bread and cheese, she would never complain about eating rabbit stew again! As she ate, she watched James in the bath. Her heart ached, it felt as though it was going to burst right out of her chest, and she knew right then and there, how very much she truly loved him.

James glanced her way to see if she had fallen asleep again. She was looking at him, but not seeing him. Instead she had a look of bliss on her face obviously deep in thought. James stood up, dried off, and walked to the bed. He reached down to take a bite of the rabbit and noticed it already had a bite in it. Looking at the tray of food, everything had a bite in it, except for the bread and cheese. Sitting down, pulling Jayde to his side, he began to ask her questions about her captivity. With each question, some of his fear grew, and some of the fear subsided.

"Jayde, do you remember what happened after you rode off into the woods?"

"I thought you were riding up behind me. Instead it was him. I tried to scream out to you, but he hit me and I passed out. I woke up in the tower." Jayde tried to speak as calmly as she could. She could feel the tension in his arms and hear it is his question.

"Did he ever, hurt you?"

"No. He rarely spoke to me. With the exception of the same story he told me every day."

James let out a sigh of relief. "Did he tell you what I did when I was younger?"

The pain in his voice nearly broke her heart. "He told me his version of the story."

James took a deep breath and told her about that summer. Jayde was silent while James told the same story with more details. Even after he had finished, she remained silent. She must loathe him. No, she probably did not trust him any longer, how could he ever expect her to love him?
"You probably never want to see me again. You must be ill at the fact that it is my child you carry. I understand. I could not expect you to feel differently. I shall stay with Fendrel tonight. We can make arrangements for your and our child's care and future after you have rested." James could barely swallow, feeling the knot of sorrow and self-loathing like a rock in his throat.

Jayde had spent the last fourteen weeks hearing this story with fewer details and a different kind of hate from the storyteller. She felt James begin to let go of her, to get up and leave her. Jayde's hands flew out and trapped his hands against her sides. Turning to face him, she studied his hands. They were large hands. Strong and wide with long fingers. His narrow wrists extended upwards to well defined arms covered thickly with blonde hair nearly the color of sunlight. Broad shoulders that could carry the weight of the world but were weighed down by the guilt and regret of his actions twelve years ago. His neck was long and graceful and the stubble on his face was days old and nearly completely red, a shocking contrast to his golden blonde hair that topped his head.

Jayde sighed a deep breathe. "James, I do not want you to leave. I do not regret the child that I carry nor do I regret that it is yours. I do not loathe you. I am in disbelief that you could have done these things because this is not the man that I know. The man sitting in front of me is kind, caring, and honest, gives his heart completely and strives to better himself. I will not persecute you more than you have already persecuted yourself. If I could not stand you, would that somehow make you feel better? Not likely. If I loathed this child that you and I have created, would that relieve you of your guilt? No, it would only make it worse. You are not the eighteen year old boy by the river, you are a man, a husband and soon you will be a father. You must find forgiveness for yourself. My forgiveness for you will not erase your past, nor will it ease your burden of guilt. Only you can accomplish that. I love you. I love the man that you are and the man you will become. Accept your past, but do not let it define your future."

Jayde's speech left him breathless. It was honest and raw. James reached out drawing Jayde to him. Holding her, he took several long shaky breaths. For the first time, he thought back upon his past and did not feel the self-loathing. He still felt the pain, and the regret, but it was as though Jayde's words lifted his burden of hate that he felt for himself. Maybe, one day, he could find a way to forgive himself. Until then, this was a welcomed start.

He brought his mouth down upon hers gently, slowly asking for more with his tongue. Teasing and giving what he hoped she would return, he discovered her curiosity overcame her shyness. Their kisses grew until their unquenched and pent up desires drove them to frantically pull at each other. In one motion James ripped Jayde's chemise down the front to her waist. Pushing her down on her back, he took her full breast in his mouth while his hand caressed and taunted her other breast.

Jayde's hands grabbed James hair and pulled him down violently at her breast. Feeling his mouth take her breast she moaned out. Aching, she arched her back desperate for more.

James tore his mouth from her breast and trailed down over her belly, tearing her chemise completely, searching further down until he reached her most tender place, her jewel and gently began to lick then suck on her. Her gasp, arching hips up to him and feeling her nails nearly cut his skin trailing from his shoulders down his arms was reward and encouragement to continue. Plunging his tongue inside of her, he again was rewarded with her gasp. As he continued to plunge his tongue within her, he used his thumb to rub her jewel until she cried out. Then lifting his body above her he thrust his shaft deep and hard into her. Thrusting into her deeper and harder until they both screamed when they reached their climax. Rolling off of her and collapsing by her side, James held her hand.

After several minutes, James asked softly, "When did you decide that you loved me Jayde?"

"I have always loved you. It took me until this day to understand what I had always felt. To be able to give a name to the pain in my heart when you were near, when we fought, and when we were separate." Jayde's answer was confident. Rolling to her side, she threw one leg over James's body, tangled her hand in the hair at the nape of his neck, and looked him in the eyes. "Never have I loved another as I love you, and never will I love another. Do not doubt this, James de Seaton. I can give you nothing more pure than my love. Take warning however, if ever you harm my love for you, it will never be able to be repaired."

There was a twinkle in James's eyes after hearing her words. "I swear to you my love, I will cherish and protect your love with my life."

Weeks of such little nourishment, winter weather with no warmth, and cold stone floors to sleep on, left Jayde weak. Laying in James's arms, Jayde fell into a deep, dreamless sleep instantly with a smile on her lips, almost missing James' words.

Smiling and kissing Jayde's forehead, James wrapped his arms around her, bringing his hand back to rest on the small bump that provided a safe place for their growing baby. Closing his eyes, James too, fell into a deep sleep.

Chapter 9

James and Jayde rested for one more day before beginning their journey home. Lord Simon provided them with enough food for their travels. The group of three were all very eager to go home and made their gratitude and goodbye brief. They pushed themselves and their horses to get home as quickly as possible, eager to get back to the safety of their own home and day to day life.

It was midday on the fourth day of traveling that Era came into view. Jayde stopped her horse at the top of the hill and stared. James and Fendrel on either side of her, the three looked down on the town, but only Jayde saw the beauty below. There were orchards, farms, homes, a river, and a lake. There was a sounding horn in the distance to announce their presence and as the three of them began to ride down the hill, four knights rode up to great them. Immediately recognizing Lord James, one knight turned and blew his horn once to signify that the Earl of Era was finally home.

People in town began to rush to the main road to catch a glimpse of the group who had been gone for so long, most of them getting their first glimpse of Lady Jayde. As the trio began their procession through town, Jayde's exhaustion started to show. After so many weeks of starving and being pregnant, the unusually warm day in April and the overwhelming cheers from the people, Jayde started to become dizzy. Clutching the saddle and her mare's mane, the world began to spin, and the people became blurred. She could feel herself falling, it almost felt soft and welcoming. She felt strong arms holding her and there was a hush among the people. Jayde slowly opened her eyes and looked into James concerned face.

"It is just the heat and the baby, I will be fine when we are home and I can cool off." Jayde reassured him.

People near them in the crowd started to whisper to the person next to them. The rest of the walk to the castle, James held Jayde in his arms and instead of cheering the people smiled and waved, worried that their loud cheering had somehow overwhelmed the delicate looking Lady Jayde. Finally, at the castle, a small child ran out in front of the horses holding a bouquet of wild flowers.

"These are for Lady Jayde." The little boy said, holding out the flowers and showing off his grin with his first missing tooth. Jayde wiggled out of James's arms and slid to the ground. Kneeling down in front of the boy, Jayde accepted the flowers and inhaled the beautiful scent.

"Truly, they are for me?" Jayde quietly and bashfully asked. The little boy nodded vigorously. "Then I shall cherish them forever." Reaching out, she hugged the little boy then stood up and walked forward toward James. Dismounting, James took Jayde's empty hand and continued to walk to the stable boy waiting to take their horses. Turning around, Jayde waved to the little boy, and giggled as he puffed his chest out with pride. The people cheered louder than ever as the three walked into the castle. Unknown to Jayde, her simple and honest reaction to the little boy, won the hearts of the town.

Once inside, Maggie came running grabbing both James and Jayde going on about how happy everyone was that they were finally home. Touching Jayde's even thinner frame, Maggie exclaimed, "Child! You are but skin and bones! Sit, Maria's cooking will fatten you up nicely. Maria! Serve up some food for Lady Jayde! She needs some fattening!" With that Maggie was off to order people around and to personally see to it that only the best was ready for Lord James and Lady Jayde.

Smiling at his wife, James led her to a chair so that they could eat together. Fendrel came in a moment later joining the couple at the table at Lord James request.

"My Lady, how are you feeling now?" Fendrel's concern was in his voice. Watching her fall from her horse on the ride through town reminded him of just how dangerous and painful her capture had been.

"I am tired and weak, but rest and Maria's cooking should help return my energy and strength in no time." Jayde gave a most reassuring smile to Fendrel. During their journey home, Jayde had listened to the men tell of everywhere that they had searched for her. Had it not been for the storm, she would most likely be lying dead in the abandoned castle hidden in the trees. She shuddered at the recollection of Blaxton's final words to her. Words that she had not shared with her husband. Were James and Fendrel correct? Would Blaxton come back to finish what he started or would he accept defeat and leave them alone to live their lives?

Fendrel embarrassingly watched as James reached over and took Jayde's hand in his, gently caressing it until Maria and Maggie brought a feast out for them. He could not help but feel as though he was being left out on some big secret. Nor could he fight the slight pain of jealousy for the love that the two obviously shared. Watching for a moment more before averting his gaze, Fendrel recognized a change in his friend. One that he could not name.

Jayde looked at the feast that had been brought to them. With wide eyes, Jayde began to laugh. She laughed so hard her sides ached. With James and Fendrel staring at her, "Please say that we are expecting company! We cannot possibly eat this feast alone! Even though I am exceedingly hungry, I cannot imagine finishing an entire pig between the three of us! James, please, invite people, your knights, to sit and enjoy this meal with us." Recalling how the knights at Adonia ate with them, he sent a servant out to call the men in. He knew his knights were not accustomed to eating with him in the hall and would be uncomfortable.

Jayde watched as the knights filed in quickly and stood along one wall looking uncomfortable and unsure.

Leaning towards James, Jayde asked "do your knights not eat their meals with you?"

Stifling his laugh, James replied, "No, they eat on the fields or in the barracks."

Shocked, Jayde scolded him. "If you do not treat them as family, how can you expect them to love you and be loyal to you like family?"

Giving in to the laugh that he could no longer contain, James rested his head in his hands, laughing as Jayde stood up and began to address his knights.

Looking at the mass of uncomfortable, smelly, sweaty men, Jayde too struggled to contain a giggle. "I can see that you are all very uncomfortable at the moment and I can only assume that you were not given any reason to have your training interrupted. Rest assured, not one of you has done anything wrong." Jayde saw a few smiles from some of the knights who had accompanied her to Adonia. Continuing on, "Some of my earliest memories are in the hall at Adonia. The knights that trained in my father's fields always ate their midday and evening meal with my family. I am afraid that I cannot allow for you to eat anywhere else. It would feel lonely not having the hall filled with familiar faces. After discussing with Lord James, it is agreed that we would like to invite you all to join us for the midday and evening meals from this point on. You train as a family, then you eat as a family. We, are a family, all of us and I expect you to remember that, both on and off of the field. Now, if you would please humor my request, take a seat and eat." Slowly the men made their way to the tables but remained standing. Finally, Jayde sat down. Only after she took her seat did all of the knights sit as well. Maria and Maggie brought wet hot towels out for everyone to wipe their hands with. Then they returned with even more trays of food. Jayde sat back a moment to listen and watch. The knights were relaxed a bit and were talking amongst each other. Smiling, Jayde remembered happier times in her childhood, before her mother passed, of scenes very much like this one. With time, she could make new memories and traditions here in her home at Era with her new family.

James and Fendrel spent most of the midday meal discussing the next few days of training on the field and of new weapons to work with. Fendrel stopped mid-sentence while discussing introducing the long bow to the men and chuckled. Following Fendrel's eyes, James looked to his wife whom had fallen asleep in her chair. Fendrel stood up to quiet the knights as James carefully scooped Jayde's sleeping body into his arms and carried her up to their room. Laying her down, he lightly kissed her head and covered her up before stoking the fire and returning to his men below.

James spent the remainder of the afternoon trying to focus and train with his men. When Jayde invited the men to join them for meals, she changed them all. The men seemed more willing to listen, give opinions and trained harder than James had remembered. It almost seemed as though their comradery was better, the bond stronger. Despite the positive change in the men and all of his efforts to concentrate on training, he found himself looking towards the doorway searching for Jayde. Finally, the day ended and everyone parted to get ready for the evening meal. Taking the stairs two at a time, James went to their room searching for Jayde only to find their room empty. Panic setting in, James called out to her. Turning around he collided with her spilling the pitcher of wine down her dress and knocking it to the floor where it broke into several pieces.

Jayde was not only startled by James nearly knocking her over, but by the look on his face as well. Grabbing his arms to steady herself, she then reached up to his face to steady him.
"James, what is wrong?" The look of panic on James face frightened her as much as being run into.

Relief poured through James body after running into Jayde in the doorway. He could feel his body shaking realizing how vulnerable they still were. Reaching out, he grabbed her hands, pulling her to him crushing her to his body, calming his racing heart.

"James, why are you acting this way?" Jayde inquired.

"I had not seen you all afternoon, then you were not here." James still held her tight.

"I went to get you wine to quench your thirst after training this afternoon."

119

"I just feel as though we are not rid of Blaxton yet and I was worried." James smoothed her hair back and kissed her on the mouth.

Maggie opened the door to the bedchamber nearly dumping the first buckets of hot water onto Lord James and Lady Jayde whom were standing in the doorway.

"Heavens above! I nearly drenched you both. Lord James, can you not keep your hands off of Lady Jayde for even a moment? At this pace, the two of you should have little feet running through this castle in a year! Get yourself ready to bathe. That hall is going to fill quickly and all will be waiting to dine until you arrive."

James scooped Jayde into his arms and mocking Maggie, "Oh Jayde, I just cannot keep my hands off of your ravishing body. Heavens above, I must have you here and now, without delay. I care not who watches or who waits below..." chuckling he watched as the flustered Maggie waddled away with the now empty buckets as more servants carried water up to the room.

James undressed and bathed quickly while watching Jayde change out of the wine covered dress and into a clean one envisioning what he would like to do to her indeed ravishing body.

Coming from behind him, Jayde kissed the top of his clean head and said she would meet him below. James tried to grab her, but she stepped away from him too quickly and nearly ran out of the room. Carefully walking down the stairs, Jayde indulged in the delicious smells wafting from the kitchen. Standing back a moment, Jayde watched as the servants began to set up for the evening meal. Looking around the room, Jayde noted all of the work that needed to be done to the hall to make it as warm and beautiful as the smell of the meal cooking. Tapestries needed to be repaired, nests cleared from the rafters, and the floors to be scrubbed. The walls seemed bare despite the poorly hung tapestries and panes of colored glass that needed replacing. There was much to do in this room alone. From the hill the castle had appeared large, she could only assume there must be many more rooms to be discovered and if half of them were in this condition, there would be repairs that needed to be made through Christmas.

Tables were being brought in and cleaned off, benches and chairs brought to the tables. Candles and candelabras were being brought out and placed around the room and upon the tables. Seeing that the servants were handling their tasks and preparing the great hall for the evening meal, Jayde left to find music for the evening.

She recalled seeing a man with a lute in his hands when they were arriving through town and now she meant to find him. Stopping at the stables, she asked a stable boy if he knew of the man she spoke of. The boy directed her to the well, where several young ladies gathered and giggled. Making her way to the well, she found the young man lounging on the grass with his lute next to him, two pretty and blushing young ladies kneeling at either side of him and six more ladies standing around him all begging him to play another song.

Clearing her throat, "Excuse me, are you a skilled musician?" Jayde stood waiting patiently for the young man to answer her.

Stumbling to his feet, pulling his hat into his hands, "yes, my lady, I am a skilled musician. Do you wish for me to sing you a sonnet?"

"No, thank you. I wish to know if you will entertain us for the evening meals?"

"Yes, My Lady. For just this evening meal or for many evening meals?" He stammered, growing more nervous, hoping that he might actually use his talents to earn wages finally

"Let me hear you this evening and we can discuss it more tomorrow. What is your name?" Jayde felt a friendly soul standing in front of her and she could not help but to smile at the young man.

"My name is Pycard, My Lady." Pycard was so excited he forgot all about the swarm of young girls around them. In truth, he had never laid eyes on a woman as stunning as Lady Jayde.

"Very well, Pycard, you should claim your Lute and immediately present yourself to the hall. After the evening meal, you may sit down and eat your evening meal with the servants." Jayde turned to walked back to the hall to see how work was progressing. James should be down soon and his knights should be filling the hall soon as well.

"Excuse me, Lady Jayde, what mood would you like for me to set for the meal?" Pycard wanted to secure his future and not upset the Lord or Lady. Did they want a light and happy mood? Perhaps a somber and serious evening?

"Make the evening light and happy. Everyone is home, and healthy. Let us keep it that way." Jayde was starting to feel exhausted again. She needed to return to the hall and sit.

Jayde walked through the hall to the kitchen to see how well it was functioning. As she got closer, she could hear the argument and the sounds of pots and spoons flying across the room. Walking into the kitchen, Jayde saw evidence of a battle. Maria stood with a large knife pointed in the direction of a short fat man. The short fat man stood with both hands held out in Maria's direction. There were bits of food thrown against and sliding down a wall, plumes of flour still floating in the air, and a pot of gravy starting to bubble over the fire. There were platters of meats and roasted carrots, potatoes, parsnips, decorated with sprigs of rosemary.

Pitchers of Ale and Wine lined the table near the door as did several cups and stacked plates.

The hall would be filling up soon and this war inside the kitchen needed to end immediately.

"Maria, let's put down the knife. Tell me what this man has done to upset you so much." Jayde was hoping this would diffuse the situation and allow peace to return within the warm kitchen walls.

"This pompous ogre thinks he knows more about cooking than I! He comes in here, samples my cooking then tells me what he thinks I should add. Tonight he decided to add spice to my gravy! Go back to the smithy where you belong! How dare you come into my kitchen and pretend you know anything about my art! I should go to your smithy and take one of your branding irons to you!"

Turning red and pointing one long, meaty finger at Maria, Thomas shouted, "You, woman, do not belong in a smithy, you belong with the pigs!"

With that comment, Maria's flick of her wrist sent the knife flying through the air and lodged into the wood brace on the wall behind Thomas with the handle touching his head. Thomas's face was no longer bright red, but a ghostly white.

"If you ever comment or adjust my cooking again, I shall not miss." Maria then turned around to pull the bread out of the brick oven.

It was all too much for Jayde. Far from being recovered or completely healthy and what little energy she did have was being consumed by this growing blessing, everything went black and Jayde collapsed to the floor.

Pycard had followed Lady Jayde to the hall and had begun to start strumming his lute when he heard the commotion from the kitchen. Setting down his lute he walked into the kitchen in time to see Lady Jayde collapse to the floor. She looked dead. Reaching down he scooped the petite woman up in his arms and rushed into the hall calling out for help.

Fendrel was laughing with Luther when from the corner of his eye he saw a scrawny boy carrying a lifeless looking Lady Jayde and calling for help. Rushing over he took the small body from the boy's arms and taking the steps two at a time burst into the chamber of James and Jayde.

James had just finished getting dressed when his chamber door burst open. Fendrel stood there with the ghost white and limp Jayde in his arms. "Lay her down on the bed!" James growled as he shut the door behind them.

Anna had turned around from lighting the final candles when she saw Fendrel running up the stairs with her darling Jayde. Running as fast as her short legs could take her, she chased up the stairs only to be greeted by a door slamming in her face! Who did they think *they* were! This was *her* mistress! Throwing open the door she shoved Fendrel so hard to the side he stumbled nearly falling to the floor. She then pushed Lord James out of the way as well.

"My Lady, Jayde, are you okay? Wake up dear friend! One of you make your selves useful and fetch Maggie, some cool water and linen! Anna is here now my friend, I am here."

Neither James nor Fendrel wasted any time doing as they were told. James returned with Maggie moments after Fendrel returned with linen and a bucket of cool water.
Maggie wasted no time, dipping a linen in the cool water and placing it on Jayde's forehead.

"Come on darling, wake up. I have put so much time into healing you and nursing you back to health. Wake up." Maggie and Anna continued to vigorously rub Jayde's hands and arms hoping to recover her from her faint. Finally, after several minutes, Jayde's eyes fluttered open.

"What happened?" Jayde struggled to sit up only to have her arms give out from under her.

"My Lady, you fainted in the kitchen. You do not remember?" Fendrel was even more worried than he had been when they arrived home earlier that day.

Sighing, Jayde closed her eyes recalling the events of the evening. "Yes, I remember. Maria threw a knife at the Smithy's head just before I fainted. I was so tired and so hungry. I was coming in to sit and rest a moment when I heard the argument so I went in to calm everyone down."

"Maria threw a knife at Thomas?" James and Fendrel asked in unison.

"He was adding spices to her cooking and telling her what she should be doing." Jayde again sighed.

Anna ladled some water and brought it to her young mistress to drink. "Maggie will see to it that food is brought to you so that you can stay in bed and rest."

"No, please, I need to be downstairs tonight. I need to be around people." Keeping her eyes closed, Jayde struggled to keep the tears from falling and from sounding hysterical.

"I will carry you down to dinner and back up. No more walking for the night. Do you understand me?"

"Yes. Thank you James." Jayde looked up at James with so much loneliness it broke his heart.

With a bargain made, Anna and Maggie left the room confident that their delicate young mistress was in good hands.

James lifted Jayde into his arms kissing her on the top of her head before turning to the door that Fendrel held open. Slowly, carefully, walking down the stairs, both men halted at the last steps, in awe of what awaited them. Picking her head up off of James's chest, Jayde looked at the scene awaiting her. Every single knight was on a knee waiting for news of their mistress. While James's chest puffed with pride, Jayde smiled and opened her heart to this new family before her letting her tears slide down her cheeks. As James carried her to her seat, each knight bowed his head to her as she passed, all of them waiting to stand up until she had been seated. The knights took their seats and looked to their mistress for her health and reassurance. Jayde wiped the tears from her eyes and once again smiled at everyone.

James stood. "Each of you has amazed me today. In all of our time together, I have never witnessed you train harder, and never have I seen any of you show concern like you all have tonight. I am proud of you. I am grateful for each of you, and am confident in the strength and loyalty of the family that we are. Come, let us enjoy this feast and entertainment!" James lifted his cup first to Jayde, whispering "thank you" to her, then turning to his men and lifting his cup to them.

The men in return held their cups up to Jayde, then James before drinking and beginning their meal. The evening meal was delicious. Roasted rabbit, succulent beef, and pheasant accompanied by the roasted vegetables and roots. Everyone ate their fill and enjoyed conversations and the sound of music that Pycard played on his lute.

Sitting back, holding Jayde's hand, James recalled when the hall was last filled with people and music. He had been a young man, his family had been healthy, and the pressure to grow up had not been so urgent. Now, because of Jayde, the hall his mother had taken so much time and effort to make warm and happy, was healing, as was his heart. Gently squeezing Jayde's hand, James leaned over to her, kissing her smiling cheeks and whispered to her.

Jayde could not contain her joy. The last time she had been this complete, was before her mother's death. Sitting here now, she was surrounded by knights who cared for her as their family, a husband whom she loved more than life and the sounds of music and laughter. Smiling, she gently touched her small belly. Life could not possibly be better than this.

"Jayde, you are the best thing to happen to me. You are my sun in the sky, the rain that quenches the earth, the air I need to live. I love you more than I have ever thought possible." Jayde turned her head to face him. Pressing their foreheads together, Jayde closed her eyes and enjoyed the intimate moment, a moment that ended too soon when she yawned. Laughing quietly, James whispered, "Looks like it is time get to get my two favorite people to bed." Standing up, James placed one arm under Jayde's knees and the other around her back. Lifting her up and holding her tight to his chest, they both paused, breath catching as the entire Guard stood up for their departure. Smiling, Jayde waved and bid everyone a good evening. Once they were out of sight, they could hear the Guard sit back down and resume the quiet conversations they were previously having.

Once upstairs in their chamber, James helped Jayde out of her dress and settle into bed, holding her tight to his chest caressing the bump that their child created in her belly. Falling asleep quickly, neither felt any alarm despite the danger camping in the forest.

Blaxton was seething sitting in the forest watching the castle knowing that somehow, James de Seaton had everything he wanted while he had nothing. He would return to the ruins of a castle, and make his final plan. This time, there would be no failure for him. He would kill James de Seaton. But first, he would have some fun.

The guard of Era were all overjoyed at the safe return of their Lord and Lady. Feeling that Lord James had been triumphant, the danger having passed, no one was looking for the shadow that slipped out of the woods and along the wall disappearing under the full moon.

Chapter 10

It was dark and Jayde was cold. She could hear him whistling and hear the soft steps as he made his daily visit. This could not be! James, where was he? NO! Jayde could feel her soul dying as the very breath in her body let out. Just let me die!

"Hello my little flower. I see you survived my time away. Let me tell you a story…"

Jayde tried to lift her head to look up at him through the iron bars in the door. Her body was too weak, she could move nothing. This was it, this would be her last moments, never be held or kissed by James again.

"What? No greetings today Flower? No fight in you? Have you given up? Go ahead, let go, die. I am eager to return your lifeless body to James and watch him suffer as I have for so many years. Give up flower, give up…"

Jayde could do nothing. She could not move, she could not speak, and she could not breathe. She was dead…

James was exhausted. He had been up through the night trying to put out a fire near the edge of the forest. It looked as though some one had been cooking, leaving the embers to flame with the wind in the night.

James sent the guard to the hall for hot food and drink while he dragged himself up to check on Jayde. She was probably already up and pacing, worried or scared, not knowing where he was. The thought of him opening their chamber door to see her running to him covering him in kisses and delicately touching him to make sure there was not a single hair upon his body harmed caused him to smile. Taking the last eight steps two at a time, James opened their door. Instead of seeing his worried wife, he saw her lying in bed, pale, motionless, and drenched in sweat. Crossing the room in three strides he knelt on the floor touching her forehead and trying to wake her. Jayde continued to lay there motionless, her typically pink lips slightly blue. Fear gripped James's heart and he began to gently shake his lifeless wife.

Jayde could hear him open the door and walk to her. The room was so small, he reached her body in three strides. She knew his hands where on her shoulders, yet she felt nothing. He was calling her name, pleading with her to come back to him. It was strange that he wanted her alive, that he needed her. His voice was different though. It was familiar. It was James! He had come for her finally! She must not give up! *Breathe!* Jayde commanded her body to breath. Nothing happened. She just lay there on the filthy stone floor. Again, she tried to will herself back to her body. She could *feel* his warm hands on her body. She could hear his voice. *Just one breath* she told herself. All it would take was one breath…

James could see her chest rise and fall, with no sounds of air. Just the motion of her body trying to survive.

"Breath my love! Breath!" As if on command, Jayde gasped for air. Then again. Her eyes flew open darting about the room like a crazed and wild animal. Finally seeing James, Jayde threw her arms around his neck giving in to body racking sobs of relief and desperation. James, cradled her in his arms the way you would a child. Sitting on the bed, rocking her back and forth, smoothing her hair and whispering, "Hush my love, I am here. You are safe. Just breathe, just breathe." What just happened? Was she ill? Was it the baby? "Jayde, are you okay?"

Jayde could feel James heart pounding in his chest. It almost matched the pace of her own racing heart. Trying to calm down and taking deeper breaths, Jayde could only nod her head. Jayde could still see the terrifying images despite her closed eyes. Squeezing her eyes shut tighter, she held on to James more tightly as well. Nothing could rid her memory of the images and feelings she had just experienced.

"Jayde?" James could feel her shaking with fear. Leaning back a little and looking down upon her face, he tilted her chin up towards his face. Looking at her face, he saw that the beads of sweat were gone. Her lips were no longer the deadly shade of blue but the perfect rose that they should be. Color had returned to her face, but her eyes remained squeezed shut and her body continued to shake. "Jayde" James whispered. Then with his thumb he caressed her lips, traced an eye brow with his finger tip, then down her nose. Finally, he caressed her cheek with his rough knuckles, soaking up the sensation of touching her silky soft skin. Slowly, Jayde opened her eyes, staring up into James's eyes. Her vibrant green eyes were almost cloudy, as though a storm were brewing in them.

Jayde looked up into James's eyes to find the comfort and love she so desperately needed. Looking back at her were James's confident hazel eyes, filled with love and worry. His forehead was creased with concern and there were black marks streaking his face. Now it was Jayde's turn for concern.

"James! What happened? Is everyone alright? Are you alright?" Jayde asked her questions without pause for an answer.

"I am fine my love. It is you that I worry about. When I entered our chamber, you were lifeless. You were not breathing, you did not respond to my voice, and your lips were blue. You appeared dead. I have never been so terrified in my life." Closing his eyes and bowing his head slightly, allowing his forehead to touch hers, his whisper was filled with pain. "I thought I had lost you again." Jayde's body involuntarily shuddered when the images flooded her mind again, but she dared not share those with James. Refusing to allow Jayde to be out of his sight for even a moment, James carried her out to the stables and mounted his horse with her seated in front of him.

Luther, Walker and Fendrel were waiting for James at the stables and followed behind Lord James and Lady Jayde while casting confused glances at each other. The knights could not understand why Lord James was bringing Lady Jayde, still in her sleeping gown, with them to the burned woods, but they were smart enough to not ask. Since November of last year, when Lord James had married, Lord James had changed. Fendrel could not help but to reflect on how his friend had changed in the past six months. Many of those changes benefited all of the knights, but there were some changes that Fendrel questioned and worried that they could cloud Lord James judgement and ability to care for his castle and knights. However, the knights and people of Era seemed to appreciate and respond well to the changes that they had seen in Lord James. Fendrel knew that the people of Era had quickly fallen in love with Lady Jayde and he too was eager to see what she had planned for the town and the people who lived there. Fendrel's thoughts drifted from Lady Jayde, to Lady Jayde's petite maid Anna. It seemed that Anna and Lady Jayde were somehow connected. When Lady Jayde was hurt, Anna fretted and often knew something was wrong before any words were even said. The two women were as good of friends as he and Lord James were. Lost in his own thoughts, he did not notice that everyone had stopped and that they were all staring at him as he sat there with a grin on his face. Shaking his head to clear his thoughts and the images his thoughts were leading him to, he finally heard the roar of laughter from the men and sweet giggle of Lady Jayde.

Grinning sheepishly, Fendrel dismounted and gruffly told Luther and Walker to dismount and get to work clearing the debris. Still laughing the two men did as they were told while Lord James rode ahead slowly making sure that there were no embers for the wind stir up and create another fire with.

Despite how silly James was acting towards her, Jayde felt more loved and protected than she could ever remember. She had small flashes of memories of her parents fawning over each other like this. They were so happy and beautiful. Jayde wondered if she and James appeared that happy and beautiful to others watching them. Suddenly, a cold shiver ran up Jayde's back, and she could not help but to look over her shoulder. James had dismounted his horse and was walking the area near her looking for any glowing embers. "James…" Jayde called out uneasily.

James was so absorbed in his search he barely heard her small voice. Jayde called out to James again, this time getting a reaction.

James could hear the concern in Jayde's voice and suddenly had the uneasy feeling they were being watched. Pausing for just a moment, his head jerked up and he jumped back as an arrow sliced through the air

missing his head and lodging into the tree to his right.
Spinning around and mounting his horse behind Jayde,
he curled her into a ball and covered her body with his
as he gave a shout for Fendrel, Luther and Walker.
Within seconds, Fendrel, Luther, and Walker had their
swords drawn and were rushing to where James had just
fled. Walker saw the arrow and pulled it from the tree
and looked in the direction from where the arrow was
shot from, following its path towards the hilltop.
Fendrel and Luther followed his gaze and all three
mounted their horses taking off at a neck breaking pace
to try and catch the person responsible for attempting
their Lord's life.

Jayde could barely breathe under James's protecting
body but dared not move out of fear that she might fall
out from under his arms. What had happened? Had she
felt someone watching them? Why were they trying to
kill James? Her mind raced, trying to process the last
minute of their morning. Suddenly she felt James arm
lift her and felt herself falling in the air only to land in
the strong arms of a knight. She heard the sound of a
horn being blown and saw hundreds of knights running
to their horses and rushing out of the gates and
following closely on James heals. There were six
knights surrounding her and the seventh knight was still
holding her in his arms as she was carried inside. Once
inside, Jayde was carried up to what looked to be an old
solar where she was sat in a chair as the six other
knights checked every crevice of the room, including

behind a tapestry that not only was in desperate need of a cleaning and repair, but also hid a door and stairs that Jayde had never seen before. One knight stood directly in front of the hidden door and tapestry, one stood at the window, another in the far corner, a fourth at the main door, and the other three knights left the room, closing the door and stood guard in the hall. Everything seemed to flow flawlessly, as though this very scenario had been practiced hundreds of times and the knights were always at the ready. Jayde recognized the four knights that were in the room with her. She had seen them many times close at James's and Fendrel's side talking in hushed voices. They were always seated apart from each other at meals, and always seemed the least relaxed. Alistair stood at the window, Cederick at the tapestry, Rylan in the corner and Devon at the door.

Standing, Jayde began to walk towards Alistair and the window in hopes of catching a glimpse of James. Instead Alistair took a step towards her and asked if there was anything she needed. Jayde simply shook her head no and sat back down feeling frustrated and helpless. When there was a sharp knocking on the door, all four of the knights startled and drew their swords while Jayde sat calm, jumping and allowing her nerves to take charge would not help any of them. The door swung open to a now startled Anna holding a tray of food.

Pausing briefly, eyes darting to each knight, Anna straightened herself and walked into the room setting the tray of food on the table. Looking Lady Jayde directly in the eye, she saw her mistress was worried and annoyed. Letting a small giggle escape, Anna began to leave, stopping when she felt Jayde's hand touch her arm.

"Stay with me a bit please Anna?" Jayde asked her dearest friend. This was unbearable. Did these knights not know that James was fine? She was sure of it, she could feel it in her bones. To Jayde's relief, Anna smiled and quickly sat down across from her. Looking at the feast in front of her, she wondered how Anna had managed to carry up so much food. "Will you share this meal with me?" Jayde asked her friend. Jayde did not see the glances from the knights in the room, but Anna did.

Anna was famished, and the meal smelled amazing. Sitting across from Jayde, just like they did when they were children, Anna had to resist the urge to reach out and start eating the meal that could was large enough to feed them both. When she heard Jayde offer her to enjoy the meal as well, joy filled her heart until she saw the glances from the guards. Being as proper as she could, Anna declined, "Thank you Lady Jayde, but I am not hungry." Anna's stomach gave away her lie and growled so loud and fierce that not only did Lady Jayde and Anna burst out laughing, but so did Alistair, Rylan,

Devon and Cederick. Anna then reached for two pieces of bread and buttered them both handing one to Jayde and keeping the other for herself.

Both Jayde and Anna were so absorbed in eating and talking, that the smiles being exchanged between the four men were missed. Jayde had earned a loyalty from them that was rare and unspoken. Soon, Maggie arrived carrying a tray filled with three times the amount of food Anna had brought. Setting it down on a table at the window, Maggie turned around to see the hungry eyes of four men staring in her direction.

"If I did not know any better, I'd swear you boys are staring at me!" Maggie teased making the four men blush. "Go on now, go eat something. You four need to keep your strength and wits." The four knights stood their ground, refusing to be weak enough to eat. Sighing, Maggie turned to Jayde saying, "Well, maybe you will have better luck convincing these fine men to eat something. You seem to have luck with other stubborn minds." Turning, Maggie left shaking her head smiling at the sound of Lady Jayde and Anna giggle.

"If you do not eat, the food will be wasted." Jayde simply stated.

"My Lady, we are keeping your safety, no expense to be spared, be it our lives, or empty bellies." Alistair kindly replied.

"Let me guess, these are the orders of Lord James? Well, Lord James is not here and I am not sure when he will return. The seven of you need to work it out so that all of you have something in your stomachs, and I will not take no for an answer." Trying to be firm, Jayde looked Alistair square in the eye, challenging him to defy her.

Bowing his head to such a tiny and determined Lady Jayde, Alistair could not resist smiling. Nodding to Devon, Alistair gave the men permission to go and eat, one at a time. After Devon, Rylan and Cederick had eaten, he then had the three knights guarding the door come eat as well before he finally allowed himself a small meal.

After Anna had brought a robe to her mistress she left to tend to other duties. Jayde was now alone in the solar, and Jayde finding herself bored began to explore the solar. It was beautiful and once was loved and well cared for. Jayde knew that James mother had passed away quite some time ago, but it seemed as though everything she touched or loved was sealed and never looked upon again. She would need to make sure she was careful to not destroy important memories that

James had of his parents, but she wanted to make this her home too. There were beautiful books on a shelf in the corner where Rylan stood guard. Touching the binding of each book, she wiped layers of dust from them. In a bench there was an incomplete small tapestry, and a sewing kit. The sun was setting and Jayde knew that the evening meal should be well underway by now. This was ridiculous. She made up her mind that she would refuse to be a prisoner because of a threat that had long since passed. Smoothing the folds in her robe, she walked to the door with her head held high and her shoulders back. Opening the door, she was greeted by the three knights guarding the door. Peter, Hugh and Gilbert, the knight who caught her when James went riding off. All seven knights began to protest and try to persuade her to stay in until James returned. Jayde did not want to hear any of it. Just then, the faint sounds of galloping horses could be heard. Jayde took the moment of hesitation from the seven men to run.

Jayde was racing through the hall and out to the stables with the seven knights assigned to protect her close on her heals. The ground shook from the horses pounding hooves. Jayde was overwhelmed and realized too late that she was in the path of the horses. Suddenly, she felt Gilbert's strong arms wrap around her waist and pull her back to safety. She felt his grip loosen slightly after he adjusted his arms so as to not squeeze her small bump that protected her baby. Turning her around to face him, the shock consumed his face.

"Please, do not say anything to anyone. Only Lord James knows." Jayde whispered pleadingly.

"How can I protect you if I do not know the whole truth My Lady?" Gilbert asked.

"Please, now you know. Please, keep this between us." Jayde again pleaded.

Gilbert silently nodded and gently led Lady Jayde back a bit farther to keep her out of the path of any horses. Glancing down at Lady Jayde, Gilbert was caught off guard by the intense green eyes staring back at him. Smiling gently, Gilbert and Lady Jayde shared a moment of secrecy and trust.

Jayde continued to scan the mass of knights riding in and unsaddling searching for James. Panic began to set in and she began to feel faint. Reaching out and stumbling, Jayde could feel the tears starting down her face. The world started to spin, Jayde's stomach lurched, and she could hear someone talking to her but she couldn't seem to understand the words.

Gilbert felt a tiny streak of cold graze his arm and out of the corner of his eye he saw Lady Jayde start to fall back. Grabbing her and keeping her from falling to the ground he scooped her up in his arms. He looked around at the knights assembled in front of him, and saw that they had all stood in formation and taken a knee. Fendrel stood up and walked towards Gilbert signaling him to follow inside. By the time that Gilbert had reached the Great Hall, Lady Jayde was wide awake and a hollow rage echoed in her eyes. It was almost ghostly and it sent a chill down Gilbert's spine. Without question, he quietly and carefully stood Lady Jayde up on her feet and took several steps back.

Fendrel was walking ahead of Gilbert but stopped suddenly when an icy chill raced down his back. Slowly turning around, he saw Gilbert stepping away from Lady Jayde, whom was staring at Fendrel, but not walking. Just standing there. For the first time, he feared a woman. This tiny, pale, long haired beauty literally froze his blood. Putting his hands out as though to deflect invisible blows, Fendrel quietly said, "It was Blaxton." He watched as Lady Jayde's face turned from pale, to white, to gray. She looked as though she were about to faint again.

The words echoed in her mind. She knew it was too good to be true that this madman would simply accept defeat and leave them alone. What was going to happen next? As though a bolt of lightning had struck her, she knew what she was going to do. Still looking at Fendrel, she spoke with a confidence she did not even know she had.

"Fendrel, call the knights in. We are to have an emergency meeting and the evening meal. I expect everyone." Jayde felt as confident as she sounded.

Turning to Gilbert, she nodded to him to follow her. Leading him up to the solar, where she knew they could speak privately, she closed the door behind them.

The sound of the door latching behind him made him jump. If Lord James found out that he was alone with Lady Jayde in her solar, he would kill him. "Lady Jayde, we should not be alone with a closed door. People will become suspicious of your fidelity and loyalty and people will talk."

"What is more important to you, finding Lord James alive or worrying about silly gossip like a kitchen maid?" Jayde asked without even trying to mask her annoyance. Watching Gilbert, all he could do was nod his head agreeing with her statement. "We keep our plans and conversations private. We share only what needs to be shared when it needs to be shared. You, Fendrel and I are the only three within this inner circle. Do not break my trust. We will return to the hall and I want every detail. How, when and if Blaxton was alone. I want to know everything." Jayde wanted to make sure Gilbert was on her side and would help keep any knights unwilling to listen to a woman, in check.

Walking towards the door, Gilbert held the door open for Lady Jayde. As she walked past him through the halls down the stairs and into the Great Hall, he could feel the tension growing. As they entered the hall, every knight stood for Lady Jayde. The emotions that filled the hall were so thick it choked him. He stood back and watched as Lady Jayde walked to the table. She was as regal as the queen herself.

Jayde walked into the Great Hall and was stunned when the mass of knights all stood as she walked to the tables. "Everyone, please sit. We need to talk about what happened today. I want every detail, no matter how small. If you heard the tune of a whistle from a bird you did not recognize, I want to know. If you saw a lone rider in the distance, I want to know. Smells, sights, sounds, anything and everything. Fendrel, you were with Lord James this morning when you battled the fire, is this correct?"

"Yes, Lady Jayde, I was at his side the entire time." Fendrel confirmed.

"Good. Now think, think about what you could smell. What did you hear? Did you see anyone or anything unusual?" Jayde pressed.

Maria had taken it upon herself to instruct the kitchen to prepare the evening meal. These men were hungry, and she knew Lady Jayde would not allow the knights to go hungry. The smells of roast meats, vegetables and breads were already dancing through the air when everyone assembled. Very quietly and seriously, the meal was carried out and placed on the tables. Even Pycard, the jongleur, was quiet tonight. Instead of playing music, help helped the servants to bring out the meal, and ales.

The moon had long since risen, the evening meal been eaten, ales sipped, and families in town fast asleep before the group in the hall were finished for the night. Jayde, Fendrel and Gilbert remained in the hall after everyone else left to go home to their families or the barracks. Sitting in the now empty hall, the three of them spoke quietly discussing the next day. It was agreed that Fendrel and Gilbert would split the knights up for training exercises. Jayde had some errand to tend to in town. The three said good night and went their separate ways for the few hours of precious sleep that they could get.

Chapter 11

Jayde awoke ready to start the day. There was much to do before the day could end, and sitting around was not going to accomplish anything. Dressing practically, Jayde met with Maria and discussed the meals for the rest of the week. The two women agreed that at the beginning of each week, the meals would be planned. Maria being the organized authoritarian that she was, could manage the kitchen just fine without needing Jayde to guide her through the week. Next, Jayde walked the fields where the knights were training hard already. Finding Fendrel, Jayde followed him to the stables where three knights were packing up and heading out for the first search party. Every day, three men would leave going in a different direction. They would spend three days searching and then return. Jayde knew that Blaxton would not choose the same location again, and searching now while training would help save them the borrowed time that was already running out. After wishing the men a safe and speedy journey, Jayde walked down to see Thomas, the blacksmith.

Thomas was hard at work when Lady Jayde came to his shop. Stunned that Lady Jayde had come down to visit his shop, he stammered, "La- La- Lady Jayde, it is wonderful to see you again. I hope you are feeling better? What can I help you with today?"

Jayde cut straight to the point. "I wish to commission you for a sword. How quickly could you have one made?"

"Well, My Lady, the man I am to make the sword for would need to come here for measurements and a description of a design if any. I could have it completed within three days, two if I worked late into the night." Thomas was curious whom the sword was for. There were no young men in town that needed a sword nor were there any pages under Lord James.

"I am ready for you to take those measurements now please Thomas." Jayde looked Thomas square in the eye waiting for the flabbergast reaction she knew was to follow.

"My Lady, what ever could you need a sword for? Surely Lord James has several knights assigned to your safety and well-being. A lady of your frame could not possibly hold a sword as large and heavy as those of Lord James's knights." Thomas could not believe what he was being requested to do!

"I know that my size and strength are childlike compared to those of Lord James's knights, however, I was told that you make all of the swords for the knights and could make a sword that would fit my size. If it is the thought of making a sword for a woman, you could always tell yourself you are making a sword for a page. When I was younger, my father's blacksmith never had a problem making a sword for me. I was barely five, but still he made one for me. It was truly beautiful. Is this request one that you can handle?" Jayde was gentle and kind with her words to Thomas. She did not want to offend him, and needed him to help her.

Looking at Lady Jayde, he guessed her to weigh no more than a twelve year old boy and no taller than one either. He would need to make a leather sheath for her as well, but this one would need to be regal. He had always wanted to etch leather.

"Excuse me for just a moment please My Lady." Thomas said rushing inside not waiting for a reply. Rushing right back out with his daughter close on his heels, "Bethany, help take Lady Jayde's measurements. I have a special project and need your help." Grinning ear to ear, Bethany grabbed the tools she would need to help her father. Somehow sensing that this was somewhat secret, he motioned for Jayde to step inside the shop as far as possible. Within minutes, he had Lady Jayde's measurements and was ushering her out of his shop. "I will send Bethany to you tomorrow night when I am finished. Bethany, close the shop, we have work to do."

With that, Jayde left Thomas and Bethany and made her way to the castle in time to sit and have the midday meal with the knights. Everyone seemed focused, eating quickly and excusing themselves back to training in the fields. Jayde finished her meal then went to the solar to work and wait for the seamstress to arrive for their appointment. After studying the needlework in the bench, Jayde decided to work on James mother's unfinished work. What had been done was beautiful, hopefully what she added would be just as beautiful. Just then, there was a gentle knock at the door.

"Lady Jayde, it is I, Diane, your seamstress." The voice from the other side of the door called.

"Come in please," Jayde answered setting the needlework down. "Please, close the door. The matter in which we are to discuss is private."

Nodding, Diane closed the door. "Hello, My Lady, it is a pleasure to meet you."

Smiling, Jayde motioned for Diane to sit next to her. "Diane, have you ever made men's clothing?"

"Of course My Lady." Diane was confused. She was told that Lady Jayde had requested her to have clothing made for herself, not Lord James.

"Wonderful! I need you to make some for me." Jayde's excitement showed on her face.

"My Lady, I do not understand. I thought you wished for me to make you new dresses?" Diane started to feel uneasy. Something was going on and Diane did not want to be a part of it.

"Diane, I need for you to make men's clothing that will fit me. Please, do not ask questions, help me. My husband's life depends on your help." Jayde pleaded.

Diane studied Lady Jayde. It was not her duty to tell anyone, least of all Lady Jayde how to dress. Once, her mother had told her of a Lord whom had requested dresses to be made to fit him. This was strange, but she could not refuse. "My Lady, I must ask you a few questions. I need to know the nature of men's clothing you need. Clothing for dancing or riding?"

"Clothing for training and fighting." Jayde answered quickly and quietly.

Diane stared at Lady Jayde. For fighting? "Yes My Lady. What colors would you like and what fabric?"

"I do not wish to be noticed. I want to blend in with any other knight." As soon as the words left her mouth, she knew that no matter how she was dressed, she would stick out because of how tiny she was. For the first time, she wished she had more of her Father's genes rather than her delicate mother's.

Clearing her throat, Diane continued. "Yes My Lady. I have a plan, is there a deadline?"

"I need them as soon as possible. Oh, Diane, one more thing, I'd like it if I could wear my dresses over these, as a cover. Can you do that?" Jayde had almost forgotten. She wasn't sure what this mission was going to be like, but she wanted to be prepared. "How soon will you have them ready?"

"I will have a first set ready for you when you wake in the morning, another two sets before you go to sleep tomorrow and another two sets the day after that. Will five sets be adequate?" Diane knew something was wrong, but it was not her station to pry.

"Thank you Diane. One last thing, can you please not tell anyone about this? I really appreciate it." Jayde hoped she could trust this woman. Maggie said she was trustworthy, and she trusted Maggie.

Nodding, Diane stood up and excused herself so that she might get this started and finished as soon as possible. The green eyes this woman had made her feel vulnerable, as though she could see right through to her very soul. A chill ran up her back as she walked out the door and away to do her work.

Jayde sat alone in the solar and gathered her thoughts. Tomorrow was a big day. Tomorrow, she began her training. Standing and taking a deep breath, Jayde went to her chamber where Maggie was waiting for her.

"Out with it" Maggie said as Jayde walked into the room.

"Let me close the door." Jayde closed the door and turned to face Maggie. "I need you to promise that this conversation stays between us."

Maggie stood there and waited for Jayde to continue.

"Promise me!" Jayde needed to confide in someone, someone she could trust.

Startled, Maggie nearly shouted back, "I promise!"

Taking a deep breath, Jayde crossed the room to the window bench and sat down. Folding her hands in her lap and looking down, "Maggie, I am pregnant, about four and a half months. I think something is wrong however. These past few days, I have been experiencing pains deep within. I do not know what to do or whom to turn to."

"Oh dearest Lady Jayde. You have been through so much. I am sure the baby is fine. I will send for the midwife, she will confirm that you and the baby are healthy." Maggie hustled out the room and down the stairs. She would personally fetch the midwife.

Jayde waited for what felt like an eternity until Maggie returned with a midwife. "This is a very private matter. I do not want to find out that this was discussed with anyone." Jayde suddenly grabbed her stomach and groaned. There it was again, that pain deep within. It was agonizing.

The midwife gently led Lady Jayde to the bed and waited for the next contraction, then she placed her hands on Lady Jayde's belly, and waited for the contraction to pass. It was a long and hard contraction. "My Lady, you most definitely are in labor. We must prepare for this birth."

"My baby will not survive will it?" Jayde remained calm somehow.

"I am sorry My Lady, but if you are only four months along, the baby will not likely survive." The midwife tried her best to be kind and not lead on Lady Jayde.

The gravity of the moment seized Jayde like ice. She could barely breath, her sobs consumed her. She could not hear anything that was being said to her. Minutes passed into an hour and that hour passed into three hours. The pain kept coming. The aromas from the evening meal came and went and still Jayde labored. She felt like her insides were being ripped out. She could not keep quiet much longer. Finally, Jayde screamed out in pain.

Gilbert and Fendrel were concerned. Lady Jayde not only missed their meeting, but the evening meal as well to speak with the knights as a whole. They decided to search for her. As they arrived at the top of the stairs, both men heard the scream of a woman in pain. They rushed down the hall to Lady Jayde's room and burst in without knocking. The scene that they walked into was like that of one on the battlefield. Lady Jayde lay on the bed, her skirts hiked, blood was everywhere and there was a midwife covered in blood. Remembering how secretive Jayde had wanted this to be kept, Gilbert shoved Fendrel into the room with one hand and slammed the door shut with the other. Fendrel retreated to the farthest corner of the room while Gilbert rushed to Jayde's side.

"Lady Jayde, breath, keep breathing. Here, take my hand, now squeeze. Squeeze as hard as you can, each time the pain comes. There you go, breath." Gilbert coached Lady Jayde. He had no idea what he was doing but knew that in the battlefield, when a man was injured, talking to him and holding his hand helped to keep them calm. Kneeling in the pool of blood, Gilbert silently prayed for her health and recovery. From the mood in the room, he feared the worst.

Finally, late into the night, there was a faint cry as the midwife laid a tiny baby upon Jayde's chest. Everyone in the room crossed themselves except Jayde and Gilbert. Jayde marveled at the sweet fingers and toes and watched as her beautiful baby girl struggled with each breath until finally after only a few minutes, her baby girl quit breathing. Too small and too young, she had no chance of surviving. The tears came again, hot tears streaking down her face. She held her little angel in her arms until Maggie offered to bath her and wrap her in a linen. Jayde watched as Maggie delicately cradled the baby in her arms and bathed her, then wrapped the baby in linen. Turning to Gilbert, she laid the baby in his arms.

"My Lady, I must clean you up before I can lay her in your arms again." Maggie lovingly insisted.

Numb, Jayde could only obey and allowed the stripping of her blood soaked gown and the warm clean wet linen to wipe her clean. She did not notice both Fendrel and

Gilbert turn away from her to allow what little privacy there was. Finally, Jayde was clean and dressed and the bedding had been changed. She weakly sat down in bed and held her arms out for her baby girl. Softly she sang a lullaby, bringing tears to the eyes of both ladies and men in the room. "Sweet dreams my beautiful Laila."

Maggie knew that if she did not take baby Laila from Lady Jayde now that Lady Jayde might not be able to let go again. Walking towards Lady Jayde, she waited until Lady Jayde lifted Laila up into Maggie's arms.

"Promise that you will make sure she is warm. Promise that we will take her to the Rose Garden. Promise." Jayde's weak sorrow filled words cut like knives.

"Yes My Lady, I promise she will be warm and I promise she will rest in the Rose Garden. Tomorrow, when you are ready, I will help you to visit her." Maggie then turned and walked out of the quiet room with Fendrel on her heals.

Fendrel was still in shock. How had she managed to hide her pregnancy? Did Lord James know? "Maggie, what are you going to do with it?"

Stopping in her tracks, Maggie spun around to face Fendrel. He had never seen a rage in this woman's face like he saw now. "We, meaning you, will come with me right this minute to the Rose Garden and we, again meaning you, will dig a grave for this innocent baby. Tomorrow, we will plant a rose bush over the baby so that she will live to be visited by her mother as often as wanted. You will go to the stone carver tomorrow and have a stone carved with Laila's name and this day's date. Do you understand?" The last part was not so much a question as it was a challenge to defy or complain in any way.

Jayde awoke in the morning to find Maggie and Gilbert in her room. Her body ached, her heart ached and yesterday slammed into her with such force it seemed to knock the wind from her lungs. Maggie came to her side and helped to calm her while Gilbert poured some tea and brought it to her.

"Drink this child, it will help your strength." Maggie lied. The tea would do nothing for Lady Jayde's strength. All it was going to do was make her sleep.

After waking up, drinking the tea and falling back to sleep, Jayde knew what the tea was for and welcomed it. She could sink into darkness and not feel the emptiness in her heart. Finally after two days of darkness, Jayde knew she must stop this and accept the day for what it was. She knew the pain would be raw and blinding, but she had to find James and hopefully, there would be more babies in the future, though none would be as beautiful as Laila.

When Maggie walked into Lady Jayde's chamber, she was startled to see that Lady Jayde was awake. "Here, let me pour you some tea."

"No. No more tea. The tea will not bring back Laila and it will not rescue James. I need a bath Maggie, I smell almost as bad as when James found me in the ruins. This is going to hurt, but it will not kill me. Help me to be strong, but know that I welcome your support when I am weak." Jayde was determined to live today. Her little baby deserved a mother who wanted to live for her.

Maggie had a bath brought up as well as a sweet bread and broth. After Lady Jayde had eaten, Maggie helped Lady Jayde to step into the bath. "My Lady, while you slept, the Blacksmith's daughter, Bethany, came by. She asked for you to come visit her when you were well again." Maggie washed and scrubbed Lady Jayde's hair while mentioning her visitors. "The seamstress also came to visit you. Your clothing is wrapped still and in your wardrobe. She said there were strict orders that no one was to touch or open those packages. Do you know what this is about?"

"Hmmm, I shall take a look in a bit." Was all that Jayde responded with. She felt a little better after her bath. Maggie excused herself to remove the tray and bowl from the morning meal. As soon as Jayde dried herself off, she opened one of the packages that Diane had left for her. Quickly, she slipped her dress on over it and slipped out of the castle to go to see Thomas and Bethany. Arriving at their shop, Jayde knocked and called into the shop. "Hello? Thomas, Bethany? Are

159

you here?" Where could they have gone? Just then she heard a door open from behind her.

"Lady Jayde? I hope you are feeling better." Bethany said.

"I am recovering, thank you for asking. How are you and your father?" Jayde was eager to see the work they had done for her.

"Father is fine, he should be coming out any moment. I will let him know you are here. He is very excited to show you our work!" Running back into the house, Bethany called out to her father.

Moments later, Thomas appeared with Bethany and a package wrapped in linens. "My Lady, it is good to see you up. We were worried, they said you had fallen suddenly ill. I hope you are recovering well. Please come in and look at the sword you commissioned." Thomas then unwrapped the swaddled sword. The sheath was beautiful. It had what looked to be the wind blowing down the length of the sheath etched into the leather. "Bethany took care of the leather. This is her work here." Thomas said as he pointed to the sheath.

"It is exquisite. Thank you so very much!" Jayde found herself lost in a moment that was not consumed by sorrow.

Thomas continued on, pulling the sword out of the sheath. It took Jayde's breath away. The hilt was beautiful. Whisping around the handle were curls of air, much like the wind on the sheath. At the base of the blade were tiny emeralds. There was more wind swirls down the blade from base to tip and in the center of the blade, was a circle of jade. It was more than she could have hoped for. Picking it up, it was perfect for her height and strength. Overwhelmed with appreciation, she quickly hugged Thomas then Bethany before she wiped the tear that had fallen down her face.

"Thank you. This is truly a work of art. I had no idea any sword could look this beautiful." Jayde could feel the tears building up. Sliding the sword into its sheath, she paid Thomas then left with her new sword in its sheath wrapped in the linens. Jayde rushed back to the castle and to her chamber closing the door swiftly behind her. Slowly sinking to the floor, she crossed her arms over her knees, buried her face into her arms and sobbed long slow sobs. She cried so deeply, she felt drained and eventually fell asleep sitting on the floor with her back against the door.

"Lady Jayde, are you in here?" Maggie softly asked and followed with soft knocking on the door. She had seen Lady Jayde rush up here a few hours ago, but had not seen her since. She was worried for Lady Jayde. To experience such a loss so young, not to mention the stress of Lord James being missing and only recently being rescued herself, the poor child was alone. Gently, she tried the door. It was unlocked but difficult to move. "Lady Jayde?" she tried again, but a little louder.

This time she heard something on the other side of the door.

Jayde was alone on a hill blanketed in thick low fog. She couldn't even see her own feet. In the distance, she could see James, and he was holding Laila! Her beautiful little girl. She took a step forward, and watched as James took a step back. She called out to him, but he would not answer. She began to fan the fog at her feet hoping that she could see a path before her that would lead her to James. When she finally managed to fan the fog away, she saw that there was no ground beneath her feet, just air. Suddenly she began to fall through the fog and into darkness. Crying out for James, she watched him smile at her as he turned and walked away up into the clouds holding their baby girl. She continued to fall, feeling nothing but numbness until she heard someone calling for her. She needed to find the voice. It was Maggie!

Jayde snapped her head up. She took a look around, and realized she was awake, and alone in this room. This room filled with so much pain. She remembered waking up in here the first time. James kneeling by her side and crying when she woke up. She couldn't stand this room anymore. She needed to find Maggie and discover the other rooms that were available.

"My Lady, are you well? Do you need anything?" Maggie hoped she would not need to force her way into the room to check on her.

"Maggie? Oh Maggie!" Jayde jumped to her feet and flung the door open. "Maggie, I was just coming to look for you! I am so glad you found me first." Launching herself forward, she hugged the one connection to James she had. The older woman embraced her back, giving all the warmth that Jayde had missed so deeply since her mother had passed.

Maggie stood there for barely a moment before reacting and wrapping her arms around the beautiful and strong young woman. She held Jayde the same way she remembered holding Lord James the day his mother passed. "It is okay child, I am here. I will always be here for you." Maggie gently smoothed Lady Jayde's long hair as she held her tightly. After several minutes had passed and Jayde pulled back, Maggie asked, "What are you planning that is such a secret? Secret trips into town, the seamstress making clothing wrapped in paper with strict orders only you may open them, the Blacksmith's daughter, Bethany, coming and requesting your presence when you are ill. Tell me everything."

Sighing, Jayde sat down on the bench at the window. "Oh Maggie, I do not know where to begin... Five days ago..." Jayde recounted the story from when James had taken her with him in to the forest until now. She included her plans for searching for James, and her plan to train with the knights. Jayde thought Maggie was going to fall out of her seat and faint at the mention of her training with the knights. "I know what Blaxton is like, I know how he thinks. I know that after his sister

163

killed herself, something in his mind died too. He thinks differently than you and me." After a long pause, Jayde concluded her story, "I have made up my mind about this. There is nothing that you can say that will change my plans, or my actions. James would and has risked his life for me, I will risk everything for him. We have no living children to care for, all responsibilities that James and I have here at Era can and would be taken over by Lord Henry and Lord Raymond." Jayde choked her emotions. This was not the time to grieve for Laila.

Maggie sat quietly for a moment. Looking at Lady Jayde, she could see that the liquid jade in her eyes that brought so much warmth to her face now appeared to be stone. She no longer looked like the young seventeen year old new bride that Lord James had brought home barely six months ago, but instead looked like a confident, strong, young woman with more wisdom than a battle hardened old man. Taking a deep breath, Maggie stood up and smoothed the skirt of her dress.

"I am sure I have disappointed you, but this is bigger than you and I, this is love and loyalty. James would not approve of my plans, I know. He would do anything, including locking me in a dungeon, to keep me from following through, but if Blaxton kills James, then I will have nothing to live for. My father trusted my life in James's hands. Somehow, I feel like Lady Catherine has trusted me with James's life too. I understand if you cannot be a part of this, then stay out of my way." All Jayde could hear was Maggie's silence. Taking a deep breath, Jayde realized she might have to do this alone.

Maggie slowly turned to face Lady Jayde. Reaching out she took Lady Jayde's hands in her own. "Lady Catherine would have been proud of Lord James for marrying you. She would be proud of how you treat people, and how you love her son. I am proud of you for being the strong woman you are. I do not want you to put yourself in harms way, but I will not stop you. I will help you along this path that you have chosen, but I must warn you, it will be difficult and there will be many that try and get in your way. Now, what do we need to do first?"

Smiling, Jayde could barely contain her gratitude. "I need to ask you help me run this castle. I cannot spend all day in the fields, and all day here. Maria and I create each week's meals on Sunday. We could review the tasks for the servants inside and outside of the walls of this castle, on Sunday as well. I trust you to carry on as you always have before I was here. The fewer people whom know about this the better. I start in the fields today with Gilbert and Fendrel. I will braid my hair, then sneak off to the fields. After training, I will slip on my tunic over this and sit down for the evening meal as well. I will take breakfast in my chamber from now on. We can do this."

"Well, let us begin. Come, sit down over here and I will braid your hair. Are you going to wear a dress on the fields today or change?" Maggie began to braid the ever long rich brown hair.

Smiling, Jayde stood up. "Thank you for braiding my hair. I'll need you to keep Anna away, she is my dearest friend, but does not keep secrets very well." Jayde surprised Maggie by unlacing her tunic and revealing the garment underneath. Maggie took the tunic from her and laid it out on the bed. Jayde's gentle curves were well hidden beneath the men's clothes, except for her muscular legs. "Well, time to take the first step. Thank you again."

"I will be here waiting for you after training to help you wash and ready for the evening meal." Maggie hugged Lady Jayde then motioned for her to be very quiet. "Only Lady Catherine knew of this hall, she kept it a secret in case there was ever a siege on the castle. Walking to the fireplace, she pulled the raised paw of the lion statue towards her. There was the familiar sound of a lock lifting and the squeak of an old hinge to a door. The large wood slab to the left of the fireplace moved slightly. Maggie smiled, and disappeared into the dark abyss beyond the wooden slab. She returned with a torch and lit it from the fire in the fireplace. "I will take you this way today, and make sure that I clean the hall and stairs myself. Each morning, you take this torch and light it, then you carry it with you lighting the other torches on your way. There is a holder for this at the end. I will show you how to latch this door once in the hall and show you how to get back in from below. Follow me Lady Jayde."

The hall was filthy. Dust, spiders, and Jayde even thought she saw mice, had taken over this hall. Jayde followed Maggie down the hall, turned sharply, walked down several stairs, turned sharply again and down a short hall before coming to another large wooden slab. Placing the torch in its holder Maggie pulled on a matching lion statue's paw and the lock on the slab released allowing the door to move slightly. "What is on the other side of this door?" Jayde questioned Maggie.

"It used to be a private garden for only Lady Catherine, now it is just a space filled with weeds. There is ivy climbing the wall here, so the slab is completely covered. You will notice that there are several lions in the garden. Lord Edward had them made and arranged here in the garden as a wedding gift to Lady Catherine. Her family's crest was a Lion." Maggie pulled on the door until the ivy on the other side finally let go allowing the door to swing open. Once out in the old and forgotten garden, Maggie pulled another matching lion statue's paw and the door closed and the lock latched into place. Leading Lady Jayde to a gate, she pulled out a key and handed it to Lady Jayde. "This is the only key to this gate, it is yours now. Lady Catherine would want you to have it. Where are you to be meeting with Gilbert and Fendrel?"

"I am to be meeting with them in the breeding stables, unfortunately, I have absolutely no idea where that is." Jayde felt nervous and unprepared suddenly. How did she not think to ask where she was to go?

Seeing the frustration on Lady Jayde's face, Maggie offered, "I can show you how to get there from here." Maggie continued to lead the way to the working stables. "This is where all of the horses that the knights train are bred and born. Only the knights are allowed here at these stables. There will be no one from town here. Not even the blacksmith comes here. This was a good choice to have your secret meetings. My Lady, I will leave you here to walk the rest of the way alone. The fewer people that know about this, the better; as well as the few people that realize that I know, the better. Be strong Lady Jayde. I will be waiting for you this evening." With that, Maggie disappeared back to the castle.

Jayde took a deep breath, and carrying her sword down to the stables, she followed the barely visible path down. She could hear Fendrel and Gilbert talking as she walked up and decided to stop and listen for a moment.

"Are you sure this is a good idea? Lord James will kill us if he finds out." Fendrel's nervousness and doubt could be heard in his words.

"If we do not go through with this, he might be the one dead. Lady Jayde understands this mad mind of

Blaxton's more than we ever will. She has been exposed to the craziness that fuels his rage. She is smart, do not underestimate her." Gilbert was quick to defend Lady Jayde.

"Look how small she is! She could not even lift a sword above her head let alone wield it in battle. How much of us taking her to battle will be us wasting our resources protecting her?" Fendrel was getting frustrated now.

Gilbert tried again to soothe and persuade Fendrel, "She is stronger than she looks Fendrel. Have faith in her. Helping to strengthen her is the point of this. Think of it as training a page."

Fendrel could not hold back any longer. "No! I will not be a part of my own death sentence. You may train her, I will not stop you nor will I confess to anyone of this plan, but understand this, if we are able to save Lord James, he will forever hate you. He may even cast you from his knights. You will no longer be one of his most trusted. Do you understand the risk you are taking? What is in it for you?"

Gilbert could not answer Fendrel. In part, he knew that Fendrel was correct. This plan was his death sentence. Once Lord James was rescued, he knew that there would no longer be a place for him here. Why was he so eager to go along with Lady Jayde's plan?

Just then, both men startled, as Jayde walked into the stables, never having made a sound and warning them of her presence. Even the horses in the stables had not seemed to notice or be bothered by her presence.

Fendrel saw the smaller sword in her hands. Groaning, he threw his hands in the air and stormed out leaving Gilbert alone in the stables with Lady Jayde.

"Thank you for doing this. I know this is inappropriate for you to be training me alone, but I appreciate it more than you could know." Jayde nervously stood there in the doorway of the stables watching Gilbert.

Gilbert could barely speak. Lord James would most definitely kill him if he could see his wife now and hear the thoughts in his head. She was beautiful. The tights clung to her legs like a second skin and left nothing to the imagination. The shirt fit perfectly, too perfectly. It gave just a peak of her milky white shoulders while the front was open enough to tease him with the gentle curves of her breasts, disappearing into the linen fabric that peaked on her wind hardened nipples. The shirt cinched perfectly at her waist and barely covered her butt. Knowing that he could not act upon his thoughts, made his erect and bulging manhood ach leaving him feeling frustrated. Maybe Fendrel was the smart one, leaving while he could. This was a bad idea, his thoughts were going to kill him before Lord James could. More gruffly than Gilbert meant to be, he ordered her to follow him. Taking her out to the horse paddocks below, Gilbert began training her. He knew he would have to train her harder and faster than any page, he only hoped she could handle it. The truth was that no matter how close they got, they would at best be one step behind. With Jayde, they could be one step ahead.

Chapter 12

The days had turned into weeks without any clue as to where Blaxton had taken James. Every few days, another group of knights left and another group returned with more disappointment. Many knights had started to hint that Blaxton had already killed James and that all of this preparation was pointless. Gilbert did his best to shelter Jayde from hearing any of these conversations of doubt, but Jayde still heard some of the whispers.

Each day was exhausting. Jayde could barely function at the end of the day and several nights Jayde fell asleep in the middle of the evening meal. Maggie would usually wake her late the next morning before helping her to get ready for another day of training. Jayde's legs were a covered in bruises from training and falling. Her body had gained exquisite curves from all of the training and her strength had improved so much that Gilbert had mentioned that once she could stay atop a horse while wielding a sword he would introduce her to training with the rest of the men.

Gilbert had taken to sleeping in the breeding barn since he had started training Lady Jayde. On hot nights he could sometimes still smell the fragrant rose oil that she used in her soaps. It was hard enough to keep his hands off of her, not to wrap her tiny body up in his arms and make love to her. Nearly every night he was haunted by visions of her coming to him in the night seeking solace and love and accepting both from him. She had never led him on, never given him any reason to believe that she wanted him. From the night she had born Laila, they shared a secret bond that went unspoken but not unnoticed. The next week of training was going to be hell for him. She knew how to ride a horse, he had watched her. In fact she knew how to do a lot of fighting. She was better than most of the men in archery, was skilled with hand to hand combat and was a master with her dagger. Tomorrow, he would begin to work with her sword skills while riding. Tomorrow he would fight every urge to not turn her around in the saddle and make love to her right there, riding off into the woods to start some hidden future.

Jayde awoke early today. Today she would test her skills at riding and swords. She knew her advantage was also her disadvantage. She was petite. She could hide against the sleek body of a horse and more easily dodge the blows from another rider. For her personally, she wanted to know if she could do all of this without a saddle. Then she would feel prepared. Maggie came in with breakfast, braided her hair then left to go about ordering servants around. Jayde had requested that all of the Blue Banners with lions and wind swirls be cleaned and readied for use and it was Maggie's priority until every last banner was ready. Both Maggie and Jayde sensed that war was closer than any of them thought. Taking a buttered roll with her, she ran out the secret passage and all the way down to the barn. Gilbert was nowhere to be found which is exactly what Jayde wanted. He was always trying to protect her, hold her back. She could do more without him watching over her. Slipping into the barn she bridled her horse and led him out to the training field that Gilbert had set up for her. Grabbing the young stallion's mane and jumping, she seated herself onto the horse. She took the stallion around the paddock at a trot, then canter before charging ahead at a gallop. Drawing her sword, she swung it at the target, weaved the obstacles, and took her dagger out and throwing it at the next target striking it on the bullseye. Ha! Slowing down to a trot, she turned around and started towards the barn. Coming down the hill was Gilbert and he looked mad.

Gilbert was coming around the castle after getting a roll from the kitchen when he watched Jayde charging on a young stallion bareback. What was she doing? She was going to get herself hurt or killed! He arrived in the barn before she did and was fuming.

Jayde arrived in the barn and slid off of her horse just as Gilbert grabbed the reins and led the horse to his stall taking the bridle off before closing the stall door. The air was charged more than usual and Jayde shivered a little in fear. She backed up against a wall hoping that the storm would blow over. Instead, it seemed to make it worse.

Gilbert threw the bridle on a bale of hay and spun around to see Jayde against a wall. "What were you thinking? Why were you not using a saddle? You could have been hurt!" Gilbert was yelling as he advanced to Jayde. "Damn it!" Gilbert was standing directly in front of Jayde. He could feel her breath on his chest. Reaching out, he cupped her chin and tilted her face up to look him in the eyes. The vibrant green eyes with tears streaming down her cheeks startled him. All of his anger left his body and instead all he could think about was kissing her delicious rose red lips. Without any more thought Gilbert brought his mouth down to hers.

Jayde began to silently cry the moment Gilbert began yelling at her. What did she do that was so wrong? All she wanted was to find James and bring him home. She wanted him to take her in his arms and hold her, kiss her temple, hold her hands and make love to her. She wanted to argue with him and laugh with him. She missed him so much, her body shook. Gilbert was now standing so close to her there was barely any space between their bodies. He reached down and lifted her chin to face him. She tried to stop the tears, tried to not show any weakness. That was part of the training, do not expose your weakness. Then his mouth was on hers, one hand at the nape of her neck and the other at her waist drawing her to him. Jayde's heart raced with panic. She tried to pull back, but Gilbert deepened his kiss thrusting his tongue into her mouth. It was nothing like kissing James. Her panic grew until fear consumed her mind and she began to desperately push against Gilbert's shoulders.

Gilbert felt Jayde's head tilt back, so he deepened his kiss. He barely felt the tiny hands pushing against his shoulders at first. Realizing that Jayde was not enjoying this kiss, he shoved himself back and away from her. What had he done? He knew that she did not care for him the way he cared for her. If she had fallen and been hurt, he did not know what he would do. He needed to distance himself. "I am so sorry Jayde, Lady Jayde. My Lady, I think our training together is over. I have given you everything I can and now you need to be with the rest of the men training. I will speak with Fendrel immediately. He will be waiting for you in the fields with the knights. Good day My Lady." Without even looking at her, Gilbert left the barn. He had become too close. He allowed it to become too personal for him.

Jayde stood against the wall for a while after Gilbert had left. What on earth made him kiss her? She was a married woman, in love with her husband, searching for a way to save him. Oh God! What will James think when he finds out? He will hate her, he would kill Gilbert, would he throw her out? Her stomach rolled over. She couldn't think. She needed to get away from her thoughts. She grabbed the bridle, put it on the stallion and went back out to the field. She worked her horse and herself hard. The pair were soaked with sweat when Maggie appeared at the stables. Stopping her physical self-torment and training she turned the horse and trotted over to Maggie. "Maggie, is everything alright?" Jayde dismounted and tied up the stallion giving him a break for water while she brushed him down a bit.

"My Lady, you were not present at the midday meal and Gilbert looked angry. Is everything all right? What has happened?" Maggie knew something was wrong. She had never seen Gilbert so happy training anyone before and had seen Lady Jayde find a confidence and authority that seemed to amplify her beauty.

"Everything is fine. I just got lost in time. I will go to the kitchen now and find something." Jayde was hoping that she was convincing. She did not like lying to Maggie.

"Lady Jayde, I brought you a meal. You should sit, eat, rest, and tell me the truth. I might be old, but I am smart." Maggie did not like knowing that Lady Jayde felt like she needed to lie to her.

Jayde saw the sack of food that Maggie had brought. She was so hungry she sat down on the ground and shoved a piece of meat into her mouth. She grabbed the jug of ale and poured a cup for herself. Finally after getting some food in her stomach, Jayde looked at Maggie, all she could do was shake her head. The tears started again. "Oh Maggie, I do not know how to fix this. Gilbert was angry with me this morning. I was riding my horse without a saddle. I know I can do anything in the saddle, my father taught me when I was young. I needed to know that I could stay atop of this beast without a saddle. I had to make sure that I am prepared for battle as well as make sure that I could have the respect of the other knights. I rode to the barn knowing he was angry. After I dismounted, he grabbed my horse, put him in a stall and was yelling. I tried not to cry, it was just too much. All of these weeks training, being exhausted, searching for James, I just could not take any more. Then he kissed me. I pushed him away, he apologized and left. What have I done? What will James do? Maggie, I did not think I invited or enticed Gilbert, what have I done?"

Maggie was in shock, this explained so much. Lady Jayde was the reason Gilbert had been so happy and now today, why he was so miserable. Lord James would have to challenge Sir Gilbert to defend Lady Jayde's honor and the challenge would be to the death. No one else knew though, so maybe there would not need to be a challenge. "Lady Jayde, you have done nothing wrong. This is not what you need to think about or spend your time and energy on. You must stay focused. I have worked hard to keep people from knowing of our plans. So far everyone believes you are simply stressed and worried. When you show up to train with the knights, word will travel fast. Be ready to face doubt, criticism, hate and obstacles. Are you ready for this?"

Taking a deep breath and truly hearing what Maggie was saying, Jayde replied, "I am as ready as I can be. It is time to test my strength and the loyalty and trust of Lord James's knights. Thank you Maggie. It is time for me to ride this beautiful beast and see how the men will react. I shall   see you after training." Jayde stood up and mounted her stallion taking their time to ride around to the knights training fields.

Maggie rushed back into the castle only to find a near drunk Gilbert sitting alone in a dark corner of the hall. "Sir Gilbert, should you not be out in the fields training?" Gilbert snorted in reply. "Sir Gilbert, I need to have a word with you. It is of exceptional importance."

"Nothing is important anymore, everything that once was important is gone. I just want to finish my ale and go." Gilbert sounded more drunk than he actually was and he did not care. Let everyone think he was drunk instead of heartbroken.

"Sir Gilbert," Maggie started quietly, sitting on a chair next to him. "Sir Gilbert, I spoke with Lady Jayde just a while ago." Gilbert's eyes flew up and gave away his sobriety and Maggie noticed. "Sir Gilbert, I realize now that your recent joy has been you falling in love with Lady Jayde. You must know that she cares only for Lord James in that way. She is riding over to the training field right now. You must stay by her side. We both know how strong Lady Jayde is, but she could still be over taken by any of the knights whom are not as honorable as you. Something is coming, Jayde will fight side by side with the knights, but without their respect, she will be in danger. There are several knights here that would not stop simply because a woman pushes away. Instead they might even find it a challenge. You must protect her. I do not know or understand what it is that you two share, but you share a bond with her that no one else does. Why is that Sir Gilbert? Can you explain it to me?"

Gilbert took a moment before answering. "It was because of Laila. I held Lady Jayde's hand until she held Laila. I was there when Lord James should have been and that is the intimate bond that we share. The bond of life and death. I will protect her with my life until Lord James is able to take that responsibility back. Then I am leaving. I cannot watch her happiness knowing that it is only a matter of time before I try to give her my love again." Gilbert stood and walked out towards the training fields.

Walking out he heard the commotion before he could see it. There were knights standing in a circle, laughing. Pushing through, he saw Lady Jayde in the center on one knee. Her braid had been pinned to the earth with a sword. Rage filled him. "What the hell is going on here?" He bellowed.

Jayde's eyes locked with his and gave him a warning to not intervene. In one fluid motion, Jayde grabbed her dagger in her left hand and sliced upwards while in the other hand pulled her sword from its sheath. Standing she jabbing the knight whom had pinned her braid of hair to the ground at his jugular with the tip of her sword. In that instant there was stunned silence. Within moments, nearly one hundred knights surrounded Lady Jayde and the unfolding scene. The look on Lady Jayde's face was a mix of confidence, strength, and triumph. The knight at the end of Lady Jayde's sword looked down at the ground. Still pinned to the ground was Lady Jayde's braid, cut off by her own dagger.

"My Lady, I give you my apologies and my loyalty." The knight said, dropping to his knee while Lady Jayde's sword still pressed to his neck.

"I demand that you think about whose side you will fight for. Lord James is in danger. He needs for you to work together. You need me to save him. Not only am I small enough to squeeze into tight spaces, which believe it or not will be useful once you realize the kind of place that Blaxton will be holding Lord James, but I know first-hand how Blaxton's mind works. I am smart and strong, you will learn from me as well as I will learn from all of you. This can only happen if you trust me and respect my authority. I trust there will not be any further challenges?" Jayde knew she would have had to earn their respect, she just did not realize it would be by cutting her hair to her shoulders. Everything has a price though.

By the end of the day, every person training on the fields was exhausted. Jayde had challenged each and every person to do their absolute best, then asked more from them. This time, she did not even bother to go up to her chamber and change her clothes to keep the façade. As she walked in to the great hall, servants stared at her hair. Enough people had witnessed the scene in the fields today and word traveled fast. Since cutting off nearly four feet of hair today her hair seemed to have become even shorter as it slowly returned to the bouncing curls she had when she was a young child.

Tonight, there was no wine, but only ale to toast to and quench their thirst from such a long day. Maggie grabbed Gilbert by his ear as soon as the knights walked in. "You promised you would protect her! She was held at the tip of a sword and her hair was cut? How is that protecting her?"

"My God woman! Calm yourself. No such thing happened. A knight challenged Jayde's authority, he pulled a sneaky move on her and pinned her braid to the ground. Jayde used her dagger and cut her own braid off all while drawing her sword and holding him at her mercy at the end of her sword. She actually made him bleed! I do not think that Jayde realizes it yet, but the other knights tied off the now cut end of her braid and have it hanging in the stables as a reminder to all of their allegiance, and as a reminder that looks can be deceiving. In my defense, I tried to step in to help her, but one look from her stopped me. Jayde is very fierce and I think that her actions today were unfortunately necessary to earn the respect she now has."

"LADY Jayde, that is what you meant to say, was that LADY Jayde is fierce. Now hearing the truth in the matter today, I unfortunately must agree with you. I am glad to hear that at least this will be easier for Lady Jayde. You must still stay close to protect her, but Gilbert, be careful how you speak otherwise you will give away your affections of Lady Jayde and the consequences of that would be life changing for not only you, but Lady Jayde as well. Trust me when I say that Lady Jayde has already lost everything good in her life, please do not take Lord James's love and trust from her, or the love and trust of the people of Era." Maggie wanted to caution Gilbert, to protect himself as well as Lady Jayde. She knew that when a man as loyal as Gilbert gave his love, he gave it completely and could only give it once. She hoped it was not too late. Maggie excused herself and went to fetch jugs of ale to set upon the tables for Lady Jayde and the knights.

Gilbert stood up uncomfortably and walked over to the chair next to Lady Jayde. She had requested that he sit with her at meals, and he would not reject her offer. The only other empty chair was the one to Lady Jayde's left, where Lord James should be sitting. Gilbert was pretty quiet throughout the evening meal. He could not let their friendship be ruined because of his actions earlier that day.

"Lady Jayde, I must apologize again for my actions this morning. I care for you more than I should, it is true. I cannot change my heart, but with my heart and my head, I will watch over you and protect you until Lord James is safe and able to protect you. My Lady, I must excuse myself now, it has been quite a long day and I fear I am more tired than usual." Gilbert bowed his head and left the table, leaving Jayde feeling alone.

Suddenly, exhaustion caught up to Jayde. Standing up, she was about to excuse herself to retire to her chamber, when Fendrel jumped up and cheered.

Fendrel could hear the quiet conversation between Lady Jayde and Sir Gilbert. He had noticed, along with several other knights how close the two seemed to be. He was startled that Gilbert would leave so early, but after hearing the conversation, he understood. Seeing Lady Jayde stand up he knew what it would look like to some of the eyes that were watching and he knew that all of the hard work that Lady Jayde had done would be lost. It would look as though they were having an affair. He glanced to his left and saw the panic on Maggie's face, knowing she saw what he did and assuming she knew more. So Fendrel did the only thing he knew how, he jumped to his feet and gave a cheer. "To Lady Jayde! Never has there been a knight like Lady Jayde!"

The hall roared with laughter that was deafening followed by the toast, "TO LADY JAYDE! NEVER

HAS THERE BEEN A KNIGHT LIKE LADY
JAYDE! SPEECH! SPEECH! SPEECH! SPEECH!"

Jayde was already standing. Confused, she looked at
Fendrel and realized he had heard everything and that
he was saving her from something she did not
understand. Smiling her best fake smile ever, she
picked up her cup of ale and raised it in the air. The
hall silenced. Jayde began to speak, but was interrupted
by a few knights calling out.

"Where are you Lady Jayde? Small but MIGHTY!"
The hall roared again with cheers.

Laughing, Jayde stood in her chair, she did not think it
was possible but the cheering actually became louder.
She waited a moment for the men to quiet down. "I
know that we are facing a lot of challenges right now. I
know that you accepting me to train with you is
difficult. I appreciate your open minds. You must not
be easy on me. I expect you to respect me, my
authority, and I expect you to train as hard with me as
you do with every other knight. If you think that this is
our biggest challenge, I am sorry to let you down, but it
is not. We still have no idea where Lord James is. It
has been three months. Summer will be ending soon
and with the end of summer comes cooler fall nights.
Where ever Blaxton is hiding with Lord James, know
that it will not be someplace nice, well-kept and clean
like it is here at Era. It will be the worst conditions and
Lord James will have been starved and tortured both

physically and mentally." Jayde took a deep breath and hesitated before continuing. She was unaware that Gilbert was hiding in the shadows listening and watching her every move and those around her. "I know that many of you are aware that I was in danger before Lord James and Fendrel returned with me. Six months ago after returning to my father's estates, Blaxton took me and held me as his prisoner. Blaxton held me in a tower that had holes in the rafters, and provided me with a stale piece of bread and slice of cheese every other day for four months. I had no fire, bed, blankets, or even a chair to sit on. The rain fell into the small room I was confined to, as well as snow and hail too. The wind was colder than any winter wind I had ever felt. I began to give up hope of ever getting home to Era, Lord James, and all of you. I began to think that I was going to die in that tower before I could ever tell Lord James of the child that I carried." Suddenly the men looked at each other in disbelief.

One knight stood and spoke up. "My Lady, with the greatest respect, I must confess that I will not fight you, train you or allow you to travel with us being pregnant. I have sworn my life and loyalty to Lord James, you and your child are an extension of Lord James and it is my honor and duty to keep you safe." A chorus of 'here here' was echoed through the hall.

Jayde held up her hands and continued. "I would not expect or ask you to make that exception and I am proud to know how you feel and know of your allegiance to Lord James. The night after Lord James was taken, you were all told that I fell gravely ill. There was some truth to that. On that evening, I brought a beautiful baby girl into this world and held her as she took her first and last breaths. Although I did not have Lord James at my side, I was not alone. Two of you were with me and gave me strength to survive and heal so that I could help to find Lord James. Without those two knights, Maggie and the midwife, I do not know that I would have had the strength to see the morning light. In a few days, I will travel with some of you and we will find where Lord James is being held. Once we find him, I will send for the rest of you, as well as Lord Raymond and Lord Henry. I cannot imagine that Blaxton will be doing this alone again. He does not strike me as the type of man to repeat his mistakes. He will have learned from what he did wrong with me and instead will be stronger, smarter and more dangerous. Rest while you can men, when I call for you, there will be no rest until Blaxton is dead and Lord James is safe." The hall filled with cheers. "On that note men, I must say good night. I hope that you all rest well, we train harder tomorrow than we did today." Jayde stepped down and retreated to her chamber where she barely managed to change her clothes and climb into bed before falling asleep.

Gilbert stayed hidden, and waited for the hall to clear out before he quietly crept through the hall and out to the breeding stables. Once he was outside the castle, he let down his guard as he walked through the garden of roses. There he stopped and laid the wreath of daisies that he had strung together atop the carved stone. He stopped at the barracks and gathered a change of clothes before heading down to the stables to get what little sleep he could before the morning.

Fendrel hid in the dark kitchen waiting to follow Gilbert from his place of hiding. Where did he go each night? He knew that Gilbert had not slept in the barracks since he began training Lady Jayde. Were the two having an affair? Had she just made fools of them all convincing them that she too was loyal while sleeping with a knight? It would not be the first time a wife had slept with someone besides her husband, but Lord James was his friend, they grew up together. Fendrel was so absorbed in watching Gilbert that he did not notice the quiet figure also hiding in the hall.

Maggie sent Anna out to follow Gilbert and keep an eye on him. What Anna found was the handsome Fendrel sneaking around as well. Anna and Jayde grew up together learning how to move with stealth so as to not wake or alert Lady Ethna. They used to sneak out with Anna's brothers when they would hunt boar. They learned how to remain quiet, move quickly, climb trees and Anna's brothers had even taught the girls hand to hand fighting. Jayde and Anna had always believed that no one else knew. In truth though, Lord Dario, Jayde's father, not only knew about their adventures, but actually encouraged Anna's brothers to train the girls.

Anna and Jayde had even hunted and killed their fair share of boars that often were prepared and cooked for the evening meals. Anna followed Fendrel through the rose garden, and down to the breeding stables, where she watched as Fendrel hid in the shadows watching Gilbert. Bored, Anna sat down on a stone just out of sight from the stables waiting for either Fendrel or Gilbert to move. She tipped her head back to look at the stars. When she brought her head back down, she saw Gilbert snuff the torch he used for light. Just then something to her left moved. Before she could focus in on it, Fendrel stepped out scaring a scream out of Anna.

Fendrel had not noticed Anna following him until he was about to leave after watching Gilbert and feeling confident that Gilbert was not going to try and slip away for a late night rendezvous with Lady Jayde. Suddenly he did not trust Lady Jayde or her supposed love for Lord James. When he turned to leave his hiding place, he barely saw the figure sitting on the edge. It was a tiny figure, a woman. He knew it! Lady Jayde did not love Lord James. Was the child even Lord James's child? That might explain Lord Gilbert stopping and placing flowers on the child's stone. He was going to confront Lady Jayde and make her be truthful to him. Sneaking around he crept up on Lady Jayde. When he jumped out of the bushes to scare her, not only did he startle the woman sitting there, but he was startled himself as well. "Anna! What are you doing here?"

Anna covered her mouth as she let out a surprised cry. She was angry at herself for being careless and angry at Fendrel for sneaking up on her. Whispering, Anna replied, "I should ask you the same thing! What are you doing following Sir Gilbert around?"

"I am making sure that Sir Gilbert is not sneaking off for a rendezvous with Lady Jayde. I am making sure she is indeed as faithful as she claims." Fendrel replied.

Anna stood up and slapped Fendrel across the face so hard it actually hurt her own hand. "How DARE you accuse My Lady of such dishonesty. I will not stand here and allow you to ruin everything she finally realized that she has. She finally has a family. Do you dare to think that she would throw it all away for a fling in the hay? Lady Jayde nearly died giving birth to Laila, Lord James child. What keeps her getting up and training harder than any of those pansies you call knights out there is the focus to find Lord James. I listen to her sleep each night. She talks in her sleep, calling to him, crying. She wakes up unrested, and trains hard because she knows that Lord James life depends on it. Believe what you wish, but keep your lies to yourself!" Turning on her heels, she disappeared into the darkness and into the castle to find Maggie.

Maggie was just about to leave and return to her own home when Anna came rushing in. Hate was written across Anna's face as she blew into the hall. Grabbing Anna by the arm and tugging her into the kitchen, she waited patiently for Anna to calm down. "Anna, start at the beginning. What did you see?"

Anna was enraged. It was difficult to tell her story without allowing her anger to get the best of her. "Then Sir Fendrel had the audacity to accuse Lady Jayde of having an affair with Sir Gilbert! Maggie, how could he suggest something so horrible? Lady Jayde is one of the most honest and most loyal people I've ever met. Looks like Lady Jayde needs someone to protect her from those that are supposed to be loyal to her after all. What are we going to do?"

Maggie thought for a moment. "Go and get some rest dear. I will take care of everything. We will protect Lady Jayde together." With that, Maggie went and woke the seamstress.

Jayde awoke just before dawn to the sounds of someone shuffling around in her room. Jumping from her bed and reaching her sword, she spun around pointed it at the noise. It was Diane, the seamstress. "What are you doing in my chambers?" Jayde demanded. Before Diane could answer, Maggie quietly slipped into the room only to jump back at the sight of Jayde holding Diane with a sword.

"For goodness sake, Lady Jayde, please, put that thing away!" Maggie whispered.

"What is going on here?" Jayde asked, lowering her sword but not putting it away.

"My Lady, after evening meal last night, I asked Anna to follow Sir Gilbert. What Anna discovered was that Sir Fendrel must have overheard something that Sir Gilbert said to you because he too was following Sir Gilbert. He then confronted Anna and accused you of having an affair with Sir Gilbert." Maggie stopped talking and froze. The color in Lady Jayde's face turned crimson with rage.

"An affair? An affair! Has he not seen how hard I have been training? I am BETTER than half of the men on those fields! Why would I go through this pain and conditioning? Only to have an affair? A man does not want to hold the body of a boy at night, he wants a woman, with curves and soft delicate hands. I have no curves left, my hands are stained from reins, and my fingers are callused. I look like a young boy! Even if I had ever wanted to be have an affair, altering my body to look like a boy would not be how I would go about having one! How dare him! Is this what all of Lord James's mistresses do? Do they all train on the fields then lay with any man that casts her a lustful eye!" Jayde was more than consumed with rage. Dressing quickly, Jayde grabbed her dagger and sword. "Maggie, go to the barracks or send someone to wake ALL of the men. I expect everyone in the fields immediately. Should anyone dare to defy my order, give me there names, I will make an example of each one." Then Jayde stormed down the stairs and out to the fields.

Nearly every knight arrived in the fields still dressing. The air was charged and no one had ever seen Lady Jayde's delicate face look like stone before now.

"It has been brought to my attention that some of you believe that I am dishonest." Several knights started to glance around staring hard at anyone whom might dare to own those thoughts. Jayde looked at Gilbert, then turned until she found Fendrel. "Some of you believe that I am not a faithful wife. Answer this, why would I put my body and mind through HELL if I were not loyal? I could simply let Blaxton have Lord James, wait for him to die and marry again to my supposed true love. Do you not think that would be far more practical for me if I was having an affair? Some of you believe that I am not skilled enough to be here on these fields. I will be openly challenging several of you on various skills today. I promise I will win each challenge. I can make your lives hell, a hell like you have never experienced before. I will push each of you to train as hard as I have and am and I will break you. So I suggest you decide your position here. I suggest that you all find a way to grasp the absolute gravity of this situation. When we leave to rescue Lord James, it will be a war. I will be the one to slice Blaxton's head from his body. That is MY right and MY honor. I will make sure he pays for the damage he has caused. Stay out of my way. Do you all understand me?" Not a single knight spoke a word but all nodded in solemn agreeance. They knew that whomever Lady Jayde called out first was whom spoke so poorly of her.

"Fendrel, get your horse and your sword. I am challenging you. MOVE NOW!" Jayde grabbed the bridle of her young stallion and without any stump to boost herself, she mounted the horse bareback.

"My Lady, I must insist that you saddle your beast. It would be an unfair challenge for you to not have anything to hold on to." Fendrel called out as he mounted his horse.

Jayde kicked her horse forward leaning into the sleek neck of her magnificent beast. Just before reaching Fendrel, Jayde swung her right leg over her horse's back and jumped. She tackled Fendrel knocking him from his horse and rolled quickly to her feet and brought the tip of her sword to Fendrel's neck. Jayde spoke so quietly that only Sir Gilbert and the few other knights standing nearest to them could hear, "Do you doubt my skills or loyalty to my husband now Sir Fendrel?" Jayde barely controlled her sneer as she spoke to him.

Fendrel struggled to grasp how he was on his knees with Lady Jayde's sword at his neck. Everything happened so fast. First, Lady Jayde was atop her horse, then she disappeared as her horse charged him then she appeared again and knocked from his horse and now she had him at sword point in front all of the knights! Her eyes locked with his, and Fendrel knew in that instant, that he had made a fatal error. Not only did he loose the respect of every knight on the field, but he had also lost any trust from Lady Jayde. He could hear the hate in her voice when she spoke.

Jayde knew at this moment, she was alone. She could no longer turn to Sir Gilbert as a friend and she could no longer turn to Sir Fendrel for advice. This was it, it was time for her to step into James's place and lead. "Get up." Jayde turned around, sheathed her sword and swung herself onto the back of her horse. "I expect each and every one of you to be able to mount and dismount your horses without a saddle on, before the end of the day. If I see you not training, I will assume you are bored and an expert at your station and I will find something far more challenging for you. Do not disappoint me." Jayde turned and rode her horse back to the stable and tied him up. Then she went into the castle and sat down for rolls and broth, alone, at the large table in the magnificent and empty hall. Taking pity on herself, she realized that she always seemed to be alone when life was at its most difficult. She had grown accustomed to that feeling, but after so many years, it still had not dulled the pain. Finishing her meal, Jayde stood and sent for two messengers. She sent a note to both of her brothers that she had a plan and needed them. She explained that searching the traditional way was getting her nowhere and she was tired of waiting. She needed them to come to Era and bring their toughest knights, she also requested that the remaining knights be at the ready when they were called. Then she gave the messenger instructions that if they could have the notes to both brothers, within one and a half days, she would double their payment. Both men set off on their horses in different directions at a full gallop. Jayde then returned to the fields with the men to train.

Jayde first checked in on the men whom were working on mounting and dismounting their horses without the use of a saddle. There was progress, but still more practice was needed. The men who had managed to complete that challenge had moved on to other training. After a few hours, Jayde moved on to the men training in archery. Jayde first worked with the men using longbows. This was yet another skill that her father had secretly made sure that she had mastered. Jayde corrected a couple of men, improving their aim and then moved on to the men training with the contraption. Although Jayde had used the crossbow before, she was far from being an expert. She took a few tips from the crossbowman and hoped she would never have to operate the crossbow. The horn was sounded to announce that the midday meal was ready. Everyone quickly made their way to the hall, thus far today, they had trained harder than they had in a very long time and it showed.

The midday meal today was cold smoked meats, breads, and fresh fruits. Although there was quiet conversation between the men, it was noticed by many that Lady

Jayde did not talk with anyone and barely ate. She seemed distracted and truthfully several men were hesitant to talk with her, they had seen a wild animal like rage in her today and it had scared many of them. Her vibrant green eyes had flashed like lightning, her cheeks pinked in the wind and her lips were the color of crimson. There was a confidence about her as she walked among the knights and dared anyone to defy or challenge her.

After the meal, everyone returned to the training fields. Jayde trained more with the crossbowman after the meal before calling everyone to the main field. There she watched as each of the knights showed whether they had managed the task of mounting a horse bareback or not. While a majority of the knights managed to acquire this new skill, there were still two dozen knights struggling. For those men, she instructed that they would meet in the morning in a smaller field where she could watch them practice and teach them the skill she required them to master.

The knights seemed to be in a better mood at the evening meal and even the jongleur played lighter music tonight. Jayde however remained stoic and deep in her own thoughts. She quietly ate her meal, drank ale and continued to pick apart the puzzle that consumed her every moment of existence. When Henry and Raymond arrived, she would have a private meeting with the two of them and they would look at the places that the knights had already searched to look for what they had missed. James was out there somewhere, and she was going to find him. Finally, she could take no more and left the joyous group. Anger and sadness surged through her veins as she walked into James office. It felt as though the knights whom had sworn their loyalties to James, had begun to forget him and had conceded that he must be dead. She must get them focused and to get them focused meant finding war. Entering James office door and closing it behind her, she looked around. She had never been in here before and felt almost as though she were invading his privacy. The room seemed to match his personality and it was comforting. The tapestry on the wall was a hunting scene, the fabric on the chairs were of deep blue with gold trim drawing out the blue from the tapestry. The cherry wood desk was large and solid, but not overpowering the room. There was a matching bookshelf in the corner that had deep shelves and were filled with what looked to be rolled maps. Jayde investigated the room wondering if there were any secret passages leading from here as well. When she reached the bookshelf, she noted that it seemed to move, but could not find the trigger to open the door. Tired, Jayde took the torch she had brought in from the hall with her and left the room just as she found it. Jayde retired to her room where Maggie had sent a bath up for her. It was lovely. The steam was still wafting in the air as Jayde climbed in and sank to her chin. Her muscles ached from weeks of training making the bath feel even more relaxing than it ever had. Jayde still struggled to get used to her new hair. It used to be long and straight, but now that it was short, it was curly. The harder she trained and sweat, the tighter the curls got. Her father had curly hair. After washing every nook and cranny from the tips of her toes to the top of her head, Jayde leaned her head back and searched for peace in her heart. The everyday torment and guilt for the loss of Laila nearly drove her mad at night. Laila was in her dreams every night and she could not imagine having to tell James. His heart would break. She remembered the joy in his face when he discovered that she was pregnant, his face could have lit up the entire room. Maggie and the midwife had reassured her that this loss was not hers to bear. This happened most likely due to her captivity and that Laila could not grow strong enough. Still, she agonized over what she could have done differently. Jayde was deep in her thoughts when she heard a soft knock on her door.

"Who is it?" Jayde called out.

"My Lady, it is me, Anna." Anna's familiar voice responded.

"Come in." Jayde smiled as her friend walked in the room.

Anna closed the door behind her, and reached for a linen to help Lady Jayde dry off with. Anna wiped down Lady Jayde's arms and back before wrapping her and sitting her down on a bench. She picked up a comb and began to comb Lady Jayde's hair. After just a few pulls, Anna could not help but laugh.

"What?" Jayde could not help but to laugh as well despite not knowing what they were laughing over.

"Your hair! I go to comb it and there is hardly anything to comb!" Anna started to cry she was laughing so hard.

Jayde turned around to face her friend. As silly as it seemed, she needed the laugh. Jayde started to laugh harder and before either women knew, they were clinging to each for support laughing so hard they had tears rolling down their cheeks.

Maggie was about to leave for the night when she heard the sounds of cackling. Curious, she followed the sounds upstairs to Lady Jayde's chamber. Then she heard what sounded to be gasping, in a panic she threw open the door only to find Lady Jayde and Anna gasping for air in between bursts of laughter. Smiling and shaking her head she quietly closed the door and left to go to her own home and fall into a deep slumber herself. Walking home, Maggie could not help but cry, knowing this was the first time in months that young Lady Jayde had laughed. She deserved so much more happiness than life had given her thus far. She hoped and prayed every night that Lord James would be found soon and help to bring back love and joy to this castle with Lady Jayde.

Chapter 13

James had lost count of the days. At first the days were filled with pain, and the nights disappeared when he would pass out. Then Blaxton changed it up and filled his nights with pain and torture and left his days to escape into darkness. It was different this time. There was no castle, just tents and trees. There were men camping with him and from the sound of it, they were bandits. They all seemed to follow Blaxton to a certain extent. Some of the bandits he recognized, and thankfully they did not recognize him. There were women in the camp, but they were women who only came at night. He could not make out where exactly he was, and the men and women in camp were never allowed near him. He slept outside like an animal exposed to the elements, left to sleep off the concussions, where the bugs infected his open wounds. During the first several days, or weeks, he was chained standing up, shackles hanging from the tree above with just barely enough slack for his feet to touch the ground. He must have not been doing well because he woke up one day with just his bare feet shackled and laying on the ground.

James did his best to listen to people talking as much as he could. From what he had heard and could make out, Blaxton had gathered up this group of men to wage a war against Lord Simon. Several nights ago, Blaxton had become particularly drunk and was raging about what a fool Lord Simon was. Somehow Blaxton found out that Lord Simon had assisted James and Fendrel when they were searching for Jayde. It added to Blaxton's hate for James and now was gathering power against Lord Simon. To make matters worse, Lord Simon was ill, and was not recovering. Lord Simon did not have any sons and his daughters, from what James remembered from their stay with Lord Simon, were barely old enough for marriage. James had heard Blaxton promise one of the daughters to the gruff looking man who was always at Blaxton's side, after he was finished with them. James had to force himself from throwing up what little bits of food he was able to eat. Blaxton was no longer avenging his sister, but seemed to have actually gone mad. There must be a way for him to get a word of warning to Lord Simon. If he could do that, maybe he could get word to his brothers.

James tried for days to find a tool left laying around to open the shackles. Only once did he get close to an actual tool, but the bandit who had left it behind returned to claim it before James could sneak over to it. James tried to twist his feet out of the shackles but only managed to cut both ankles. This time, Blaxton noticed the blood dripping down James's feet and stopped to inspect James and his wounds.

In a rage, Blaxton grabbed James by his shirt and drove his fist into James's face. "You played me for a fool! You made me believe you were too weak! Get up! Get up and fight me!"

James tried to clear his head and jumped to his feet only to feel a fist slam into his temple. Everything went black.

"You! Get over here and clean him up. I expect him to be ready for another round in the morning!" Blaxton screamed at one of the few women brave enough to stay at the camp during the day. "I will teach him who is better and stronger. I will break him before I kill him. Then maybe I will return for that fairy of a wife and make her mine."

Jayde was training on the fields again, this time with her sword on her horse. She refused to saddle her horse. In truth, the saddle was too heavy for her and she did not want to appear weak and ask for help, and it was by far more comfortable for her to ride bareback. It had been four days since she had sent the messengers for her brothers. She was just about to charge the target on her stallion when the horn sounded. Looking up to the hill, she saw the beautiful and familiar family crests standing tall next to an army of men. Excited, she abandoned the target and rushed her horse up the hill to greet Lord Henry and Lord Raymond. Lord Gilbert chased after her concerned for her reckless abandon in not waiting for the responding friendly call of the horns.

Henry and Raymond caught sight of the little figure racing up the hill and started to laugh. Their laughter ended when they saw the rider from the woods emerge on her heels. Drawing their swords, both men kicked their horses forward followed by their knights only a moment after. Either Lady Jayde was trying to escape this man or she had no idea he was coming up behind her.

Jayde looked up in time to see her brothers draw their swords and charge at her! What was going on? Did they not recognize her? She pulled back slightly on her beast and her moment of hesitation was all that it took. Suddenly she was falling from her horse and slamming into the ground. Stunned, she looked into the face of Sir Gilbert, panting and yelling at her.

"Do you even know who these people are? Just because they have our crest does not mean they are friendly! You must wait for the responding horn!"

Just then, one set of hands had Gilbert by the neck pulling him from her and another set of hands scooped her up and handed her to a knight on a horse. It was happening so fast. Henry was holding Gilbert, and Raymond was about to plunge his sword into Gilbert.

"STOP! NO!" Jayde screamed as she jumped from the arms of a knight, throwing, her body between Raymond and Gilbert. "Raymond, you do not know what you are doing. Please, just listen. This is Sir Gilbert, he is to protect me at all costs. From anyone whom might be any threat, whether they are family, friend or enemy." Turning, Jayde placed a hand on Henry's forearm. "Please, Henry, let him go. I swear to you, I tell the truth." She heard hundreds of swords being sheathed, and the most important sword, the one in Raymond's hand, seemed the loudest.

"Gilbert, I am sure you remember Lord Raymond and Lord Henry, Lord James younger brothers? I sent for them. They are here because I asked them to. Thank you for taking my safety seriously. I promise I will wait for the horn next time."

Embarrassed, Gilbert bowed his head to Lady Jayde, and mounted his horse galloping into the woods where he could remain hidden. He let his emotions for Lady Jayde once again get the better of his judgement. She was safe, he knew she was safe and she had known she was safe. He could not let this happen again. If Lord James were not missing, he would have left already. Lord James was not the kind of man to share his wife with anyone and let them live. Even when Lord James had taken a mistress, when he found out she had been with one of his knights as well, he refused to see her anymore, arranged a marriage between the mistress and the knight and then cast them out of Era. Lord James had then brooded for weeks until he came back from a trip about six months prior to his marriage to Lady Jayde.

Lord Henry had recognized little Lady Jayde as she came galloping up the hill despite her inappropriate clothing and lack of hair. She was still beautiful. Her hair was short and tight with curls, and the men's clothing fit her too well exposing long, muscular, curvy, sexy legs that hugged the back of that black beast in a way that made nearly every knight on the hill feel the tightness of their groin grow as she charged the hill. It was graceful the way she rode the stallion, almost seeming as one with the horse. His trance had only been broken when he saw the other rider, then instincts took over. James would kill him if anything happened to Lady Jayde.

Lord Raymond did not recognize the rider as Lady Jayde at first. He saw a feminine looking page come flying up the hill. When the rider looked up at them, he recognized the eyes and started to laugh. Those eyes were unforgettable. She looked like a wild kid, turned loose, escaping some horrible tragedy as she approached them. When he saw the man emerge from the woods, ice ran through his veins and blood was all he could see. Had Lady Jayde hesitated for even a moment, he would have rammed his sword through the knight and possibly even Lady Jayde. He would need to speak with her about that later, after they were within the walls of Era.

Lord Raymond was the first of the three to break the solemn silence that engulfed them. Grabbing Jayde by the waist, he pulled her to him and squeezed her in a big brotherly hug, placing a kiss on her forehead. Playfully he tousled the curls atop her head.

Recovering the breath that had just been squeezed from her, she did not anticipate the hug from Lord Henry that lifted her from her feet and spun her around in a circle.

"What has happened to your hair?" Lord Henry seemed almost sad.

Smiling, Jayde laughed, "It got in the way." Then she grabbed the reins to her horse and mounted it as she heard Raymond start to offer her help. "Come on, let us get you all settled and fed. It is just about time for the midday meal and there is much that needs to be discussed and plans to be made." Jayde led the army through the streets of Era as though she were leading children. The fear on the peoples' faces as they saw the knights, dissolved when they saw the smiling and confident Lady Jayde.

Henry and Raymond exchanged looks as they went through town. The people had never been this happy, not since their parents had passed. In fact it seemed as though the town had grown and was thriving. Could all of this be because of such a tiny little girl?

"Sebastian, would you please see to it that the grooms assist in placing all of the horses someplace and make sure Maria gets all of the assistance that she needs to prepare the midday meal. We have quite a large number of guests." Sebastian smiled and nodded to Lady Jayde before turning and making some order from the chaos.

Walking into the castle, Jayde found Maggie and asked that some food be brought to Lord James office promptly and then gave instructions that no one was to disturb them. Without waiting for Maggie to say anything, Jayde turned and led Lord Henry and Lord Raymond up to the office. Once the door was closed,

Jayde pulled down a map and started to place markers on it. The markers were areas that had been searched so far. Showing Henry and Raymond the marked areas, she then pointed to a wooded area a hard day's ride from Lord Simon.

"I am unclear as to why, but this area has not been searched yet. I doubt that Blaxton will repeat himself, so I feel like this would be a place that would draw him in. I want to go here." Looking up, both men had very serious faces.

"The reason your men have not searched these woods is because they are said to be haunted." Henry said as he pointed at the woods on the map. What did she mean when she said that she wanted to go there?

Raymond could not hold his question back any longer. "Jayde, why are you dressed like a man?" Raymond blurted out.

Realizing that she must look ridiculous to them, she knew she owed them an explanation. "I have been training with the knights…" she looked both men in the eyes when she spoke. "And I will have you know that I am as good as or better than most of the knights out there." She waited with her head held high for the words of chastise. Instead, what she saw was two grown men turning red, with tears streaming down their cheeks, desperately trying not to laugh.

Henry and Raymond could not hold back any longer. Both let out the bellowing laughs they were holding in. All three of them laughed a good hard laugh until finally Jayde recognized how similar the two men's laughter was to James, then her laughter turned to tears. Crumpling to the floor, she let go of all of the tears that she had been holding on to for the past few months. Henry and Raymond had no idea what to do, so they simply stood there and let Jayde cry. They would ask Maggie later what else had been going on. The way that Sir Gilbert had looked at Jayde when they had arrived made them uneasy.

Finally, Jayde recovered her emotions just in time for Maggie to bring in a tray of food. "Oh dear, I am so sorry, I forgot the ale. I will return with some shortly." Maggie flustered and turned to rush back down.

"Let me help Maggie, I will come with you and get the ale." Lord Henry kindly opened the door for Maggie. After so many years of Maggie keeping them out of trouble, being a shoulder to cry upon, and standing proud of the men they had become, getting the ale himself one time would not kill him. Plus now he could pick her brain a little. Closing the door behind them, he questioned her. "Maggie, what is Sir Gilbert's role in the safety of Lady Jayde?"

Maggie stopped in the middle of the hall at the top of the stairs. "Sir Gilbert was instructed by Lord James to protect Lady Jayde always. He held Lady Jayde's hands when she brought Laila into this world and stayed by her side when Laila left this world. Then he trained her so that she could carry out her plans to find Lord James."

"Wait, who is Laila? And what is it you are keeping secret?" Lord Henry's suspicion of Sir Gilbert grew. Why was Maggie protecting Sir Gilbert?

"I am sorry My Lord, you must ask Lady Jayde about Laila. I was unaware that you did not know." Maggie left Lord Henry at the top of the stairs as she slipped away to get the ales.

Turning, Henry stormed back into the office nearly slamming the door shut. "Who is Laila?" Henry demanded.

Jayde stood there looking at him in shock. How did he know of Laila?

Henry watched the pain rip across her face, and instantly regretted his question.

"Laila is my daughter. She is in the rose garden." Jayde's voice was barely above a whisper.

Henry began to question if Laila was Sir Gilbert's child. That would explain why he was so protective of her. The anger of her betrayal to his brother could not be contained. He crossed the room backing her against the wall. In a deadly tone he asked, "Was the child even my brother's or was it *Sir* Gilbert's?"

Jayde's world began to spin. She saw the door open and saw the shock on Maggie's face, and the horror on Raymond's. She felt her hand swing out and make stinging contact with Henry's face before she slid to the ground in soft sweet clouds of black.

Chapter 14

Jayde awoke in her bed with only Maggie sitting on the bench. Sitting up, she tried to clear her aching head.

Maggie jumped to her feet, and came to Lady Jayde's side with a cool wet cloth. "My Lady, how does your head feel? Do you think you could take a little broth?"

"My head is sore, what happened? Where are Lord Raymond and Lord Henry?" Jayde felt exhausted and hungry.

"My Lady, you fainted and hit your head on the desk. I have never seen Lord Henry look like death before, but after you slapped him, and rightfully so, you fainted and as you fell your head hit the desk, he thought he had killed you. They wished to speak with you when you woke, I can tell them that you are not well enough tonight and that they must wait until morning if you wish?" Maggie had grown so fond of Lady Jayde, it often felt as though she had raised the girl herself. She was often more protective than she needed to be of Lady Jayde.

"Thank you Maggie, I appreciate it, but I am well, I shall speak with them tonight. However, please I beg of you, could you please find me something more to eat than just broth?" Even as Jayde spoke, her stomach growled.

Smiling and chuckling, Maggie nodded and rushed off to do as she had been asked. As soon as she opened the door, Lord Raymond jumped to his feet.

"Is she okay?" Lord Raymond was worried sick. He had been sitting on the floor of the hall outside of Jayde's room all afternoon and evening waiting to make sure she was not going to die. Henry however had disappeared.

"She is awake and quite hungry. She is willing to speak with you two, but if either of you upset her the way Lord Henry did earlier, I will not hesitate to take a switch to your behinds!" Maggie then huffed off to get some of Maria's delicious meal and bring it back for the three of them. Neither Lord Henry nor Lord Raymond ate the evening meal either this evening. Maggie gave the meal request to Maria then stepped out to the rose garden to place a lily on sweet Laila's grave as she did every evening after everyone had eaten. Sitting in the dark on the stone bench, was Lord Henry.

"Is she alive? Did I kill her?" His voice was rough and his eyes red from the tears he shed privately.

"She is awake and waiting on you." Maggie was at a loss for words. She was not at liberty to scold him, yet she could not console the little boy sitting before her. She placed the lily at Laila's stone, crossed herself and said a prayer.

"You are who has put all of the flowers here?" Henry asked.

"I bring the lilies. Sir Gilbert brings the wreaths of daisies, and Sir Fendrel brings the lilacs. We were all there that night with Lady Jayde." Maggie choked on the words, fighting to hold back the torrent of tears she dared not shed.

"What does Lady Jayde bring?" Henry was almost afraid to ask.

Taking a shaky, but deep breath, Maggie answered Lord Henry with sadness. "Lady Jayde has not been able to visit Laila's stone. She dreams of her baby every night, calls out to her, calls out to Lord James and cries, but during her waking hours, she is unable to visit."

Standing, Henry kissed the loving face before him on the cheek. Then went to the kitchen to carry the trays of food that waited up to Lady Jayde. At the door to her chamber, he saw Raymond. Handing Raymond a tray and the ale, he knocked on the door and waited for Jayde to call them in.

"Come in." Jayde called out, assuming it was Maggie. She was surprised when Henry and Raymond entered her room carrying food and ale.

After setting the tray down, Henry walked to Jayde's side, bowed deeply to her, took her hand in his and kissed the back of it. "Baby sister, I beg of you to forgive my ignorance and offense. I was taken by surprise that you were pregnant and made assumptions of you that were inappropriate and not true."

"Thank you for your apology. I accept. Your worry is not unfounded however. I fear that my training with Sir Gilbert has led him to feel more fondly for me than he should. I know this because last week, I went down to where we trained early in the morning, while Sir Gilbert was still eating his morning meal. I prefer to ride Gallivant without a saddle but Gilbert does not think it is safe." Jayde's story was interrupted by both men choking on their ale.

"Galavant is what you call that beast?" Raymond asked.

"I can see who won the argument regarding the saddle…" Henry chuckled.

Jayde however remained serious. She knew that the next bit of information that she shared, would enrage her brothers and endanger Gilbert. "Gilbert caught me charging a target with my sword drawn while riding Galavant bareback. When I rode back to the stables to hear his lecture, I was surprised when he took Galavant and put him back in his stable. Then he turned to me and began to shout about the danger I put myself in. Suddenly, he stopped shouting and kissed me." Jayde saw the blood rise to both brothers' faces. Quickly, she continued. "We ended my training with him immediately and since then, he has stayed away from me except when I pass him on the training field and today on the hill. He of course apologized and promised it would never happen again. You must leave him alone. He has a job that he must finish. When we go to war, he will be the extra eyes watching my back making sure that I get to Blaxton."

"How do you know of Blaxton?" Raymond asked. It occurred to Jayde that her pregnancy was not the only thing that had been kept a secret from Raymond and Henry. Between bites of food and sips of ale, Jayde told them everything from the beginning. By the time the story was over, both men sat back in their chairs now understanding all of the events leading up to now.

Standing, Raymond gave Jayde a hug. "Little sister, sleep well, we train hard tomorrow and ready for our trip." Then he left and retired to his room where a bath sat waiting for him.

Henry remained seated after Raymond left. "Sweet little sister, I will stand beside you, I will fight with you, and I will lay my life down to save you. I beg of you to think about the sacrifice we will both make. I beg of you to be certain that you are able to do this. I do not want to sacrifice my brother's life for yours, but will if you are in any danger. Do you understand?"

Nodding, Jayde replied, "I understand better than you realize. I do not think you realize how hard I have trained and the sacrifices I have already made. I know you do not care for Sir Gilbert, but you must trust him. You must trust that he will die for me, to make sure I am able to drive my sword into Blaxton and bring James home. He does not eat with us because he is afraid to betray himself again and put me at risk of losing the respect I have earned from the knights."

"Whose trust will you betray when you are able to bring James home? Will you betray the trust of a man who loves you despite you being married to another or will you betray the trust of a man who loves you but has barely spent any time with you as your husband? You see, you must betray one of them. If you betray Sir Gilbert, James will likely kill him. If you betray James, your betrayal will likely kill him. Do you know where your loyalty will lie?" Henry was careful this time to not sound emotional when asking the tough questions.

Without blinking and without hesitation, Jayde answered with confidence. "I will never betray my husband."

Relieved, Henry then asked, "Does Sir Gilbert know where your loyalty is?"

"I do not doubt that Sir Gilbert knows that my loyalty is in James. If there were any doubt, he would have pursued me. I have already had this conversation with Sir Fendrel. You should ask him in the morning how I answered his doubt." Jayde was suddenly tired. "Lord Henry, I cannot imagine that you are not tired. I am exhausted and wish to ready for bed."

"Of course." Standing and giving Jayde a hug, Henry turned to leave. "Good night little sister. Sleep well, we shall see your training in action tomorrow." With that Henry left and found that he too had a bath waiting for him in his room.

For all three, morning came too quickly. Jayde was the first out to the stables, as usual, and was already breaking a sweat when the fields started to fill with the seventy-five knights from Lord Raymond, the eighty knights from Lord Henry, and the one hundred knights that were in constant training at Era. With two hundred fifty-five knights watching, Jayde led Galavant to the center of field.

"I want to remind all of you that we are family. The man you train next to may be the one to watch your back. The fields are crowded, I know. Do your best to work together not against each other. Train hard, I will be training with you. If any of you have a problem with this, please find Sir Fendrel, I am sure he can set you straight. I will expect that all of you will be in the hall for the midday and evening meals. Oh, Sir Fendrel, Lord Henry wishes to speak with you regarding last week's, ah, situation." There was some laughter as Jayde rode down to the breeding stables where she used to train with Gilbert. She needed some privacy and some time to think.

Fendrel hung his head slightly and walked to Lord Henry. Lord Raymond joined the two men in the center of the field. He had no idea what this was about, but he did not want to have to hear it second hand. By the end of the story, Lord Raymond and Lord Henry were laughing so hard they had to lean on one another to keep from sitting on the ground. Fendrel could not take any more laughter, "My Lords, if there is nothing else, I should return to training." This of course set the brothers into another round of laughter. Fendrel headed off to the archers fields.

"To think! Something so tiny could land someone as big as Fendrel!" Henry gasped.

"Then she held him at the tip of her tiny sword!" Raymond finished. The two men continued to laugh. They agreed that they needed to find Lady Jayde to congratulate her on her very hard earned respect from the knights. But first, they would spread the tale. By the time the evening meal was ready, everyone would know and it would not be a struggle to get the one hundred fifty-five other knight that they had brought to get behind following a woman, no matter how petite she might be.

The brothers searched everywhere and could see no sign of Lady Jayde. Starting to worry, what if Jayde had been correct and Blaxton had changed. What if he had come back for her as well? Lord Raymond and Lord Henry mounted their horses and raced up the hill to search for Sir Gilbert. Reaching the point where they had seen him exit they began to call out to him. Within moments, he appeared.

"What is wrong?" Gilbert asked.

"Where is she? She was on the training fields then she rode off without any one and now we cannot find her." Henry's voice was laced with worry. "We need your help to find her."

"Have you checked her Solar?" Gilbert pushed.

"We have checked every room of the castle. We have checked the stable, the training fields. We are at a loss." Raymond tried to stay cool.

"Have you checked the breeding stables?" Gilbert knew that Lady Jayde had found some peace while training there. He could see it in her face when she would arrive for training.

"What breeding stables? I do not remember any breeding stables." Raymond tried to remember anything like a breeding stables from growing up.

Gilbert offered, "I can take you there if you would like, but I will not stay."

Both Lord Raymond and Lord Henry nodded their heads in understanding. Then spurred their horses to follow behind Sir Gilbert. He took them around the training fields so that no one would notice the small group. He led the men down the path that overlooked the breeding stables and valley below. From their point, they could see Lady Jayde training down below, and could see her once secret path leading from her garden. Without another word, Gilbert turned his horse around and returned to his camp in the woods.

Lord Raymond was about to start down the path, when Lord Henry put his hand out to halt him. "She came here for a reason. Only she and a few other people know of this place, so either she was coming here to meet someone or she was coming here to find peace. Let us just keep our distance and watch for a little while."

Jayde rode Galavant up and down the field mostly at a gallop. Frustrated at the lack of progress and lack of motivation, Jayde spun around throwing her dagger at the target. Walking up to the target, Jayde had to pull on her dagger with all of her might before the dagger finally came free of the wood beneath the target. Sighing, Jayde urged Galavant forward to the edge of the field and looked out. The view of the valley below was beautiful. The river snaked through the valley disappearing into the woods below. Funny, she did not remember seeing the river on the map. Could that be it? Galloping into the stables, she tied Galavant up, and ran up the hill following her path into the garden. She had to look at the map and see if this river was on the map and if it led to or near those woods, this could possibly be how Blaxton has come and gone unnoticed.

Raymond and Henry were getting bored. She had done nothing but run her beast up and down the field. Both men sat up when she threw the dagger at the target

down the field. The dagger sank into the middle of the
face of the scare crow looking target. Impressed by her
aim and ferocity, they watched with interest as she
struggled to remove the dagger from the target. She
seemed defeated as she sheathed the dagger and
retreated to the edge of the field. A breeze stirred and
gently tossed her soft curls about her head. They were
about to get up and leave when Raymond noticed that
Lady Jayde's head snapped up and she raced to the
stables then up the other hill towards the castle.
Mounting his horse, he kicked his horse forward down
the steep slope towards the field and stables. Tying up
his horse with Henry seconds behind, they went chasing
up the hill after Jayde calling out to her.

Jayde had just reached the garden where the secret
passage was when Jayde heard her name being called.
It almost sounded like James! Spinning around her
heart in her throat, she saw Lord Henry and Lord
Raymond running up the path. Her heart broke into a
thousand pieces and it must have shown on her face for
when Lord Raymond reached her, he put his hand on
her shoulder.

He could see the sadness on her face, and knew it was
because of Henry. Placing a hand on her shoulder, he
said, "Henry and James have always sounded similar.
They both sound like Father, but James is the spitting
image of him and sometimes it is hard to be around
James because he reminds me of our Father. I promise,
we will find and bring James home." Raymond had
never shared the truth in his avoiding James to anyone

before. He knew he must keep his promise to Jayde at all costs.

Henry slowed down watching Raymond place a hand on Jayde's shoulder. He could see them talking but felt like it was too intimate for him to hear. Slowing down to an easy walk, he let them say their peace. Finally approaching the pair, he questioned Jayde.

"Little sister, are you well? Why were you running off?" Henry had never seen his baby brother so at peace before. It seemed as though a huge burden had been lifted off of his shoulders. He could not help but wonder what was said between the two.

"The river below, do you know where it flows to?" Jayde asked, her voice filled with hope.

"As children we were always forbidden to play by the river. Then after our parents and brothers passed away, Raymond and I were sent to live with our Uncle while James took over Era. What are you suspecting?"

"I need to look at the maps. I wonder where that river leads. If my hopes are correct, I know exactly where Blaxton is and how he managed to get in and out of Era unseen. Follow me." Jayde turned and practically ran through the dead garden to the Lion sticking out of the wall. Pulling the paw forward, she heard the familiar sound of the latch give and had the pleasure of seeing the surprise painted on her brothers' faces. Reaching through the ivy, she pushed the still hidden door and disappeared. Patiently she waited as both Raymond and Henry finally braved what they did not know and followed her into the wall of the castle. Taking the lit torch from the wall, Jayde led the still shocked men up the stairs around the corner, up the next set of stairs and down the hall before reaching the door. Finding the latch, she opened the door into her chamber and left the torch in its resting place in the secret passage. Without speaking a word, the passage was left and Jayde carefully opened the door to the hall. They all knew what people would say if anyone saw the three of them leaving Lady Jayde chamber. After making sure no one was around, Jayde then led the men to James's office. Finally, they could speak. Grabbing a map of Era and the surrounding lands, they followed the poorly represented river and discovered that it indeed led to the edge of the wooded area still unsearched. Hope filled Jayde's heart and tears spilled down her cheeks. Overjoyed, she jumped and hugged both Raymond and Henry.

"When do we leave?" Jayde could not bear the thought of wasting any more time.

"We must send out a search party in the morning to confirm our suspicions. Then we may attack with every able body we have." Henry tried hard to not let Jayde suspect his true plans. If they could go and get James without allowing Jayde to come along, they would all live to see the sun rise again. He knew that if James learned that his wife was allowed to fight in a war, they would all have to face his wrath.

Jayde smiled and agreed with Henry. She must make sure he felt as though that were the perfect plan. She would eat a light meal this evening and then feign exhaustion. Then she could sneak down to the river with Galavant and go search for James herself. With any luck, she could be back before dawn and Henry and Raymond would never know. Tucking the map back onto the shelf, the group left and returned to the fields where they all separated only to plot on how to deceive the others.

The day seemed to drag on as though Father Time himself were plotting against her. Jayde tried to focus but by midday, she had managed to slice her hand with her dagger. She retired Galavant to his stall hoping he would rest for their long evening ahead. Leaving the fields, she mumbled to Sir Fendrel that she was not feeling well and needed to rest.

Finally, it was time for the evening meal. To ease any suspicions, she forced herself to sit calmly and eat with everyone else. When Raymond questioned her barely eating, she explained that she was just nervous about tomorrow. As if planned, Raymond suggested that she retire early and get as much rest as she could. It took everything inside of her to not jump up and shout with joy at what a marvelous idea it was. As demurely as she could, Jayde bid everyone a peaceful night and slowly walked up to her chamber. Waiting until she knew most of the knights were well into their second pints of ale, Jayde slipped out through her secret passage and down to the stables where Galavant was anxiously waiting. Silently she slid on to his back and led him out the back and up the hill near the woods where Sir Gilbert had taken to residing. Hoping he was still in the hall eating, she passed down the hill and through the town as quietly as possible. Once at the river, she needed to figure out how deep it was and if Galavant could navigate it.

"Where do you think you are going My Lady?" Gilbert asked.

Jayde had to cover her mouth to hide her scream from being so startled by Gilbert. "Would you believe me if I told you that I have been aching to take Galavant on an evening ride before fall turns into winter?"

Gilbert simply shook his head. "You believe that you have found him. Where are Lord Henry and Lord Raymond? Are they aware of what you are trying to do? Alone in the dark?"

"No. You and I both know that they would never allow me to do anything remotely dangerous. If only they knew how dangerous stitching was." Jayde hoped that her attempt at humor might soften Gilbert.

Just then, Lord Henry and Lord Raymond appeared from the darkness and were startled by finding Jayde and Gilbert at the river.

"What the hell do you think you are doing?" Henry practically shouted at Jayde.

"Exactly what it looks like I am doing. I knew that the two of you had something planned and that your plans did not include me. I will not be left behind!" Jayde defended her actions. "I can either go with you or I shall go without you."

"I cannot allow you to put your life in danger like this!" Henry tried to argue with her.

"Allow? ALLOW! Just exactly who do you think you are? YOU are not MY husband. You do not own me or make any decisions for me!" Jayde was offended by his typical male beliefs.

"You are my responsibility when my brother is not able to protect you!" Henry was starting to get louder.

"If it had not been for me, you would not be here right now! You should be grateful to me for asking you to be a part of this!" Jayde exploded.

Raymond was near Gilbert watching Henry and Jayde have their go at each other. "Is she always this stubborn?"

"Always. Sadly, Lord Henry still has not realized that she will win and somehow in the end, will make him feel like it was all his idea. That is how training started." There was pride in Gilbert's voice. For someone who looked and sounded tiny and dependent upon a big strong man, she was wildly strong and had a voice that could boom louder than Lord James' ever had. His heart ached being so close to her, knowing he could not kiss her soft lips, caress her shoulders with his lips, follow the curve of her thighs. He knew that when this was done, his heart would turn to stone from the pain of watching her find happiness and love with another.

"I have absolutely no idea why or how my brother could have married someone as stubborn and dangerous as you! You will ultimately get us all killed because you want to prove something?" Henry was starting to get sucked in.

"No, I will be saving your necks because you will be too busy being a closed minded old man and worrying that a woman who is stronger and more skilled than half of the knights on that field might actually be RIGHT!" Jayde refused to back down and refused to lose this fight. "I thought you were different, like James. I thought that you could see beyond tradition and beyond gender and see that I had brains and could use them! I thought you were encouraging my help! When I do find James, and believe me I will find him, he is going to ask how his brothers helped. Tell me Henry, will I be telling him of how difficult you made this and how you delayed us finding him? Or will I be singing your praises for trusting my instincts and having faith that I would not be a problem?"

"Of course I can see beyond gender! Do you think I cannot see the strength both physically and mentally that you bring? We are all impressed by you Jayde. You have earned the respect by some of the most battle hardened traditional men I have ever met. Having you as a part of this rescue would only be an asset. I worry about my own neck it is true. But I do not fear the enemy. I fear your husband more than I have ever feared any enemy I have *ever* faced." Henry had calmed down quite a bit finally. "I know that you have somehow made this my choice, and no, I will not deny you to come with us, but you must do as I say. Do you understand?"

Jayde smiled. It sent chills down the backs of the three men. It was a smile that said she would follow orders as long as they were what she thought was best.

Shaking his head, and wiping the sweat from his brow, Henry knew he had been beat by his sweet little sister-in-law. "We should start our journey. We will follow the river and get as close as we can. Then we will need to go by foot the rest of the way, see how close we can get.

The group rode as fast and hard as they could in the dark. The tension was thick and seemed to charge and drain each of them simultaneously. They stopped for nothing, they did not speak, and in fact they barely even looked at each other. Gilbert was nervous for what awaited them, and for Lady Jayde's safety. Henry was nervous that they were going to be caught and no one

would know where to look for them or their bodies.
Raymond remained stoic, but feared that once there,
they would not be able to hold Jayde back from finding
and killing Blaxton. Jayde tried to focus on how much
time had passed. Her mind continued to worry that they
would find James dead, or so wounded that if they left,
they were going to leave him to die. Looking down her
chest to the package securely hidden under her shirt, she
hoped she could find a way to get it to James. She had
packed a poultice for any wounds, a child sized dagger
that Jayde had asked Thomas the blacksmith to make
that could easily be hidden, and a sliced orange. The
orange had been an afterthought. She knew that if
James was still alive, he would be starving,
malnourished and weak. An orange could give him the
small boost he would need to survive a few days until
they could rescue him.

The moon had risen high by the time they neared the
woods were they suspected Blaxton might be hiding.
Turning the group around, they rode towards the
mountain where they could safely and secretly tie their
horses up before sneaking into the woods. Quietly and
carefully, they scouted the edge of the woods to find the
best place to enter.

Finding a perfect point to enter at was like throwing a
dagger at a map, and so the group quietly entered the
woods. The woods were quiet with only the sounds of
the wind pushing through the trees. Jayde's heart began
to sink. If James was not here, she had no idea where
she would search next. She had exhausted her men

searching for James these past few months and now most of them had given him up for dead.

The silence was deafening roaring in their ears until they heard the faintest of sound. At first, Raymond thought his mind was creating the noise, then Henry seemed to hear it too. When Jayde bumped into the two stopped men, she cleared her mind of everything and strained to hear what ever had caused her brothers to stop without warning. After a moment, the group smiled at each other as the familiar sounds of a distant camp seeped through the woods. Hope restored to each of them, they had to restrain themselves from running towards the noises.

Jayde's heart was bursting inside her chest, and tears slowly started to slip down her cheeks. They were so close. One wrong step and everything would be for nothing. She could not help but hold her breath with each step the group tried to make in unison. They were close enough now to see the glow of the fires and to be seen by anyone who happened to look around. Retreating to the safety of the woods, they agreed to pair off and travel around the camp, looking only, not interacting. If they found James, they agreed it would be best to leave him there until they could come back with their army.

Raymond and Gilbert went around the camp to the east, while Henry and Jayde crept around to the west. Jayde stayed a few paces behind Henry always keeping a vigilant eye out for any sign of James. After only a few minutes, Jayde's short legs separated her from Henry's long strides completely. Gathering her thoughts and taking a deep breath to slow her racing heart, a tent set slightly farther from the others in the camp caught her eye. There was no fire in front of it, and only what appeared to be a small light coming from inside. Creeping closer, Jayde could hear a voice that she knew would haunt her until the day she died. It was Blaxton! He was arguing with someone, no, just yelling. Whomever the poor soul was that was getting the tongue lashing, remained quiet. The sound of a fist hitting the skull of another human made Jayde's stomach roll. Lying flat on her stomach, she held her breath and the tent flap flew back and Blaxton emerged dragging an unconscious body. He looked even more crazy than she remembered him appearing before, but not weaker. In fact, he looked stronger and physically healthier. She waited until Blaxton had blown out his light before she made any moves. Carefully, she stood up and walked towards the heaped form of the man Blaxton had left in the dirt. Slowly, she sank to her knees, and cradled the bloodied and bruised face of James. He was barely recognizable as the man she had married just nine months ago. His long once strong arms looked weak, and were covered in wounds and bugs. Reaching down her shirt, she pulled out the package she had kept so carefully hidden and untied it. Immediately taking the poultice out, she quickly covered as many wounds as she could see using all of the poultice before she could cover all of his wounds. Taking an orange wedge, she gently squeezed a piece, watching the juices drip into his mouth knowing that it must sting the wounds around his lips. The seconds ticked by so slowly, time almost seemed to stand still. Finally, James swallowed the juice and licked his parched and cracked lips. Encouraged, Jayde squeezed two more wedges of the orange hoping the juice would give him strength.

James thought he was going to die, his world was cold and black. He was floating in darkness, when he noticed the scent. It was rosewater, like what Jayde used at home. Searching the darkness, he could not see her. This was it, the end, how was he supposed to protect Jayde from this monster if he was dead? In the darkness, he began to feel the pain of his head throbbing. He was not dead, yet. If he could just hold onto that pain, he might be able to survive another day. The scent of oranges filled his mind. It was so strong he could taste it. So sweet, but it seemed to sting. How could a memory sting? Slowly James tried to open his eyes, but only managed one, since the other was swollen shut. Confused, he tried to focus. There was an angel smiling at him, she reminded him of Jayde. He tried to protest, telling her he was not ready for this, that it was not his time, but she just smiled, brushed a curl from his forehead, and quietly shushed him.

Jayde could feel her heart breaking again as she held James head in her lap. Suddenly his head shifted in her lap, and slowly he opened an eye. He was looking up at her but did not seem to recognize her or actually see her. She smiled through the tears falling down. He was trying to say something to her, but if Blaxton heard, they would both be dead. Shushing him, she gently pushed a tight curl back from his swollen eye hoping he would wake up enough to see her.

There was a noise in the tent behind her that sent her heart racing. Quickly Jayde pressed the tiny dagger into James hand and felt his fingers tighten around it. Leaning in to his ear, she whispered, "I am here my love, I will take you home soon. Wait for me." Then she kissed his forehead before running back to the safety of the woods with her package of goods clutched to her chest. As soon as the shrubs hid her, she felt a hand clamp over her mouth and then another hand jerk her back against a tall strong body. Jayde knew that if she fought, she could expose Henry, Raymond and Gilbert as well. Going stiff, she could feel anger coursing through the arms that held her. All she could do was pray it was not Blaxton.

Henry was going to kill her. What was she thinking! If Blaxton walked out of that tent right now, Jayde would be dead and so would James. He held his breath when he heard Blaxton roll over in the tent and nearly died when Jayde came darting past him. He guessed that just grabbing her arm might cause her to fight him and reveal their presence, so he clamped his hand down tight across her mouth and secured her body to his, her body went rigid. Good, at least she was not going to fight him. Bending his head forward, with his mouth next to her ear, he very quietly whispered, "Jayde, it is only me, Henry."

Jayde heard the familiar and comforting voice, and turning around, she threw her arms around Henry's neck and buried her face into his neck. She was trying to keep it together, but she could feel her body and heart's betrayal as she felt the sobs rising up her throat choking her as her body shook.

Henry was surprised when Jayde suddenly turned in his arms and buried her face in his neck. He could feel the hot tears that fell from her eyes soak his shirt and he could hear her trying to smother her gasps for air. He knew he had to get as far from here as he could quickly. He had already found Raymond and Gilbert and told them to meet him at the edge of the woods while he went back in search of Jayde. He knew they would be waiting. Still holding her tight to him, he quickly and quietly moved to the edge of the woods where Gilbert and Raymond paced aggressively. "Shh, it is okay now, we are safe." Henry was hoping that the calm in his voice would help soothe her pain. Instead she quit trying to silence the sobs.

Jayde clung to Henry as though her life depended on it. In truth, her life did depend on holding on to him. She was afraid that if she let go, she would sink to the ground and bury herself right now. James did not even recognize her. His wounds were so deep, his face so swollen. She could feel the violent shaking, could hear her own soul shattering sobs. She needed to pull herself together. If she did not stop the tears, shaking and pain, James would die. She slowly let go of Henry's neck and felt her feet hit the ground. She could hear her mother's words echo in her mind, to be brave, to survive. Jayde slid her hands to Henry's chest and pushed. Looking down she watched her feet take a step back. The gap between her feet and Henry's was small, be brave, survive.

She forced herself to take another step back, then another. Lifting her head and looking Henry in the eyes, she took a deep breath, stood tall and pulled her shoulders back. The face staring back at her startled her.

Henry felt lost and overwhelmed. Jayde clung to him like a child clings to their mother, then suddenly let go. The moment she let go, he felt fear take her place sending shivers up his back. What if there was nothing they could do? What if they were already too late? Henry stared at Jayde with wide scared eyes as she somehow found her own inner strength to stand and push away from him. Suddenly he felt like he was going to crumble. Fear took over and he reached for her hands.

"Tell me that we are going to save him Jayde. Please, say it is not too late. Please." His words were barely more than a whisper, but all three people who stood there in the moonlight heard his words loud and clear, as crisp as the Fall morning air.

Jayde looked up into the face of Henry, but the always confident man that she was expecting to find was no longer standing in front of her. Instead, a scared little boy stood before her asking for answers that she did not have and grasping for strength to be brave, and to survive. He held on to her hands tightly as though this was the only way he could breath. Gently, she smiled at him, offering him hope and strength as though she had some to spare.

"Let's go home and gather the men, dawn will come soon." The group of four left as quickly and quietly as they had arrived at the edge of the woods.

If Blaxton had only realized that such power and determination could be concealed in a creature so wild and so small, he would have known that she would not stay at home as a proper woman should. He would have guessed that she would be waiting for the right time to strike and that her strike would be lethal. If he had only realized, he would have had men guarding the camp, and would be ready for her when she came.

Chapter 15

Jayde, Henry, Raymond and Gilbert rode hard and fast returning to Era. They watched as dawn approached and the sun broke over the horizon. Finally arriving at the castle gates well after the morning meal had been enjoyed and the men sent to the fields to train, they were startled at the eerie silence. Stopping at the top of the hill, there was not a single man out training. Waiting a moment for riders to come galloping up the hill to welcome them, realizing that there was no one, filled each of them with fear.

"What has happened?" Raymond voiced what they were all thinking.

"Let us go slowly and quietly. Stay close to the forest, no more talking. Stay together and keep Lady Jayde safe at all costs." Gilbert carefully led the group down and around the quiet town to the river's edge. Finally reaching the place along the river where they had left the night before, Gilbert stopped them. "Henry, you will come with me. Raymond, stay with Lady Jayde, if anything goes wrong, go straight to Adonia. Henry, we go by foot." Both men dismounted and quietly crept up to the castle wall, then disappeared from sight. After minutes had passed Raymond and Jayde heard the loud battle cries from within the walls. Kicking her horse forward, Jayde rushed around the castle leaving her horse in the secret garden not caring if Raymond had followed her or not. Running to the wall she found the lion's paw and pulled as hard as she could.

Raymond heard the shouts as well, but recognized them as welcoming shouts. He was stunned when Jayde took off as though she was escaping the Devil. Spurring his horse forward, he barely caught up to her before she disappeared into the walls like a ghost. Recognizing that she had found a secret passage, he secured the door behind them calling out to her to stop.

"Jayde! Jayde! What are you doing?" Raymond called.

Reaching the door to her chamber she whispered, "I am getting to my sword so that we can save them!"

Raymond grabbed her by the arms and turned her around. "Brave little sister, they are okay. The cries that you heard were not battle cries, but welcoming cheers. Follow me, I will show you. Bring your sword if you would feel better, but I can assure you, you will not need it."

Jayde rushed to grab her sword and followed Raymond through her chamber to the balcony and looked down into the hall. Below, were all two hundred and fifty knights with Henry and Gilbert hoisted on their shoulders and passing them around. Anger began to rise from deep within Jayde as she slowly walked down the stairs stopping just six stairs from the bottom. She stood there and waited to be acknowledged by the knights, Henry or Gilbert. They were celebrating. What were they celebrating? There had been no victory, James was not safe and at home. What was there to celebrate?

Taking a deep breath, Jayde screamed at the top of her lungs, "SILENCE! Your behavior is appalling! Celebrating? Really? Tell me, any of you, what are you celebrating? Has the Lord of this manor returned? Is he safe? No he is not! Right now, he is laying on the ground in the woods being subjected to repeated beatings, starvation, and a lack of attention to gaping wounds where maggots are feasting. What? You were happy to see that Lord Henry and Sir Gilbert were safe and alive? Have any of you stopped to ask where they have been? Where we have been? You make me ill. Everyone outside to the fields. NOW!"

As though the castle were on fire, men were pushing and shoving, running out to the fields. Even Gilbert had left the hall and went outside with the rest of the knights. Jayde slowly walked to the center of the hall where Henry stood alone.

Henry stood right where the knights had left him and watched as Jayde slowly made her way towards him. As she reached where he stood, he instinctively took a step back. The anger and rage seemed to course through her veins and flow from every pore of her body.

The air was so thick he could barely breathe and although he had never seen green fire before, he was sure he was witness to it now as Jayde's eyes seemed to burn right through him.

"Lead the way Lord Henry." Jayde spoke slowly and quietly struggling to control herself.

Seeing an army of two hundred and fifty knights lining the training fields facing the center was an impressive sight. Lord Henry led, followed by Lady Jayde and Lord Raymond.

"Lord Henry, Lord Raymond, I ask that you join the ranks with your knights." Jayde waited as her brothers walked from the center of the field to the edge and fell into ranks. Jayde began to pace about the field, struggling to understand these men. Stopping, she turned to face the rows of men. "Some of you came with Lord Henry from Adonia and I have known you since I was a child sneaking off into the fields to train or into the woods to hunt with Anna. Some of you have come with Lord Raymond and have never met me, but all of you have known, met, or spent time training with my husband Lord James. Have you all forgotten who he is, the Lord of Era? Have you forgotten why you are all here? I will not lie. Housing two hundred and fifty knights is far from easy and the longer you are here, the longer it takes to find Lord James, the greater the strain on Era. The people who reside in the small houses below and have opened their homes and resources to you have done so willingly without complaint because they love Lord James and wish for him to safely return home to them. I have watched as some of you have slowly forgotten the face of the man you proclaim to serve. You have relaxed, become comfortable and have lost sight of what our mission has been. The mission is now. Last night, while all of you were warm, enjoying music and drinking ale, Lord Henry, Lord Raymond, Sir Gilbert and myself rode through the night and found the camp where Lord James has been kept, tortured, and starved. Last night while all of you were fast asleep, protected from the elements, Lord Henry, Lord Raymond, Sir Gilbert and I rode home and watched as the moon set and the sun rose. Tonight we bring home my husband. Tonight, you will all risk your lives to bring him home. All of you go, pack your weapons and prepare for our fight this evening. There will be no midday meal today, there will be an early supper. After supper, we will inform you of our plan, then we ride. Do not let me catch you engaging in anything that does not prepare you for war. I will see you all this evening. Lord Henry, Lord Raymond and Sir Gilbert, meet me in the hall immediately. The rest of you are dismissed." Jayde turned on her heels and swiftly walked back to the Great Hall. Walking into the kitchen, she found Maria ordering people about preparing for the rest of the day.

"Maria, there has been a change in plans for today's meals. There will be no midday meal. There will be an early supper, and please have enough dried fruits and meats packed and ready for travel for two hundred and fifty four people. Tonight, we bring Lord James home. Also, please have a small tray of dried fruits, cold meats, cheese and bread brought to the table for Lords Henry and Raymond, Sir Gilbert and myself. Thank you." Leaving the kitchen, Jayde found Maggie ordering servants to bring down all bed linens to be washed and hung to dry while ordering other servants to bring clean linens up to the room and place them on the beds.

Maggie was giving orders to the girls for the bed linens when she saw their eyes grow wide. Looking over her shoulder, she saw Lady Jayde leaving the kitchen and approach them. Lady Jayde had become a bit of a legend amongst the servants and townspeople. She had gained their respect by her daily sacrifice and training to bring home Lord James. Maggie turned to face Lady Jayde and await her instructions.

"Maggie, I need for you to inform all of the knights that they are to bring a provisions sack to the kitchen and leave it with Maria. They may retrieve them as we leave this evening. Tonight, we will bring home Lord James." Jayde watched as Maggie teared up a little then nodded before turning back to the servants and send them on their way. Then Jayde turned and walked to the table where Henry, Raymond and Gilbert stood waiting for her arrival. Jayde sat down first and waited for the men to follow before starting to discuss the plan of attack for the evening. They would divide the group of knights into four smaller groups. Henry and Raymond would both take a group of seventy-five knights each, while Jayde and Gilbert would take smaller groups of fifty knights each. Henry was going to lead his group of knights around the forest camp to the north, Raymond would bring his group along the river on the west, Gilbert would bring his group from the south and Jayde would lead her men from the east, closest to Blaxton and James. Henry and Gilbert would strike at the same time to force the encampment to split and be distracted while Raymond and Jayde would wait just a couple of minutes to attack from within the camp and attack the enemy at their backs. Once their positions were established, Jayde would split from them and locate James, try to remove any shackles or chains and wait for Henry, Raymond or Gilbert to join her and take James to safety. Henry, Raymond and Gilbert agreed that Blaxton would most likely join his men in their fight and leave James unguarded but shackled, believing he was safe. Jayde knew better however and knew that once they attacked, Blaxton would know and be waiting for her when she went to James. She knew that if she corrected the men, they would change the plans and she would not know if James was safe until the battle was over. It was better this way. It was better that she got to face Blaxton, to show him that he did not win the first time, and that he would not win this time either.

Maria brought out a large tray of foods and the group paused in their discussions long enough to eat their first meal since the evening before. After eating, they made four lists of knights names and Gilbert ran the lists out to post them on the wall of the stables. Gilbert returned to the hall where Jayde, Raymond and Henry awaited. Finally, it was time to discuss the hour in which they wanted to travel. It was agreed that they would leave at the time they would usually sit down for the evening meal. Not so late that it would be dark out, but not so early that they would arrive in daylight giving themselves up and taking away their element of surprise. As they were finishing their conversation, the knights began to come in to leave their provision sacks in the kitchen with Maria. The four of them parted ways to pack and rest before their long night ahead.

As Jayde began to climb the stairs to retreat to her chambers Maggie called for her to wait.

"Lady Jayde, wait, please." Maggie was trying to catch up to Lady Jayde and trying to catch her breath. "My Lady, do you have a sack for provisions?"

Jayde thought for a moment and realized that she had nothing more than a sword, dagger and men's clothing. "No, I do not. Do you know where I could find one?"

Smiling, Maggie knew just the one to give Lady Jayde. "Yes My Lady, follow me to the solar." Maggie led Jayde to the solar and to the bench where Jayde had found the unfinished work of Lady Catherine. Maggie lifted the bench seat and began to pull items out setting them on the floor.

Jayde watched as Maggie pulled out multiple unfinished projects of Lady Catherine's wondering what was so important right this minute.

"Found it!" Maggie exclaimed as she jumped up. It was the same as she remembered it to be, plain like those of the knights, but embroidered on the inside of the flap was 'CMS.' Walking across the room to Lady Jayde, she held it out to her. "This sack belonged to Lady Catherine. She used it when she would sneak out to battles that Lord Edmond was fighting and bring herbs and poultices for the sick or injured. She would gather herbs from her garden and carry them in this sack before making cures for the people in the town. Now, you need a sack and I cannot imagine anyone else using this very one."

Jayde smiled as she gingerly traced the initials and felt the strong, soft fabric. "I would be honored, thank you."

"Good. I will take it down to the kitchen and set it aside for you to retrieve when you leave." Maggie took the sack and started to rush down to the kitchen. She stopped in the hallway and turned to face Lady Jayde as she was walking towards her chambers. "Bring my boy home alive please Lady Jayde." Maggie could feel the tears that started to fall down her cheeks. She waited long enough to see Lady Jayde nod her head before turning and rushing down to the kitchen.

Jayde did not have the heart to confess James true condition to Maggie. It would do no good, and in truth, she was afraid to tell Maggie. She was afraid to disappoint this woman whom seemed to love her and trust her. Turning back towards her chamber, she felt as though the weight of the world was on her shoulders. Entering her chamber, Jayde leaned on the door as she closed it. Jayde looked at the bed, and without further thought, she walked over to the bed, spread her arms wide and fell forward into the depths of the soft mattress.

She groaned as she heard the soft knock at the door. Was there no peace or rest to be had? Maybe she could ignore it and they would go away. She waited, the soft knock persisted. She heard the latch lift and the door begin to open.

Raymond, Henry and Gilbert were all awaiting Lady Jayde in the hall wondering what could be keeping her. Raymond volunteered to go check on her. He knocked on the door and waited. There was no response. He knocked three more times before finally he heard a noise from within. It sounded as though she was groaning. Slowly, he lifted the latch and pushed the door open a little. Peeking around the edge of the door, he saw Jayde face down in her bed still fully dressed in her clothes from yesterday, looking unconscious.

"Jayde? Are you well? Everyone is assembled in the hall below. Jayde?" Raymond smiled and thought for just a moment that it would be best if she could stay and sleep only to wake to see James sitting on the bed waiting for her in the morning. He knew they could not do this without her though. As much as he and Henry would like to think that they were the masterminds behind this, they both knew that without Jayde, they would still be trying to organize the group of knights waiting below.

Jayde heard her name being called and slowly awoke feeling as though she had not slept at all and feeling the pounding in her head. Jayde opened her eyes and pushed herself up. Turning around, she saw Raymond's familiar face.

"This had better be important. I desperately need some rest." Jayde was trying to find patience with her brother.

Raymond raised his eyebrows, "Jayde, it is time for supper."

"Truly? I could not have slept that entire time. Thank you for waking me. Let's eat and prepare to bring James home." Jayde slipped her dagger in its sheath, and her sword as well. Taking a deep breath, she followed behind Raymond as he led the way down to the hall. As Jayde came into view of the Hall, the sight that was before her sent shivers up her spine and left goose bumps on her arms. Standing shoulder to shoulder, row after row were two hundred and fifty knights, all standing, waiting for her. Against the rules of war, Jayde had convinced all of them to go into battle not wearing any armor. She remembered reading in one of her mother's books about the Scottish people and how they could fight without being heard. They wore shirts and kilts and soft shoes, but no armor. So there before her, were two hundred and fifty men, wearing shirts and britches, putting all of their faith and trust in her. Jayde continued down the steps and to the center of the hall. She took a deep breath and struggled to keep her emotions to herself. Taking another look at these men, taking the time to look them in their eyes, she nodded her approval, then went to her seat and sat down for supper. Peacefully and nearly silent, the knights followed her lead and found seats at the rows of tables. Henry sat in the seat to her left and Raymond in the seat to her right.

From the kitchen, Maria emerged with a tray of dried meat and brought the tray to the table where Jayde, Raymond and Henry sat. Once they tray was set down, almost as though it had been rehearsed, every single maid walked into the hall carrying trays of dried meats and placed them on the tables. Just as quietly as they appeared, the disappeared back into the kitchen. When they reappeared, the procession was the same with trays of dried berries, fruits, and cheeses. Finally, ale was served. It seemed as more of a ceremony for a king and queen instead of the last supper that it would be for some of them.

Slowly, everyone began to eat the foods before them and before long quiet conversation started. Jayde ate because she knew she needed to nourish her body, not because she felt hungry. Watching Henry and Raymond she could see that they too, were deep in thought, eating for necessity only. Finally, the group became quiet and somber, leaving very little food on the tables and everyone was staring at her, as though she might possibly call off the mission. Time seemed to stand still. Looking at each of the faces staring back at her, she stood and walked towards Maggie who stood with tears streaming down her face holding the sack that once belonged to Lady Catherine. Jayde slowly looked into Maggie's eyes, as she held out her shaking hands for the sack.

Maggie had studied Lady Jayde's every move. Proudly, she watched as Lady Jayde stood and made the first steps to rescuing Lord James. As Jayde crossed the hall, each footstep filled with growing bravery and confidence, Maggie noticed the Knights stand one by one and follow Lady Jayde. Handing Jayde her sack of provisions, she reached out and hugged this brave young woman. "Be safe. Come home alive and bring all three boys home with you. We both know there would have been no hope if you had not taken charge." Maggie whispered to Lady Jayde before turning to get another bag, saving herself from breaking down in tears.

Soon everyone was gathered out on the fields in their groups ready to ride. As the sun began to set, the four groups rode out with their only goal to save James and kill Blaxton.

Chapter 16

Once Jayde was alone with her men near the edge of the forest, she pulled them together and informed them of the changed plans. She alone would go to James, they would push forward and keep Henry and Raymond safe. She informed them that they would not see Blaxton fighting with his army of bandits, that he would have other plans. The group agreed, then dispersed to their positions. Jayde slipped away to the edge of the forest waiting for the signals that would indicate the battle would begin. At first she did not see James and fear began to overwhelm her. Taking another look around she saw a figure on the ground that was unmistaken as James. The camp was quiet, it was long after time for the evening meal, and most everyone was already asleep or laying down. Blaxton's tent was dark and she could hear the soft sound of his breathing. If only she could smother the life from him while he slept, she could then easily get James to safety. The signal was made and within minutes, the sounds of men screaming, fighting, and dying filled the air.

Jayde waited to make a move until she saw Blaxton barge from his tent holding his sword. Jayde had moved all of her men far away from James. She wanted Blaxton to feel watched, insecure and on edge. She wanted to have the upper hand, and element of surprise when she emerged from the trees. She watched Blaxton start to run towards the sounds of his men, then stop and slowly retreat back towards James and his tent. Slowly, Blaxton turned and faced her, searching for her, for anyone to be standing there waiting for him, but she remained silent and hidden. He turned again, shrugged his shoulders and called out softly, "Well, what are you waiting for? Have you come to avenge the woman? Or have you come to rescue his body? Come forward, show yourself. Pathetic."

He was trying to hide his fear, but Jayde could hear it, she could see it. Slowly, so as to not make a noise she walked from the trees and stood in plain sight waiting for him to turn around and face her. Finally, he did. Shock, fear and even impressed seemed to cross his face.

"What a surprise. Have you come back to me knowing the truth in his past?" He laughed a mad man's laugh. "No, you still love him." He said the last with pure hatred and disgust.

He took a step towards her, then another. He was now close enough that if he lunged to his left, he could strike and kill James. If he lunged forward however, he would be able to strike her. Jayde pulled her sword from its sheath. "I am ready, are you?" Jayde asked. Her voice was calm, deeper, and strong. It was a foreign voice that she had never heard before. She accepted it, lunging forward slicing through Blaxton's left arm and placing her body between Blaxton's and James's. Blaxton laughed at her. "You think you can fight me? You think you have the strength required to protect him? I shall take great pleasure in finishing what I started."

Blaxton and Jayde began their fight. Jayde was far better trained than Blaxton had expected and she had cut him several times already. He lunged, catching the top of her shoulder sending blood dripping down her arm.

Her shoulder burned for only a moment until the pain slipped away. Recovering, she spun around hitting his sword so hard it nearly flew from his hand. The sounds of their swords striking, blended in with the sounds of the war lost in the darkness.

Blaxton struck back driving his sword into the soft flesh just above her left hip. When she gasped and looked down in horror at her hip, he took his moment and struck her with his fist at her cheek, sending her to the ground.

Jayde felt the blow to her head, but could not grasp what exactly it had been. Fighting through the haze that seemed to blanket her she looked over her shoulder searching for Blaxton. She watched as he walked toward James's lifeless form on the ground.

"NO!" Jayde screamed jumping to her feet.

Henry found Raymond frantically searching for Jayde.

"Raymond, calm down, what are you screaming for?" Henry and his flank of men had decimated the group of bandits from the North as had Raymond from the West and both had sent their men toward the South to assist Gilbert. Henry had not seen Jayde or many of her men. "Henry, I have come across several of the men from her flank, most were injured or worse, and those that were able to fight were working their way towards Gilbert. Jayde was nowhere to be found. I am worried." Raymond was still searching into the darkness for Jayde hoping she would come walking towards them. "I knew she would pull a stunt like this. She promised she would not go after Blaxton alone. Come, I think I know where we should start. We will go to where she found James." Henry led the way running with Raymond close on his heels. Coming around the Eastern edge of the camp the scene they stumbled upon was moving too fast for them to do anything more than stare.

Blaxton was standing over James with his sword drawn ready to strike and Jayde was on her knees behind Blaxton. Jayde's scream made the bones of everyone who heard it brittle and blood freeze. Everyone except Blaxton. Blaxton smiled as he brought his sword down to strike James. In that moment, Jayde jumped to her feet with her sword drawn back beyond her shoulder, then bringing it forward with all of her might to the back of Blaxton's neck.

Henry and Raymond watched as Jayde's sword sliced through Blaxton's neck sending his head to the ground with his body collapsing immediately after. Blood splattered over the body of James and backwards over the front of Jayde.

Jayde stood in shock as she watched the still smiling head of Blaxton hit the ground with a sickening thud and roll away as his body collapsed to the ground. She could not think, move, or speak; she just stood there staring at the corpse in front of her.

Raymond moved first, rushing to James's side. Placing his hand over James's mouth and nose, he could feel the shallow breaths, grateful his brother was alive. Glancing at Henry and nodding, he waited for the slight nod from Henry that told him to go. Carefully lifting his now emaciated oldest brother in his arms, he ran towards his horse at the west side of the forest never looking back. Time was of the essence, and this had been discussed between he and Henry while Jayde rested that morning. Should anything happen, he was to move James and Henry would take care of Jayde. Henry called out to Jayde softly. Taking slow steps to her, he called her name again. Still there was no response at all. Gently, he reached out and put his hand on top of her hand that held her sword. Jayde finally looked him in the eyes, her face filled with horror.

Slowly, Jayde looked up to Henry's face. She had not thought, simply reacted. He was going to kill James. She had to do something, anything. If she had simply injured him he would not have stopped until he had killed them both. She had to end it all by ending his life. Would Henry understand or would he condemn her? He could not, he followed her willingly. Would he?

"I did the right thing Henry. You would have done the same thing had you had the opportunity. HENRY! You know I was right that -"

"Jayde, calm yourself. I am very proud of you and am impressed with your bravery, quick thought and strength. I could not have acted any better myself. Are you injured?"

Jayde had not thought of herself. Beginning from shoulders to knees, Jayde began to pat herself checking to be sure she was indeed whole. Wincing as she touched her left shoulder and crying out as she touched her left hip. Looking down, she saw the sticky red wet stain covering her hand and dripping down her leg. She did not recall being injured.

"Henry? Am I bleeding?" Jayde stood in disbelief. How could she have not known?

Henry watched in horror as they both realized the dark stain on her shirt and britches was not dirt, but was blood, and it was her own. He watched as the color drained from her face and shock and doubt suddenly overwhelm her. Jayde's knees buckled and Henry caught her before she collapsed to the ground. Henry gave a low and long whistle as he carried the now limp Lady Jayde to their waiting horses.

Gilbert was waiting for them at the horses and nearly fainted with panic when he saw Henry carrying a bleeding Jayde in his arms.

"Relax Gilbert, she will be okay. I need to return to Era with her immediately however, will you be fine to finish and lead the army back?" Henry spoke as calmly as he could. He could not tell Gilbert the truth about Jayde's condition. Although Gilbert had made it very clear that he would never pursue Lady Jayde again, Henry knew that if Gilbert found out that Lady Jayde was injured, he would break the rules and give away his true feelings for her.

"Yes, I will be fine to finish here and lead our Army home. We shall see you by the midday meal. Godspeed Lord Henry." Gilbert breathed a sigh of relief before returning to the forest and the men.

Henry waited for Gilbert to walk back into the forest before kicking his horse forward racing against time to get back to Era. As they rode across the land, night began to fade into dawn, setting the hills on fire in brilliant hues of pink and orange finally making way for the extraordinary light of the sun bursting over the hilltops. As Henry raced through town to the stables he began to pray that he had arrived in time.

Maggie heard the pounding hooves of a horse sprinting through town and rushed out to the stables hoping and praying it was not an injured Lord Henry. She did not think her heart could take it if another of Lady Catherine's boys were injured or near death. The dangling body that greeted her however, left her feeling just as devastated. Running ahead of Henry, she led the way up to Lady Jayde's chamber with Anna close on their heels carrying a stack of clean linens.

"Lay her down on the bed and begin to cut away her shirt." Maggie ordered Henry. Then turning to Anna, "Go fetch clean hot water from Maria and tell her to have more hot water brought up. Go! Quickly, we do not have a moment to spare."

Henry did as he was instructed cutting away the shirt that Jayde wore. Although he knew that the wound at her side was bad, he was not prepared for the carnage that was exposed when Maggie began to rinse and wipe away the blood. It appeared that Blaxton had not just stabbed Jayde in the side, but twisted his sword either during the entry into soft flesh, or the exit.
"Heaven help me, James is going to kill me." Henry knew that they must save Jayde. He would rather suffer his brother's temper with a living, breathing little sister than to bear the burden of grief should she die.
Maggie saw the flap of flesh that was barely hanging on. She would need to clean the wound, trim any scraps of flesh or muscle then sew muscle and skin back to Jayde's body and hope and pray. "Anna, go to Lady Catherine's sewing bench and get me her silk threads and needles. RUN!" Maggie began the gut wrenching

task of trimming flesh and muscle while waiting for Anna to return. As soon as Anna returned, Maggie threaded the needle and began the carefully stitch flesh back to flesh.

"Anna, I will need for you to gather a list of herbs for me. If you need any help, you will ask Maria. We will need to watch Lady Jayde for several days, checking her wound and changing the packed poultice frequently." Anna took off in search for Maria with the list of herbs to gather for Maggie.

"Now Henry, let us take a look at her shoulder. It does not appear as bad as her side, however I would feel better if I stitch it closed as well. How many men were injured in the forest?" Maggie needed to prepare for the task of mending injured Knights when they returned. She did not want to think of the casualty count. Just then, one of the maids came into the room with more hot clean water that Maggie had requested.

Turning to the maid Maggie said, "I need for you to find Sebastian. He will need to organize the day and prepare the castle and town for the return of our Knights." With that statement, Maggie turned her focus back to Jayde's shoulder and shut out all other thoughts.

Henry waited for Maggie to finish stitching Jayde's shoulder before asking about James. "Have you tended to James? How is he? Will he survive?"

Taking a deep breath, Maggie shifted her gaze up to Lord Henry. "I have tended to Lord James. The poultice that Lady Jayde brought to him two nights ago helped greatly and likely saved his life. I cleaned his wounds, taking painstaking care to clean all maggots remaining out and applied fresh poultice. As to the rest of his health, I am unsure. He is severely malnourished and is clinging to life. He has several broken ribs, what looks to be a broken arm but did not require any stitches. Currently we are simply trying to get him to take some liquids. We have set his arm, wrapped his ribs and are praying. He is in your father's chambers. I will be checking on him as soon as Anna brings back the herbs I've requested. Would you like for me to send in some food and ale for you while we wait?"

Henry simply nodded as he glanced down at Jayde, noting how pale she was and how shallow her breathing. Then, he left the room walking across the hall to where his brother lay.

Henry was not prepared for the state of his brother. James looked lifeless with the only color to his skin being that of the bruises covering his body. Hesitating, Henry walked across the room, stoked the fire and sat down in the chair at his brother's side. He looked at each bruise, some so severely swollen it nearly disguised who the man lying in front of him was. The left arm was wrapped and set in a splint and his ribs were wrapped well with linens. Henry leaned back in the chair and rubbed his eyes. James had to pull it

261

together and recover. He and Jayde deserved to live a life together. To grow old together and raise a family together. It could not end for either of them like this. He massaged his temples and closed his eyes watching with horror the scene that took place just hours ago in the forest. Jayde jumping to her feet swinging her sword with all of her might, and the look upon her face that was frozen in his mind. It was a look that contained all of the hatred that could be conjured up, combined with fear and desperation.

A gentle knock at the door brought him back to present. "Enter." Henry called out. A maid came in carrying a tray with food and ale setting it at the table next to him. "Can I bring you anything else My Lord?" The maid politely asked.

"Thank you that will be all." Henry stood and washed his hands in the basin near the fireplace, before returning to the table lifting the lid from the plate of hot food. The smells were almost better than the taste. Henry had eaten nearly the entire quail without even realizing how famished he actually was. Licking his fingers, he picked up the mug of ale and drank large gulps, stopping to breathe only after he had finished the ale. Henry sat back down in the chair and watched his brother, hoping and praying for two miracles.

Maggie, opened the door to Lord Edward's chambers expecting to see Lord Henry pacing the floor eagerly awaiting her, filled with questions. Instead, she found Lord James looking better than when she had seen him last and found Lord Henry asleep stretched out in the chair at Lord James's side. A gentle smile fell upon her face as she took a blanket and draped it across Lord Henry before changing the poultice on each of Lord James's open wounds. Feeling his forehead, he did not feel hot, or damp from fever and his skin glowed slightly, a welcome sight from the ghostly grey he came home with. Poultice and time would be the only way that Lord James would survive. And prayers, lots of prayers. Maggie left the room and went down to the kitchen to find Maria.

Maria was preparing more fresh hot water when Maggie walked into the kitchen.

"Maggie, Sebastian is waiting for you in the Hall, I have broth simmering in the hearth for Lord James and fresh water boiling for Lady Jayde. Anna showed me the herbs she had that you requested and I helped her to find the last two. They are in a basket there on the counter, washed and dried. Is there any word on the knights?" Maria asked as she continued to work on cutting linens and getting pots of water filled in preparation for the possible injuries that awaited them to mend.

Maggie hesitated before speaking. There was no new news to give the castle and saying as much would do nothing but feed the fear that weighed on each person. "Thank you Maria." Maggie grabbed the basket of herbs and went to the Hall to sit with Sebastian.

"Sebastian, thank you for waiting for me. I hope you have not been waiting long." Maggie was eager to figure out what their plan was going to be.

"I only sat down a moment ago. How is Lord James doing? Did I hear correctly that Lady Jayde and Lord Henry have returned as well?" Sebastian was hoping to find out if Maggie had any information from Lord Henry or Lady Jayde of the knights who had yet to return.

Maggie realized that neither had the information that they both were seeking. "Lady Jayde and Lord Henry have both returned. Lady Jayde is wounded and Lord Henry is resting while watching over Lord James. I have not heard any news yet of the other men. I am hoping and praying they all return safely, but am afraid I will most likely be disappointed. I think we need to prepare for several injured men, and I would like to know what our plan shall be when our knights return."

Sebastian sat for a moment to think. "We need to have plenty of linens cut, water boiling and ready to use. What herbs did you use on Lord James, can you make more of the poultice? A lot of it?"

"I will send Anna to gather more herbs. I will send a maid out to the families in town asking for as many women who can sew and request that all that are able to help come here to the hall. Maria is already cutting linens and has several pots of water ready to boil. What should Maria have prepared for food for the knights that come back and are able to eat?" Maggie felt as though she were the Constable instead of Sebastian.

"Yes, um, have Maria get something prepared for the men that are able to eat, they will need their strength. Wonderful. I shall check in with you again when I hear the men return." Sebastian suddenly stood up and left quickly without looking back.

Maggie sat quietly for a moment trying to understand what had just happened. Standing, Maggie went to Maria to convey the message of food as well as more linens and to prepare her for women from town to be arriving hopefully soon. She then sent a maid to fetch Anna and sent several maids to town to speak with the families in town and request help. Standing in the kitchen she began to prepare the herbs for the poultice for Lady Jayde.

Chapter 17

The hour for the midday meal came and went and still there were no returning knights to fill the halls, injured or hungry. The town and castle began to worry.
Maggie had changed the poultice for Lady Jayde again and managed to get some broth into Lord James.

Raymond and Henry reviewed the battle amongst each other then returned to their posts. Henry to Lord James chamber and Raymond to Lady Jayde's chamber. After waiting for the entire morning and part of the afternoon, Henry could not wait anymore. The sun would begin to set soon, and the men should have already returned home for care and food. Leaving his post with James, Henry knocked gently on Jayde's door then quietly entered.

"Has she wakened yet?" Henry asked.
"She did briefly, however the pain she was in, Maggie gave her something to drink and she swiftly went back to sleep. How is James?" Raymond was tired and wanted nothing more than to sleep however, worry for James, Jayde and their knights kept him from succumbing to the warmth of slumber.
"James is getting stronger. Color is returning to his cheeks, and Maggie managed to get him to take some broth. He has yet to wake however." Henry took a

deep breath before informing his brother he intended to return to the forest alone to see what was wrong.

"Raymond, I am going to saddle up my horse and return to the forest. I fear that something has gone wrong and it is my-"

"Riders coming in!" The distant cry was like fresh air to a dying man. Both Henry and Raymond jumped to their feet and ran down to the hall and out towards the stables as the first group of riders came riding in.

They were fifty three riders arriving and each carried an injured man. Some men from town stood waiting to take the horses to the stables and help the stable boys get the horses fed and rubbed down. Other men from town stood waiting to take the injured men inside the hall and to the women to assess their critical needs. Immediately Maggie and Anna took control as the men were brought in. Those that were critically injured went to the table to prepare for treatment to hopefully save their lives, men that were injured but could wait were sat or laid down along the Eastern wall and those that were uninjured were directed to the western wall by the kitchen where maids began to carry out food and ale for those men to eat.

Immediately, the hall was filled with noise. The sound of injured groaning men were loudest, the injured but not life threatening men were silent as they sat against the eastern wall and the uninjured men filled the void with hushed voices that hummed like bees. Raymond and Henry rushed down the stairs into something they had never seen or heard before. It was almost as though war had taken up residence in the hall. Raymond began to search for familiar faces and was immediately relieved when he found several of his men uninjured or barely injured in the hall. Henry searched for familiar faces as well, but found few and the few faces he did find were laying on tables. As he stepped forward towards the chaos, he stopped quickly after nearly being run over by Maggie. He watched as she ran to an injured man reaching into the air. Hesitantly, Henry walked in the direction Maggie had gone.

Above all of the noise, he heard Maggie call out, "Maria! Water!"

"God, please help me! Please, someone!" Henry heard a familiar voice scream out, laced in pain.

Moving quickly now Henry rushed forward to see the carnage that covered his friend. It was Cedrick. There was blood covering him and dripping on the floor, and the skin from his left cheek was hanging down laying against his neck. Cedrick began to flail screaming in agony.

"Hold him down!" Marie ordered, and Henry obeyed without question. As Henry held Cedrick's torso down, Anna appeared out of nowhere with a small wooden pail and ladle.

"Shh, take a sip, it will help." Anna spoke calmly as she slowly poured liquid into Cedrick's mouth. The liquid had a strong and familiar smell. It was bourbon. Selfishly, he wished to take a large sip himself to numb his senses against the assault of sound that surrounded him. Looking down into Cedrick's eyes, he saw emptiness staring back. With alarm, Henry looked up to Marie and was shocked to see the sad face looking back at him. Realization that his friend had died on a table in unthinkable pain finally came to him. Hanging his head, he gently closed the vacant eyes as the priest said his prayer. Maggie and the priest left immediately leaving Henry still in shock alone at the table. The sound of other men in pain woke Henry up quickly. There was nothing more to be done here for Cedrick, his soul was at peace. Standing, Henry looked around to see where he could help next. As soon as he walked away from the table two men from town walked up and carried Cedrick's lifeless body from the hall and out of sight. Hours passed with more riders arriving with more injured knights.

Jayde awoke in such pain it nearly blinded her. The sounds from below forced her to push the pain from her mind and try to get out of bed. Crying out in pain, she immediately collapsed back to the bed clutching her side. She could still hear the sounds of pain and agony from below and taking a deep breath, she clenched her teeth and rolled out of the bed to her feet. Tears fell down her cheeks as she struggled to catch her breath. Finally, she shuffled to the wardrobe and pulled on clean britches and a shirt then struggled to open the door to her chamber. Finally, out of her chambers she used the wall to lean on for strength as she forced herself to move. The sounds from below were almost frightening and her mind preparing her for what sights she would see were nearly more than she could handle. Scanning the hall, she was shocked at the number of men laying on tables and floors. The moon was full and high shedding much needed light to aid the candles that were lit. Laying on a table, Jayde saw Sir Gilbert. Walking as quietly as a ghost, she went to his side. "Gilbert? What happened? I am so sorry." Jayde could not speak any more as fresh tears began to fall down her cheeks.

Gilbert heard Lady Jayde's voice clearly above all the rest. It was soft and gentle like a warm late summer breeze and took all of the chill from his bones. Opening his eyes, he saw her sparkling green ones staring back at him. Smiling, he gratefully accepted her tiny hands to hold. He watched as her eyes left his and scanned his injuries. Her face confirmed what he felt.

"I heard that you took his head." Gilbert struggled to smile. He had never liked seeing the worry or pain on her face and it was his duty to protect her. Not only to Lord James, but to his heart. "I bet he never thought that a petite, sweet, beautiful young woman would be his end. Then again, none of us ever do." Again, Gilbert smiled hoping to ease her pain.

How was she going to tell him how horrible his injuries were? She forced herself to laugh at his attempt of humor but could not bear to look him in the eyes.

Gilbert knew his time was running out and he needed to make it count. He let go of one of her hands and tilted her chin up so that she was looking him in the face. Despite her bravery, and maturity, the face of a sad child stared at him.

"Jayde, you should know that you have become my dearest friend. I would give my life infinitely, to give you joy and happiness. I know that I crossed the line, that I fell in love with you, and I would do it again and suffer knowing that you were someone I could never have, just to experience one of your smiles. I do not want you to suffer the burden of telling me the lie that I am going to be okay. I can feel death at the door. I will always love you Lady Jayde, and I will always watch over you and protect you from above."

Gilbert took a long difficult breath and let go.

Jayde gently closed his eyes and laid her head on his shoulder. No matter where she was, she had always known that she was safe, that he was watching her, protecting her, ready and willing to lay his life down for her. She had let him down. The truth was, that there was a part of her heart that had loved him too. He had become a wonderful friend and confidant. He had become someone to her that she herself could not explain. Closing her eyes and finally giving in to all of her fears, pain and regrets, she sobbed as quietly as she could, hidden among the dead and dying, eventually crying herself to sleep.

Henry and Raymond had been busy assisting Maggie, Maria and Anna as well as the other women in any way they could. They offered comfort to those dying or in pain, they brought supplies to tables, and found warm places for everyone to heal. Standing, Henry stretched and walked toward the kitchen to get a drink of ale. As he finished his gulp, he saw blood drippings leading from the hall up the stairs towards James and Jayde.

"Raymond!" Henry called out in panic as he raced up the stairs and followed the trail to an open door. The room to Lady Jayde's chamber was cold and dark. He felt the familiar hand of Raymond on his shoulder and knew that Raymond would watch his back as they walked into a possibly gruesome scene. Slowly and cautiously, both men continued into the room. Their eyes began to adjust to the darkness as they scanned the room. The bed was empty, Jayde was nowhere in the room and there did not appear to be a struggle.

Raymond spoke up, "Henry, you go check on James, I will retrace the steps and see from where they came." Raymond turned and followed the blood droplets down to the hall, and to a slumped over blood soaked body. Raymond recognized the cold body of Sir Gilbert laying lifeless on the table. Looking down he recognized Jayde.

"Maggie!" Raymond called as he picked up Jayde who felt as lifeless as the body on the table. Looking around as he began to rush Jayde up the steps to Jayde's chambers, he saw Maggie and Maria rushing after him. Taking the steps two at a time, he nearly knocked into Henry as he was leaving James chamber.

Henry heard a shout from below and ran from James bedside into the hall where he was nearly knocked over by Raymond carrying a lifeless looking Jayde. Quickly he threw open the door to Jayde's room and stepped back to make room for everyone to get in the room before him.

"What happened?" Maggie shouted, as Maria began to soak fresh linens in the clean, hot water. Maggie quickly took the linens from Maria and began to clean around the once again gaping wound. Assessing the injury, she could see that the stitches had ripped causing an even larger wound.

"Maggie, there was so much blood, it just pooled at her feet. Can you even save her?" Raymond's question echoed through the room without any answer back.

Anna came in and had the fire roaring within moments, giving light and adding a false sense of warmth and hope to the room. Henry sat on the seat at the window and bracing his elbows on his knees, he rested his head into his hands. This one young woman had brought so much to life again within these walls and family, and yet at every turn, something was trying to destroy it. Why? What had this family done to deserve such misery?

Maggie saw Henry sitting at the window, and approached him. He did not even look up when she placed a hand on his shoulder. Sighing, she walked away from him towards the door, there were still many men to care for before this night would be done. Stopping at the door, she turned to face the men in the room. She could feel the desperation in the air, and had no hope to give.

"Pray. Pray for her, try to keep her hydrated, and keep that fire going. I am going to check on Lord James before returning to the hall below. Anna and Maria, you are both needed in the hall." Maggie left with Anna and Maria trailing behind.

"Henry, she will be okay, she has to be. She would not fight this hard for James, for all of those men down there, and for this family if she did not intend to heal." Raymond tried to believe in his words and hoped that Henry did to. "I am going to check on James, I will be back in a while to check on you." Raymond quickly left before his brother could see that he was crying.

Henry kept a vigilant eye on Jayde through the night. Keeping a cool cloth on her head when she broke out in a feverish sweat, keeping the fire going to keep the room warm, and trying everything he could to get her to take some of the hot tea Maggie had left. Dawn came and somehow, Jayde was still alive. Despite Raymond's word to come back and check on them, he had failed to return. Instead Henry had checked on both he and James through the night as well, keeping the fire going and managing to at least get James to take in some broth. Raymond had long since fallen asleep slumped in a chair near the fire with the tray of food half eaten that Maria had brought up hours ago. Passing back and forth between the two chambers, he could hear the noises from below getting more and more quiet as the number of injured, dead and dying diminished.

The night was chased away by the sun, the last body taken away, the last man stitched, and sleep fell peacefully on nearly every person in the castle, Maggie slowly climbed the stairs to check in on Lord James. James was awake and there was a warm pink tone to his bruised cheeks.

"Lord James?" Maggie whispered, almost scared to believe he could recover.

James smiled slightly so as to not cause any more pain to what he already felt. He was so tired still. The warmth from the fire and the warmth from the broth that Henry kept supplying left him feeling as though he was in Heaven. He closed his eyes, and succumbed to the sweet sleep that tugged at him.

Maggie was so pleased she nearly cried out in joy. She stoked the fire, tucked the blanket back over Raymond and quickly left to check on Jayde. If Lord James would fight, Lady Jayde must fight too. Walking across to Lady Jayde's chamber, Maggie felt as though she had just had the best day of her life. All of that left her body however when she walked in and saw the pale figure lying in bed. Henry stood at the water bucket with his sleeves rolled up wringing a linen to carry over to Jayde.

"She is hot to the touch, but nearly as grey as the dead. I do not know what else to do Maggie." He said as he turned to face Maggie who looked as tired as he.

"Let me see." Maggie walked over to Jayde's side and felt her cheeks. She was indeed hot. Checking the wounds at the shoulder and hip, she noted that there was no sign of infection. Maggie wondered what she was missing. "Henry, help me. What am I not understanding? Start from the beginning."

Henry began recounting as much as possible until Maggie suddenly stopped him.

"That is what we are missing. She is ill! No sleep, not eating well, too much exertion, and the cold night air. She does not have an infection! I will send Maria up soon with some broth! She will heal!" Maggie spun on her heels and left without another word calling out eagerly for Maria.

Henry stood there for a moment in a daze, unsure of what he was to do next. Exhaustion plagued him, but he fought the urge to collapse and drift into a dreamless sleep. The next moment he was aware of, Maria was guiding him to the seat at the window, taking the cool linen from him and giving Jayde a bit of broth. He thought he heard Maria say "I have been saying it all along but no one would listen. The Lady of the Manor needed some meat on her tiny body. Now, they will let me do what I do best and I will fatten her up…" then he only remembered darkness.

The morning and afternoon passed before Henry awoke. There was not a part of his body that did not ache. Standing and stretching, the events from the last twenty-four hours flashed through his mind. He noted that the fire was being kept, and Maria seemed to have kept hot broth coming into the room, how much of that broth Jayde had taken though, he could only wonder. Walking across the room, Henry reached Jayde's bedside and reached out to feel her cheeks and forehead. There seemed to be no fever and the grey had finally faded to paleness. He then remembered James and quickly left Jayde's chamber and crossed the hall hoping for better news with James. To his disbelief James was sitting up in bed carefully feeding himself some soup while Maggie fussed with everything in the room.

James looked up expecting to see Raymond coming back in the room. To his surprise it was Henry.

"Maggie said you were resting, I was not expecting to see you until late tonight or tomorrow. Where is Jayde? Is she feeling better? Maggie said she was feeling ill and resting. I cannot wait to see how big she has grown with my son!" James waited for Henry to answer his questions. Instead there was an uncomfortable silence that suddenly filled the room.

Henry tried his best to keep a smile on his face, but he knew James picked up on the change in the air. James did not know any of the details of the past several months and obviously neither Raymond nor Maggie had said anything either. He glanced over at Maggie whose face screamed her apologies and pain.

"Yes, well, you both need your rest. When Jayde is well, I am sure she will be up and about back to her busy self. How are you feeling? Your ribs must be pretty tender. Is there anything I can get for you?" Henry hoped that James would not press for more answers.

James sensed there was more that Henry needed to say, but would not or could not while Maggie was present. He let it go and decided he would press him later. Instead he would ask about the troops. Hopefully later, when Jayde came to visit, he could rub her belly, and listen to all of the changes she had made in his absence. "What were our losses? Do you know how the men are doing? What has happened to Blaxton? Did you capture him?" James fired off questions without pausing for answers.

Henry took a deep breath before answering anything. "I do not know of our exact losses yet, but I will find out; although I know our losses were heavier than we were prepared for. I will also check on the living and ensure they are being cared for. We did not capture Blaxton, he was instead beheaded. He will never plague this family again. I will return shortly." With that, Henry turned and left the room leaving James with a shocked look upon his face. Henry left the chambers and nearly walked into Raymond.

"What did you tell him about Jayde, the baby and Blaxton? I did not know what to say, so I said I did not know much but that you had the answers. Then I left." Raymond felt some shame for being too cowardly to tell James the truth about everything, but relief that Henry could be there to do the talking instead.

"Nothing. I simply said that Jayde was ill but would be well soon. Have you checked on the men? Do we have a body count?" Henry asked as he began to guide Raymond below to the hall.

"Of our combined two hundred and fifty men, all are accounted for. There are one hundred eighty two alive, sixty eight dead. The wounds of the living will heal and the men will survive, for most, their injuries were minor. The hall has been cleared, soldiers dispersed among the townspeople, and everyone is resting. More herbs were collected this morning, Maria has already made poultices and is distributing them now. How is Jayde?" Raymond had done as much as he could to keep himself busy and his mind off of Jayde and James and their recoveries.

"Her fever has passed and some color is returning to her face, although I do not know if Maria was able to get her to take any broth through the night and day." Sighing, Henry rubbed his forehead in hopes of massaging the head ache away. "James will need to know the truth. You and I will speak with him after the evening meal. This will be very difficult for him. Hopefully, he will be able to see the positive in all of this. Honestly, I am finding it difficult to see the positive myself."

Both Henry and Raymond heard the footsteps of a knight as he entered the hall.

"Excuse me my lords, many of the men are asking about Lord James, is he well?" The knight asked.

Henry answered, "He is awake and feeling better. He should be up and about in another day or so to make his rounds."

The knight looked very nervous now, "And Lady Jayde, how is she? Is she recovered? Is there anything that we can do for her?"

Henry smiled slightly. These men had come to love and respect Jayde, and they were willing to sacrifice their comfort for her in their time of need as well. "Lady Jayde is resting and recovering as well. Hopefully, she too will be up and about in a few days and will be out to make sure all of her men are recovering or training." Henry thought it best to keep a positive image for everyone. Maybe the hope of the knights, and prayers of all would help her to heal as well.

Raymond listened to the conversation between the knight and Henry and it occurred to him how sheltered he had been. Suddenly, the emotions he had kept hidden and locked away the past fourteen years combined with the stress from the last several months was more than he could take. Raymond turned from the two men and nearly ran out to Jayde's garden where Laila lay in peace. Sinking to the ground, Raymond allowed himself to feel all of the loss and tragedy that had fallen upon his family. In the emptiness, he felt alone. Silent tears slid down his face and despite the warm August sun, he felt nothing but cold. A familiar hand landed on his shoulder and the realization of all that James and Henry had done to protect his childhood sank in. How had he been so selfish? Here he was crying and feeling sorry for himself when not once had he ever heard Henry or James complain.

"They will be okay Raymond. Our family will recover from this. Come now, let's get some ale and drink away your sorrow and worry." Henry was never very good at consoling Raymond as a child, James was always better at emotions. It seemed that even now, he was still not good at handling emotions, but he could help to drink them away.

"Henry, I have never thought about how our family, you and James, sacrificed so much after Mother and Father passed. You both fell into the role of Mother and Father without question, fear or complaint. I have never had to feel alone and I owe that to you and James. I have never had to have responsibilities, and I guess it all just came to me now." Raymond felt a weight being lifted off of his shoulders and began to feel like he could become a new man.

Henry did not know what to say. Neither he nor James had ever had much of a choice but to take over, Raymond was so young, it was never a conversation that needed to be had.

"Come on, let us go and ready for the evening meal." Raymond ended the awkward silence and led the way into the hall.

Chapter 18

James had fallen asleep shortly after Henry had dashed away. Slipping into blackness the torture began again. This time the images were distorted, he was small, like a child and Blaxton was as tall as the trees. In the distance he could see Jayde holding his son, swaying back and forth rocking the baby to sleep. She was crying. James stood up and tried to walk to her but his legs would not let him move. He tried calling out to her, reached his hands out to her, begging her to just look at him. Suddenly, there was tremendous light and the silhouette of his angel appeared before him. He could hear her telling him to calm down and that it was going to be okay. Again, he could smell the familiar scent of rosewater, the one Jayde liked to use. He felt so warm and comfortable as he watched Jayde and the baby slip away, and the peaceful darkness return.

Jayde had awoken to the sounds of a silent castle. She felt restless and knew the only way to free her mind of its torment was to walk. Carefully, she put on her soft thick robe of the deepest purple she had ever seen. Slowly, she opened the door to her chamber with the hopes of walking the familiar halls to soothe her mind. She had walked only three steps when she heard him calling out to her. Walking across the hall, she cautiously opened the door to Lord Edward's chamber.

There laying in the bed was James. Her heart nearly exploded as she heard him calling for her again. She sat down on the edge of the bed, careful to not hurt his injured body.

Reaching out and gently pushing a stray curl from his face, she soothed him the best she could, "Shh, calm down James. It is okay now. Everything is going to be okay." Jayde could feel the tears slide down her face and knew she had to leave the room before she began to sob uncontrollably. She knew she could only go to one place to heal, the one place she had not been strong enough to go to until now. Stoking the fire before she left, Jayde went down to the rose garden where her beautiful Laila slept.

Jayde was surprised to see Rylan, one of the knights, standing at Laila's stone.

"Sir Rylan? What are you doing?" There was a little fear in her voice, and uncertainty in her step as she approached.

Startled, Rylan turned to her and bowed his head. "My Lady, I did not hear you approach. I am sorry if I have frightened you, but we are all on rotation to stand guard at Lady Laila's resting place. I will not leave my post until the sun rises and chases the shadows and cold from this place."

Jayde's voice caught in her throat as she tried to smile and say 'thank you.' Sitting down on the cold earth,

Jayde reached out to touch the stone, and traced the letters of Laila's name. Forgetting that she was not alone, Jayde laid down on her side, with one arm supporting her head and the other still on the stone and cried for her dead daughter.

Rylan was not sure what to do. Lady Jayde suddenly laid down and cried. He had never heard anything so filled with heartbreak and sorrow. The pain laced with the cries was almost too much for him to bear and he fought to keep control, finally allowing silent tears to fall down his face as well. Eventually, the cries slipped away, and the two of them remained in silence, neither of them moving.

Henry and Raymond had remained in the hall long after everyone else had left. They sat near the fire drinking ale and discussing the future of Era and Adonia. They had convinced Maggie to go home and get some rest promising that they would keep watch over James and Jayde.

After Maggie left, Henry chuckled thinking of when they were just kids. "Do you remember when Mother and Father left all of us kids alone with James for the first time?"

Raymond began to laugh as well at the memory. "The time when he told Father that he 'was a man and could manage an estate of my own!' I remember it very well.

Thomas and Geoff were determined to kill each other on the fields and you decided you were not going to take orders from a child!"

"HA! He was a child!" Henry then remembered how they had lost Raymond and had to send for Mother and Father. "I am sorry we lost you. Where were you? How did you survive in the cold?"

Raymond burst out laughing. "Survive? Father found me wandering the woods after the evening meal and made a deal with me. He said that if I went with them on their trip and promised to never tell any of you, that he would have the Blacksmith make me my own sword when we returned. He also promised me sweets. How could I refuse?"

"WHAT! We thought we had lost you! We searched all through the night and the entire next day. James was beside himself. He thought you had drowned. I remember him having to write the note to Mother and Father requesting them to return immediately. His hands shook and he paced the hall trying to find a way to explain how he had managed to lose you." Henry began to laugh uncontrollably.

"Father stopped on our way home and covered me in dirt and mud, and even ripped holes in my shirt and britches. He reminded me of our deal. I was to wait at the edge of the wood until the last horse and rider came in and then I was to walk into the hall. I still have that sword you know." Raymond continued to sip his ale remembering what he could of his family before death came and robbed him of all the memories and experiences with his parents and siblings that he could now only fantasize about.

Henry and Raymond had never sat and talked the way they had tonight. They talked for hours about Mother and Father and the trouble that James and Henry used to get into. Henry told about how James had always been the responsible one, but before Mother and Father had passed, how James used to play many practical jokes on all of them. The fire was dying when they finally decided they should check on James and Jayde. Henry went to stoke the fire and check on James while Raymond went to do the same for Jayde.

Raymond walked into Jayde's chamber finding it empty. Hope filled his heart as he turned and went back into the hall where he waited for Henry. "Is she at least getting some rest or is she fussing over everything making sure James is comfortable?" Raymond asked as Henry came out to the hall.

"What are you talking about?" Henry began to wonder if Raymond was drunk or had just lost his mind. "Is who getting rest?"

Panic swept over Raymond's face as he pushed himself off of the wall.

"Where is Jayde Raymond? This is not a joke is it? Some poor attempt to scare me like when we were kids?" Henry was not feeling amused. In fact, he felt irritated at Raymond's sudden immaturity. He pushed past Raymond and into Jayde's chamber and found it empty. "Heaven help me, where could she be?"

The two men began to walk the castle desperate to find her. Dawn was fast approaching and they could not fail Jayde, James and Maggie. They knew they must find her. Where could she have gone though?

After what seemed like hours Henry said what they were both thinking. "We should wake up Maggie. Or maybe the Guard? She is injured and ill, how far could she have gone?"

Raymond sighed and was about to agree to waking Maggie when he had a thought.

"I know she has never gone to Laila before, but what do you think the chances are that she decided to go tonight?" Raymond was more hoping out loud than asking. After exchanging a look, the two tired men made their way down to the rose garden where they knew there would be a knight standing guard.

Approaching the rose garden with the sky turning brilliant shades of pink and orange they could see Sir Rylan standing watch at Laila's stone. Both men were startled however to see another shape there as well. Laying on the ground, curled into a ball, was Jayde with her hand resting on Laila's stone.

"My Lords," Sir Rylan greeted them as they approached.

"How long has she been here?" Henry asked as Raymond scooped Jayde up into his arms.

"All night My Lord." Rylan had stood guard through the night listening to Lady Jayde cry in her sleep for her little baby. "My Lord, I have never heard anything so haunting in my life. She cried in her sleep, a most hollow and broken hearted cry. I swear, I will go to my grave with the sounds of her cries haunting my mind."

"Henry, she is very cold. We should get her inside to warm by the fire." Raymond turned and walked back towards the castle hall with Jayde in his arms, stiff and cold but still sleeping.

"Go inside and warm yourself Sir Rylan and get some rest. Have Sir Fendrel create shifts for Laila's Guard for the cold nights. It will not do anyone any good to become ill standing out in the cold all night long." Henry turned and followed Raymond into the castle after Sir Rylan acknowledged his order.

Maggie was starting a fire in the hall when she saw Raymond walk in with Lady Jayde in his arms.

"What on earth-" Maggie began to say before seeing Henry walk in as well.

Holding his hand out to stop Maggie from continuing to speak, Henry said, "Do not ask, we do not know ourselves." Following the men upstairs Maggie tended the fire and made sure to pile on an extra blanket to help warm Lady Jayde.

"Heaven have mercy upon us, this woman is determined to test my skills!" Maggie busied herself setting large river stones at the edge of the fire to warm, then left the room to get some herbs for tea and warm food from Maria.

Henry stood near the window looking below to the rose garden rubbing his temple.

"Henry? Hello, are you even listening?" Raymond had waited for Henry to answer him long enough.

"I am sorry, what did you say?" Henry checked back into the present.

"I said that one of us would need to keep James company today and one of us would need to keep an eye on Jayde. Who do you want?" Raymond knew that they were both worried not just for James and Jayde, but for their own futures as well.

"You should tend to James today. Now is not the time to have any conversations with him regarding what has been going on, and we all know that I cannot keep my mouth shut when James is the one asking for answers. Keep him busy, play chess, discuss the weather, ask him questions about his captivity, but absolutely do not discuss Jayde with him. Can you do that?" Henry would need to think about the best way to tell James everything; Laila, Fendrel challenging Jayde, and Blaxton. This was going to be the most difficult thing he would have to do in his entire life.

Henry thought he had heard Raymond say something and turned around to ask him to repeat himself again but Raymond was gone and Henry noticed that Jayde was beginning to wake up.

Maggie went down to the kitchen and found the dried rose hips and chamomile that she had been saving for a tea for Lady Jayde. Filling a teapot with hot water, she added the herbs and placed the teapot and a cup on a tray. Then she added a plate of fried pork, and two scrambled eggs. This was a big breakfast, but they were some of Lady Jayde's favorites and they were easy and quick for Maria to make. Once she had everything she needed, she carried the tray upstairs to Lady Jayde.

Walking into the room, Maggie saw Lady Jayde sitting herself up and Henry grabbing a hot river rock from the fire.

"Good heavens Lord Henry! Stop that, you are going to burn yourself! Here, let me take care of that." Maggie said as she set the tray down on the table. Grabbing a thick linen, she scooped the river stone up and wrapped the linen around it before sliding it under the blankets near Lady Jayde's feet.

"I feel as though I am in the way. What can I do?" Henry kept stepping out of Maggie's way trying to not be a problem.

Turning around to face Lord Henry, Maggie smiled and patiently said, "Lord Henry, you should go down, get something to eat and get some rest. Yes, I know that you and Lord Raymond stayed up all night drinking and talking. Go and rest, you deserve it." Then she gently shoved him out of the room and gave her full attention to Lady Jayde.

Maggie spent the entire day convincing Lady Jayde to spend just one more day in bed and that tomorrow she could make her rounds on the field. Finally, after arguing her case for an hour, Maggie won. "My Lady, now I know it is not my station to mother you, to order you about, or expect you to do as I say, but I have worked so hard to heal you, to keep you, the best thing to happen to this family for so long, healthy that I just cannot in good conscious give up this fight with you. I am begging you, give an old woman just this one favor and allow yourself to rest and heal just one more day. Especially after spending the night on the cold hard ground. Please?"

Sighing, Jayde considered Maggie's final plea. It couldn't hurt to rest, she was exhausted and still quite sore. "Okay, just today though. Tomorrow, I will return to the fields and my men. Will you promise me one thing?"

"Yes, as long as you stay in and rest today, I will promise you one thing." Maggie was so thrilled for this victory she was willing to promise anything.

"Promise to keep me informed on James recovery and if he asks for me?" Jayde was feeling helpless. Would James ever wake up? What was he going to say when she told him about Laila? Would he condemn her for killing Blaxton? Would he still love her?

Relieved to hear Jayde's request was about James health, she joyfully agreed.

Jayde spent her entire day in bed as promised. She slept between meals and through the night with the relief of knowing she would return to the fields tomorrow. She needed to keep herself busy while waiting for James to recover.

Chapter 19

James could feel his anger growing. He had tolerated Raymond and his small talk all day yesterday because he believed that Henry was handling illnesses and soldiers. He was expecting to see Henry this morning instead of Raymond again. He wanted to see his wife, meet his son and try to get back to a regular routine. His strength would return quickly, he had been strong and healthy before Blaxton and knew that with rest and Maria's food, he would be recover. Unfortunately for Raymond, his temper had already recovered.

"Raymond, I love you. You are my baby brother. I am grateful for this wonderful time we have spent together and I look forward to all of the opportunities for us to spend more time together. However, I *insist* that you get Henry and get him now." James tried his best to control his temper, but knew that his words still stung.

"Well, I can go check on him and see if he has finished up, but you might have to wait another day -"Raymond began to say.

"NOW RAYMOND! Go and get Henry RIGHT NOW!" James could feel his blood boil and the heat from his anger flush his face.

Raymond was so startled by James outburst that he literally jumped out of the chair he was sitting in and actually ran out the door.

Raymond ran down the stairs and stopped halfway through the hall. Who did James think he was? Who did he think he was yelling at? He was a twenty year old man! He was going to take his sweet time finding Henry. He did not take orders from James! Raymond was just about to sit down when he thought about the wrath that James could inflict. Hanging his head slightly, he knew he had lost, Raymond walked out to the fields to fetch Henry.

Henry watched Raymond cross the fields with his head down slightly and shoulders slumped forward carrying a huge chip on his shoulders. He knew he could not avoid James any longer.

"His Royal Highness has summoned you." Raymond still felt humiliated at being yelled at as though he were a servant. Turning to face Henry, who was already walking towards the castle, he called out, "remind his Highness that I am his BROTHER, not his DAMNED SERVANT!"

Henry lifted his hand in the air to signal that he heard Raymond's message loud and clear as he continued to walk off of the fields. Reaching the entry to the hall, he glanced back and watched as Raymond stood by Jayde's side and hoped that he would keep Jayde from further injuring herself. Turning and walking into the hall he felt his stomach turn over. He dreaded this conversation and wished that it could be Jayde to do the talking. Slowly Henry walked up the stairs and into James room. As he swung open the door, he heard James greet him.

James heard the door swing open and without looking up from the tray of foods, he greeted his brother. "Henry, thank you for joining me. Please, come in and sit down."

Henry heard his brother's invitation but knew it was more a command than invitation. Closing the door, he did as requested.

"Where is my wife Henry." James cut right to the chase.

Sighing, Henry spoke. "She is on the training fields with Raymond."

"Why?" James could feel his anger rising again.

"She is on the fields to oversee the knights and make sure that they are continuing to push themselves and train hard. She wants to be sure they are striving for improvement." Henry felt tired already, as though he had been talking all day to James.

"Start talking Henry. Do not make this difficult. I need to know everything. Why is Jayde on the training fields and not here? Does she not ask for me? Does she not care? Perhaps she cares more for my knights than me?"

he could hear the hurt in his own voice and knew that his anger was barely hiding it.

"James, there is so much for you to know. Let me start by saying that Jayde did not ask for our help for nearly three months. She took on the burden of being the head of this manor the entire time that you had been gone. You see, after you went missing, Jayde began to train with Sir Gilbert. She rode that black beast that she calls Galavant, and worked hard every day. Eventually, Sir Gilbert fell in love with Jayde and kissed her in the training stables. From that day-" Henry was interrupted by James outburst.

"He did what! To my wife? I am going to kill him. Where is he? Wait, did she kiss him back?" Suddenly James began to wonder if Jayde truly did not love or care about him any longer. They had been married not quite a year yet, and so much had happened. What if she did not love him?

Henry waited for James to finish his outburst before continuing on. "Just let me finish. There is much more to this story and the least important detail is Sir Gilbert kissing your wife. To answer your question though, no she did not kiss him back." Henry continued on, pausing only here and there for a drink. "Fendrel challenged Jayde's loyalty to you. Jayde took his challenge to the field. They charged each other on horseback, Jayde knocked Fendrel to the ground, and then Fendrel pinned her braid to the ground with his sword. I wish I could have been there, but if you ask any of the knights, they will tell you how magnificent Jayde was. If you get a group of them telling the story together, it morphs into half-truth and half hero worshiping glory story. Jayde however tells it best; quite simply with love for her husband in her eyes. Anyway, in one fluid motion, she sliced off her braid, and held Fendrel by the tip of her sword. She refused to give up on you or let anyone else give up either. The knights keep her braid pinned above the stable entrance as a reminder of their loyalty to her and you. Some of them are even convinced that it is good luck. She was willing to give even her life for you James and in a way, she did. You see, it was Jayde who figured out where Blaxton was keeping you. She organized that group of men out there, she led us all out to the forest, and she is the reason you are alive. In the battle, Jayde knew that Blaxton would be too smart to leave you alone. She lied to Raymond and I, and honestly, had she not lied, I do not know that we could have saved you. She battled with Blaxton, and he hurt her. He was about to kill you when Jayde ended his life. She has been ill these past few days, but has asked of you daily." Henry waited for James to say something, but James just sat there looking at his hands. Henry was about to break the silence when finally, James spoke up.

"How did she end his life?" James was desperately trying to imagine his sweet little wife killing a gnat, let alone evil like Blaxton. He could only imagine the horror her dreams must bring her reliving the moment when she took another person's life. It made him sick. No woman should ever have to face the ugliness of war.

"She beheaded him." Henry answered.

James thought for a moment and became puzzled. "Where was Sir Gilbert? It was his job to protect her. Obviously he has done no such thing and instead has guaranteed his own death. You do realize that I must challenge him for Jayde's honor to the death?"

"Sir Gilbert was attacking the encampment. You will not need to challenge Sir Gilbert. After Raymond brought you home, I realized that Jayde was injured. Blaxton had stabbed her in the shoulder and side. Hours after rushing her home, our men started to return as well. Gilbert was among the wounded. At some point in the night, Gilbert died of his wounds on a table in the hall." Henry thought it would be better to keep the fact that Jayde went to Gilbert and was with him in his final moments of life. It would only fuel the anger and distrust that he could see was growing in James.

"Did Blaxton injure my son?" James could only imagine the wounds, and worry for his child consumed his mind.

"No, he did not. You do not have a son James. You had a daughter. Her name is Laila." This was the worst moment that Henry had imagined. Telling his brother that his child had died.

James head snapped up. "A daughter? Had? He killed my daughter? Oh my God, Jayde. My beautiful Wild Jayde."

"James, Blaxton did not directly kill Laila. Jayde went into labor shortly after you were taken. Maggie, Fendrel and Gilbert were there. Laila was too small to live. She was born too early." Henry's voice caught and cracked. "James, I am so sorry. I did not want to be the one to tell you."

"Where is my daughter now? Where does Laila rest?" James was much calmer and quiet now.

"She is in the rose garden. If you would like, I will take you to her now." Henry offered.

James could only nod. He accepted Henry's help and leaned on him while walking down the stairs. The sun was well on its path across the sky giving warmth to the cool and crisp morning. Henry led James to the bench at the stone.

"Raymond and I found Jayde sleeping here, on the ground yesterday morning and again this morning. It was the first time she has been able to visit Laila. Do not worry though, the Guard takes shifts and there is always someone here through the night. Jayde was protected." Henry took several steps back until he was leaning against the wall. James did not seem like he wanted to hear anymore right now.

James felt helpless. He had a daughter. Jayde was without him, he was not there to hold her hand, or whisper for her to be strong, to kiss her head and tell her how proud he was of her and how much he loved her. Oh God, Laila. She never would be held by him, her father. He had not been here to protect her. That was his job, to protect her, to comfort her. He remembered the baby in his dream from last night. Had that been Laila? Was she waiting for him to hold her and love her? He would never get the opportunity to hold her sweet little hands, or watch her take her first steps. How would Jayde ever forgive him?

Henry stood still and watched James. He watched as James lowered his head into his hands, and rub his face before looking up to the sky. Henry grew concerned when he heard James begin to have labored breathing. He pushed off of the wall and stepped forward until he heard the eeriest sound in his life. James, with his face still pointed up to the sky cried out the longest and loudest cry of "WHY!"

His word echoed through the garden and out to the fields. His heart ached for his loss and he wondered how he and Jayde were supposed to recover from this, another death. Was his family cursed? When would happiness and joy visit his family? He could barely keep his body upright anymore. Exhaustion overcame him.

"Henry, I need to return to my chamber. I cannot handle anymore. Please, help me." James felt weak already and the sadness that overtook him made it impossible to function.

Henry did as he was asked and helped James back to his chamber.

"Henry, when you go to Jayde, will you please tell her I asked for her. Please?" James could barely think straight enough to complete his sentence. He did not even wait for Henry to answer before he fell fast asleep.

James was running in the dark. There was no moon to light his way but somehow he knew exactly where to go. He could hear Blaxton close on his heals but his war instincts would not kick in. Why could he not think of what to do next? There was something heavy on his arm preventing him from moving it. He could hear Blaxton nearly on top of him!

James woke up in a panic. Glancing around him, he could see the moon was high in the sky and his sweet Angel laid in his arms. She reminded him so much of Jayde, but so different as well. Smiling he closed his eyes and drifted back to sleep. In his dream he could see his Angel standing with her back to him. She was so close, but still he could not reach her. He remembered waking up and seeing her in his arms, was that a dream too? What if it was not a dream? What if Jayde saw her in his arms, what would she think? Struggling, James forced himself to wake up. Looking around the room, he saw that not only was he alone, but it was dawn already. Where was Jayde? Why did she not come to him? Oh no, what if she had come in and his Angel was there? Who was this other woman? James could feel the frustration and anger at his confusion and unanswered questions taking hold.

He needed to find Jayde and speak with her. He needed to hold her and feel her skin on his, to tangle his hands in her hair and whisper against her neck how much he loved her. He wanted to hold her hand, to be strong for her and walk with her to visit Laila. He would hold her so she could cry and beg for her forgiveness. They could try again and this time he would not fail her. James pushed the covers back and slowly stood up on his own. Gently, he stretched in front of the dying fire. Stoking the fire and adding another log James began to get dressed. He knew that he would have to get back to normal day to day life and today was no worse a day to start than tomorrow. As he was tying his shirt, Henry walked in the room.

"What are you doing?" Henry asked as he walked in. He was not prepared for James to be walking around after how tired he had been yesterday. He had even tried to persuade Jayde to rest today so as to not exert herself. Henry was learning that Jayde was as stubborn as James.

"I am trying to heal physically, mentally, and emotionally. I need my daily routine to heal mentally, I need Jayde to heal emotionally and physically, well, time will take care of that. Take me out to the fields. If Jayde is out there, then once she sees that I am able to manage my men again, she can return to her daily routine as well, and we can get back on track to where we were going, happily ever after." James was determined to bury Blaxton's memory and never look back.

"James, I do not think that Jayde will easily walk away from training. I think she likes training. I would wait a few more days before you go out there, just rest, get stronger." Henry knew that the wife James had brought home no longer lived here. She had grown up and grown into a beautiful, strong woman. She had experienced the miracle of life and the horrors of death, and did not just survive. She flourished. "James if you go out there and order her back to the castle, you will push her away."

James heard Henry talking but was lost in his fantasy of how quickly and easily life would go back to how it was. He tuned back in only to hear Henry tell him he would push Jayde away.

"I think I know my wife best. She will be happy to be back inside and return to managing staff and whatever else she would like to do." James was digging in his heals. Then softly, unsure of its truth, he added, "And try again for a child."

Henry knew there would be nothing that he could say to change his brother's mind. He would go with James out to the fields and hopefully keep him from doing something he would later regret.

The two men walked out to the fields in silence. James kept replaying the scenes from the story that Henry had been telling over and over in his mind. He kept seeing Gilbert take Jayde in his arms, pull her close and kiss her. Then as he pumped his fists, he could see her actually swinging a sword and taking off Blaxton's head. His mind filled in the sounds of battle and when the thump from Blaxton's head hitting the ground played in his head, he actually shuddered. They reached the fields and saw knights charging one another wielding swords while another group of knights on the field were sparring with one another. Off in the distance, Jayde was asking one of the knights to correct her positioning on a stance. Only Henry recognized her.

James looked around. He did not see Jayde, but did see a new page that Henry failed to mention. "Who is that scrawny boy? To which knight does he go with?" James absently asked, still scanning the field for Jayde. The boy continued to attract his attention though. He knew this boy. He was small, had curly hair that hung just a bit below his shoulders, but seemed to have the attention of many of his knights. He started to walk a bit further, then stopped. He watched as the boy swung upon Jayde's horse. He suddenly realized that this was not a boy, it was the Angel that saved him in the forest and came to him last night! What was she going to do? He watched as she kicked Galavant forward charging one of his biggest knights.

Jayde was still feeling weak, but was desperate to return to something of a normal life. She was telling Rylan that her wrist was incredibly sore from a particular hold for sparring. Rylan showed her a better technique and then whispered the other knight's weakness, balance. Jayde mounted Galavant. She hated the saddle, but was told that they would never ride into a battle without saddles. She would have to learn to like the saddle, at least a little bit. Jayde charged the knight and at the last minute, became too scared to jump from the saddle, but it was too late. Her balance was already over the shoulder of Galavant. Suddenly she was tumbling forward, she tucked her head and tried to make herself small by curling into a ball. The other horse jumped over her body as she bounced on the ground. The fall stunned her and after one bounce she lost her strength and her body sprawled out on the ground. Her head hurt, as well as her shoulder and side again.

Henry was already sprinting as James was still trying to figure out why the woman who saved him was here. James tried running but realized that a light jog would get him there faster.

"What is wrong with you? You could have been killed, and you!" Henry turned to face Raymond now. "I gave you one task! One! Keep her safe!" Henry kneeled down and cradled Jayde's head in his arms. Softly, he asked "Jayde, are you okay? Where does it hurt?" If Jayde was further injured James would probably never forgive either of them.

James slowed down a bit, he watched as Henry exploded on Raymond. Was it possible that the Angel that saved him was in love with Henry? Was this woman that haunted his dreams, which he had felt emotionally unfaithful to Jayde for, someone that Henry was pursuing? Feeling foolish, he slowed down more and casually walked forward. He saw the head full of bouncy curls slowly sitting up and he caught a glimpse of her face. James froze dead in his tracks. Those lips, so soft and perfectly shaped, and her nose was so sweet and tiny. James filled with anger and strode forward grabbing Henry by the back of his shirt and pulling him back. Reaching down he grabbed the woman by her arms and jerked her up to her feet making her face him.

"Are you determined to kill yourself? Is it just your own life or your life with me that you hate?" James waited a moment, then yelled again. "Answer me!" James watched as she started to sway still not answering him.

Jayde was still in shock from falling. She never fell, never lost her balance. Damn that saddle! She could see Henry but could not really understand what he was saying. Then James appeared and grabbed her by the arms and was yelling at her. Her head was killing her, she could not stay upright, and she felt like she could be ill. James yelled again. As Jayde began to sway again, a ringing in her ears began and she doubled forward vomiting at James feet.

James was about to shake her when she vomited at his feet. Without thinking, he grabbed her arm and wrapped it around his neck and began walking her to the castle hall. What was she thinking? When was she going to just take her place, manage their home and raise their children? Pain replaced the anger and he realized that If he would have been careful, not been taken by Blaxton, that possibly, Laila would be here right now, holding his finger with her perfect tiny hands. Her eyes would be green like Jayde's, her lips a perfect shade of pink with matching cheeks, and sweet blonde curls. Jayde brought him back to reality when she stumbled and vomited again. James picked Jayde up and carried her the rest of the way to the castle hall.

Maggie came walking down the stairs as James was carrying Jayde in. "Heavens above, what has she done now?" Maggie muttered aloud as she hurried over to James who collapsed on the bench after setting Jayde down. "What happened? My Lady, you will not give up until you have done it all, will you? Be still My Lady, let me see what needs to be done." Maggie first checked Jayde's side, and seeing that the stitches held and there was no bleeding, she checked her shoulder. It too, was unscathed. Relieved, Maggie finally checked Jayde's head where she was holding it. "My Lady, at the pace you are going, you will have more injuries than your husband." Maggie smiled hoping to lessen the hostility. The tension between James and Jayde was thick and it made Maggie uncomfortable.

The ringing in Jayde's ears was finally subsiding. She was tired and sore and was left feeling confused and betrayed. James was here, alive, and he came to her on the fields! Then he had yelled at her, but she did not do anything wrong, so why was he angry? Before she could say anything, James did.

"Why, why are you constantly putting yourself in danger? You run off into a forest, I rescue you. Then I find out that you have cut off your hair, you are riding horses without saddles, and you throw daggers, wield swords, and go to battle! When I agreed to marry you, I thought I would be marrying an obedient quiet wife that would stay home and, and…" James was trying to correct his first mistake of yelling at her and just stopped talking completely.

"AND WHAT?" Jayde was done. She had shouldered too much for too long. "Go on! Finish what you were about to say! What, stay home and sew? Decorate? WHAT!"

James could never back down from a challenge and this was no different. His temper soared. "Stay home and have babies!" The moment the words left his mouth he regretted them. Defeated he tried to apologize. "Jayde,

I am sorry. I should not have said that. Please, forgive-
"

"I tried to stay home and have babies. But my baby was taken from me. She is dead and so am I. I have given everything I possibly can for *you* and none of my sacrifices were worth it. I am done. I will do nothing more." Jayde turned to Maggie now. Jayde's shoulders slumped and she looked as defeated as she felt. Quietly Jayde spoke, "Maggie, please have a bath sent to my room, some fresh linens and cool water. I will take my midday and evening meal in my chamber and do not want to be bothered by anyone." Jayde stood and walked up the stairs to her chamber using the wall to help her balance.

Maggie's mouth fell open at James words. She waited until Jayde left the hall before speaking. "If your mother were still alive, she would slap you across the face. I do not care if you do not like what I have to say, you deserve to be taken over a knee and spanked." Maggie then turned and set about to take care of Lady Jayde.

Chapter 20

Jayde spent the next week avoiding James except at
meals. She spoke only when spoken to, when she did
speak she spoke so softly that she could barely be heard,
and mostly, she would not allow for James to touch her
in any way. Every night she cried herself to sleep, then
woke, went to Laila, and fell asleep on the ground.
Each morning she awoke in her chambers again and if
she had not found the random leaf or bit of dirt in her
hair, she would swear it had all been a dream. She felt
alone, and consumed with sadness and rejection. She
could not live like this. What could she do? She had no
other place to go, Adonia was no longer hers, and James
owned everything. She needed to feel freedom. She
needed to take Galavant for a run.

The hell that Blaxton had put James through was
nothing compared to the hell that this past week had
been. Jayde would not look at him, would not let him
touch her and would barely speak to him. The first
night, James could not sleep and took to walking the
halls and grounds. As he was returning he found Henry
carrying a sleeping Jayde through the main hall and up
to her chambers. He had nearly attacked Henry and had

even gone so far as to accuse him of having an affair with his wife. After Henry had explained that Jayde had once again gone to Laila and fell asleep on the ground, James made sure that he was awakened from now on. Each night since then, the knight on duty would come get him to come and get Jayde. It was the only time he touched her, when she was asleep and dreaming of Laila. James knew that he had hurt her in a way that even Lady Ethna had never hurt her. He doubted that she would ever forgive him, but he would try to earn her forgiveness. He would try every day until he died.

Jayde waited to go to Galavant until after the midday meal. It was a perfect autumn day at the end of September. Jayde took Galavant into the forest, down by the river and after the sun had set, when the moon was rising she finally brought him home to the stables. It was well past time for the evening meal and Jayde could not bear another cold lonely night in the castle. She led Galavant to the breeding stables, gave him a good brushing and a bucket of oats. Jayde climbed up into the loft and laid down falling fast into a deep dreamless sleep. For the first time in weeks, neither James nor Laila haunted her dreams. She had no idea the impact her absence was on the evening meal or to James. She had no idea, that shortly after she returned, a search party was dispersed, or that James heart was broken believing that she had either been taken, or worse that she chose to leave.

"When did you see her last Henry?" James for the first time exposed his vulnerability to his brothers and his guard. He let the fear that gripped his heart be seen by anyone that looked upon him.

Henry looked at the stranger before him. Could James have actually learned his lesson? "I last saw her at the midday meal, just like you."

Raymond walked in shaking his head. "I checked with the townspeople, no one had seen her."

"Put two guards on Laila for each shift, in case Jayde returns, one of the two knights can come and get us. We will divide and begin the search. Henry, you will take the forest, Raymond, you will search up on the hill and beyond, and I will take the river. Are there any questions?" James was hoping and praying they had just missed her somehow but his heart dreaded the possibility of Jayde leaving him.

"Has anyone checked to make sure that Galavant is in his stables?" Raymond asked.

Henry answered, "I checked the stables just after the evening meal. Galavant was gone."

"What about the breeding stables? Lady Jayde used to keep Galavant there when she was first training." Sir Fendrel suggested.

James for the first time felt that he did not have the answer. Looking to Raymond and Henry he waited and hoped for their help.

"James, you check down by the river, and circle up to the breeding stables. We will all meet back here." Henry took charge of the search and situation. "If you find any signs of abduction, immediately send someone for me. Head out!"

Henry held back a moment as everyone else left the hall and went on their way. "James, are you sure you want to ride? I know you are gaining your strength, but you still have a way to go before you are fully recovered. What if Jayde returns, do you not want to be here?"

James thought about it before he answered. "I cannot sit idle waiting to know of her fate or whereabouts. If she is hurt, I need to be able to be with her, if she has been taken, I must be able to start tracking them and if she is found, I want to be there to bring her home."

"What will you do if she does not want to come home?" Henry worried about having James on the search for Jayde when his emotions were so raw.

James choked on his thoughts and emotions. "I honestly do not know. I do not know that I will be able to handle knowing that my words and actions, or lack thereof, may have driven her away."

Henry could only nod his head in understanding before placing his hand on James shoulder as they walked out of the hall to their waiting horses.

The three search parties searched for hours before returning to the hall. Raymond searched the hills, and all the hiding places he had found when he was a kid. Henry and his men searched the forest twice before returning and James had walked the river bank looking for any sign of struggle or trouble before circling back up to the breeding stables.

Dawn set the early morning sky ablaze as the group of tired men gathered in the hall.

James rubbed his face with his hands desperate to remember anything or discover something he had overlooked. "Galavant is in the breeding stables, but there is no sign of Jayde." Looking at Henry, he then said, "My God, what have I done Henry?"

"I want everyone to get some rest. We will gather again at the midday meal and plan a more extensive search." Henry ordered the group of men. Only he, James and Raymond remained in the hall.

"I should have listened to you Henry. I should have held my tongue and my temper. I am such a stubborn ass that I allowed my pride to overrule my heart and head. If I could do it over again, I would have kissed her head, checked her injuries, and helped her back up on that damned horse." James slammed his fist into the table. Henry and Raymond sat down beside him.

Jayde awoke as dawn painted the sky. It was funny how everyday Mother Nature woke up the world with a new piece of art and never was any sky the same as any from before. She never looked back at yesterday to guide her today. Jayde decided she would take this small lesson from Mother Nature. Yesterday was useless. Today is what mattered. She needed to settle this with James, and if this was to be her life, then she would have to make it work and be happy with it. Jayde left the loft and walked to the hall. As she walked in, she saw James, Henry and Raymond gathered together in the hall looking as though someone had died. James looked the worst.

Jayde rushed forward forgetting the war she battled with James. Sinking to her knees, she put her hands on his face, "What is wrong? Are you well? Is someone hurt?"

James felt the tiny hands on his face before his mind could register who they belonged to. She was alive! She was alive, touching him, speaking to him, worried for him. He grabbed her by her arms and pulled her to him nearly crushing her as he held her.

"Oh my God, you are safe. We were so worried. Where have you been?" James paused as he felt a surge of anger. "Where have you *been*?"

"James, remember what you said. Checking your temper, and your tongue…" Raymond reminded James.

"Did someone take you? Were you lost? Were you going to leave me?" James was struggling to stay calm.

"No. I took Galavant out for a ride yesterday, then fell asleep in the loft above the stables. I am so very sorry to have worried you. I did not mean to, I just could not take crying myself to sleep another night, sleeping on the ground or wake up wondering who carried me back to my bed yet again. I truly am sorry to have worried you. You look like you have not slept at all. You should rest and then we must sit down and talk." Jayde tried to be gentle and not sound bossy or challenging.

James smiled slightly and kissed her forehead. "I have been up all night looking for you. Help me upstairs."

Jayde did as she was asked and helped James to his chamber. She helped him to take off his boots, and then stoke the fire as he undressed and climbed into bed. Jayde walked over and tucked the covers in around James.

James watched as Jayde made herself busy in the room. She had tucked the cover in around him and was about to leave. "Are you not going to kiss me?"

Jayde hesitated, but decided to give him a peck on the cheek. After giving him his kiss, she turned to leave again when James caught her hand. She pulled a little hoping that James would let go of her. Instead he pulled firmly back, landing her in his lap.

"Why are you so eager to leave me? Why do you not come visit me?" James was hurt and he did not try to hide it from Jayde this time.

"I *have* visited you. You were asleep, I even laid in your arms. I heard you calling out to me, and I came to you." Jayde took a deep breath. "I am trying to leave so that you can get some rest so that we can talk about my role in your home."

"Our home. This is our home, not my home, not your home, *our* home." James corrected her.

"If it is *our* home, then why can I not do as I please in it?" Jayde challenged him.

"You can do what you please, all I ask is that you maintain the management of it." James did not see the trap he was being led to.

"I can do *anything* I want? I can practice music all day?" Jayde continued to lead him into what she wanted most.

"Yes, you can do anything you want." James was confused as to what was so difficult to understand.

"So, I can do anything I want. I can ride Galavant and race through the woods, or walk the village and check on the people and their livestock, I can train with the knights, I can sew, or redecorate the castle? Truly, anything?" Jayde held her breath while she waited for James response.

"Yes, yes to all of it. You can ride your beast of an animal, walk the village, livestock, train, sew, and redecorate. Yes, any – wait what? Train? Train! NO! No you may not train with the knights because you are not a man! You are a woman and you are my wife! I will not have my wife throwing daggers, wielding swords or going to battle! NO!" James had gone too far but knew there was no turning back now.

"You see, this is why I did not want to talk with you now. You are obviously tired and need rest. You say one thing then you become confused and say something else that completely contradicts what you have already promised. James, I had to change while you were gone. I like who I have changed into and I do not know if I can go back to being the meek girl that you married." Jayde was trying to talk some sense into him and hopefully show him who she had become.

"Meek girl? Meek?" James tipped his head back into the pillows and roared with laughter. "Jayde de Seaton, you are the farthest thing from meek that can be. You were not afraid of me in the woods when we first met.

You were not even a Lady, you jumped into my arms and kissed me! You-" James was interrupted.

"I did not jump into your arms! You jerked me off of my feet and threw my body against you!" Jayde defended herself.

"But you do not deny kissing me! You survived being held captive," James became quiet and serious, "you gave birth to our daughter without me and held her for her first and final breaths. You challenged my best knights, and won their hearts and loyalty, you even cut your hair off. My love, you are one of the wildest creatures I know. You are *my* Wild creature." Smiling he tousled her hair, loving the new soft curls, he combed his fingers through her hair. Stopping suddenly he studied her. He remembered the angel that came to him in the forest, the same angel that slept in his arms and the same angel that mounted a beast charging one of his best knights.

His breath caught and he whispered, "It was you. You were the angel that came to me while I was being held by Blaxton. It was you, my beautiful, strong, Wild Angel." James leaned forward and pulled her forehead towards his and closed his eyes. "You saved me." He felt Jayde's tiny hands full of so much love and grace caress his face.

Jayde whispered back, "Of course it was me. I could not leave you there without trying to help you in every way that was possible. I love you James. I will love you until the end of time."

Releasing Jayde, James sat back against the pillows again. "Wild, I know that you have changed. Henry has told me so much. I know what you had to do in the end to Blaxton, I know of some of the heart breaks you had to deal with alone. I know there is a lot that Henry did not tell me, and if I never know, that is okay. If you truly feel like you want to train with our knights, I will not stop you, but I will be the one to train you, not them. I ask that you promise to listen to me and let me guide you. First, I beg of you to let us both heal. Do we have a deal?"

Smiling, Jayde laid against James, resting her cheek on his chest. "Okay."

"Jayde, say it. Say I promise to listen to you." James was starting to get wise to Jayde's trickery.

"Mmmhmm." Was all that Jayde said.

Tilting Jayde's chin up to look at him, James tried again. "Jayde, promise me. Please." Looking into those beautiful eyes, James knew he had been beat. Her triumphant smile confirmed his defeat. "I do not know why I even bother. At some point you will convince me of something else and somehow make me believe it was my idea all along." James brought his mouth to hers and kissed her sweetly. "Do not ever stop keeping me guessing Wild." James smiled and wrapped his arms around Jayde. Holding her tight, he fell asleep with a smile on his face and knowing in his heart that this life together was going to be an adventure.

Jayde laid still against James chest feeling comfort and acceptance. Closing her eyes, she fell asleep listening to the steady rhythm of James beating heart.

Era – Wind

Adonia – Greek Goddess / Lord

Glossary of Characters:

Abigail – cook at Adonia
Anna – Lady Jayde's personal maid
Bethany – daughter of Thomas the blacksmith
Blaxton – deranged brother of suicide victim
Diane – seamstress
Galavant – Lady Jayde's stallion
Lady Catherine – wife of Lord Edward
Lady Ethna – second wife of Lord Dario
Lady Helen Latham – you lady Lord Raymond has a crush on
Lady Jacqueline – first wife of Lord Dario
Lady Jayde – daughter of Lady Jacqueline and Lord Dario; age 17
Lady Laila – daughter of Lady Jayde and Lord James; means Guardian Angel
Lord Dario – husband of Lady Jacqueline and Lady Ethna
Lord Edward – husband of Lady Catherine
Lord Geoff – son of Lady Catherine and Lord Edward; deceased
Lord Henry – son of Lady Catherine and Lord Edward; age 28
Lord James – son of Lady Catherine and Lord Edward; age 30

Lord Raymond – son of Lady Catherine and Lord Edward; age 20

Lord Simon – another noble

Lord Thomas – son of Lady Catherine and Lord Edward; deceased

Maggie – old nurse maid and servant to Lord James

Maria – cook at Era

Pycard – jongleur (musician)

Sebastian – constable at Era

Sir Alistair - knight

Sir Cedrick - knight

Sir Corbett - knight

Sir Devon - knight

Sir Fendrel – knight and best friend to Lord James

Sir Gilbert - knight

Sir Hugh - knight

Sir Luther - knight

Sir Peter - knight

Sir Rylan - knight

Sir Walker - knight

Thomas – blacksmith at Era

You can keep up with Dawn DeRamón on her facebook page at www.facebook.com/dawn.deramon

www.ingramcontent.com/pod-product-compliance
Lightning Source LLC
Chambersburg PA
CBHW020247200626
46816CB00001BA/163